Claw Enforcement

A SECOND CHANCE CAT MYSTERY

Sofie Ryan

BERKLEY PRIME CRIME
New York

BERKLEY PRIME CRIME
Published by Berkley
An imprint of Penguin Random House LLC
penguinrandomhouse.com

Copyright © 2020 by Darlene Ryan
Excerpt from *Curiosity Thrilled the Cat* by Sofie Kelly © 2011 by
Penguin Random House LLC
Penguin Random House supports copyright. Copyright fuels creativity, encourages
diverse voices, promotes free speech, and creates a vibrant culture. Thank you for buying
an authorized edition of this book and for complying with copyright laws by not
reproducing, scanning, or distributing any part of it in any form without permission.
You are supporting writers and allowing Penguin Random House to continue to
publish books for every reader.

BERKLEY and the BERKLEY & B colophon are registered trademarks and BERKLEY
PRIME CRIME is a trademark of Penguin Random House LLC.

ISBN: 9781984802330

First Edition: January 2020

Printed in the United States of America
1 3 5 7 9 10 8 6 4 2

Cover art by Mary Ann Lasher / Bernstein & Andriulli

Titles by Sofie Ryan

Fic
Ry

Acknowledgments

This is the seventh book in the Second Chance Cat mysteries. I'm very happy we're all still here. Thank you to all the readers who have embraced Sarah, Elvis, and those crime-solving seniors, Charlotte's Angels. Thanks as well to my agent, Kim Lionetti, and my editor, Jessica Wade, whose hard work behind the scenes always makes me look good.

And as always, thank you to Patrick and Lauren who never complain when I talk to imaginary people!

Chapter 1

Elvis had *not* left the building. He had, in fact, not left the chair he'd been sitting on all afternoon. The chair, an oak, midcentury modern lounge style with cushions upholstered in a rich burnt orange fabric, was a find from one of two storage units I'd bought the contents of back in September.

"Let's go," I said.

He yawned then looked expectantly at me.

"Absolutely not." I folded my arms over my midsection. "I'm not carrying you."

He made a huff of annoyance.

"You're perfectly capable of walking."

Since the I'm-so-tired yawn and the don't-you know-who-I-am indignation hadn't worked on me, he switched back to the I'm-so-cute head tilt. That particular move worked on pretty much everyone who walked into the store, probably because this Elvis was actually a green-eyed black cat with a long, rakish scar that cut diagonally across his nose and just a bit of an attitude, not the King of Rock and Roll—which is not to say that the head-tilt thing wouldn't have worked if he *were* the King of Rock and Roll hanging around my shop charming people.

I picked up my canvas carryall. It was heavy, packed with ten glass milk bottles, carefully wrapped in newspaper so they wouldn't break or get chipped on the ride home. They were filthy, covered in dirt, sawdust and some things I didn't want to think about since I knew the containers had been found in an old chicken coop. Once they were cleaned up I was certain that the bottles would sell. One of the things I'd learned from owning a repurpose store was that people collected just about anything, including linen tea towels circa 1964, department store mannequins and glass milk bottles.

"I'm serious, Elvis. Let's go." I made a hurry-up gesture with my free hand. "Did you forget we're having Charlotte's shepherd's pie for supper?"

The cat straightened up and his whiskers twitched. It seemed that he had forgotten. But now that I had reminded him what was waiting for our dinner, he jumped down off the chair, shook himself and headed purposefully across the floor in the direction of the workroom door. He paused when he reached it, looked over his shoulder at me and meowed sharply.

"Oh, so now you're in a hurry," I said.

Now it was his turn to narrow his eyes at me. After all, we were talking about Charlotte Elliot's shepherd's pie: chunks of beef and carrot in a rich, meaty gravy topped with fluffy mashed potatoes and a crispy crust of Parmesan cheese. I might have drooled a little just thinking about it.

Elvis was right. We needed to get home.

I locked the back door of the building and Elvis trailed me across the parking lot to my SUV. I opened the passenger door and he hopped up onto the seat before I could lift him. I set my messenger bag next to him and placed the bag of milk bottles carefully on the floor.

The sun was warm on my shoulders and the back of my neck as I made my way around the car to the driver's side. It had been the kind of fall day the state of Maine was known for. The leaves were almost at peak—colors from russet to scarlet to vibrant yellow and intense oranges that rivaled the pumpkins piled up at roadside stands. The sky overhead was azure blue with just a few clouds starting to roll in from the bay.

There wasn't very much traffic driving home, but that didn't stop my furry backseat driver from intently watching the road through the windshield and giving a sharp meow when I made a left-hand turn he seemingly didn't approve of. Finally I pulled into the driveway, got out of the SUV and walked around to the passenger side to grab my bag and the bottles. Elvis jumped out the moment I opened the car door. He headed up the walkway to the front door as I wrestled with the tote full of milk bottles, which had somehow gotten wedged under the edge of the seat. It didn't want to move. I gave a groan of frustration. I didn't want to pull too hard and break something, but I didn't want to have to carry the bottles inside one by one, either.

"Hello, Sarah," a voice said behind me. "Is there a problem with your car seat?"

I straightened up and turned around. My elderly neighbor, Tom Harris, was standing by the back bumper of the SUV, a frown creasing his forehead. He was a small, round man, no taller than five eight or so, with thick iron gray hair and small black frame glasses that gave him the stereotypical appearance of a college professor.

"Hi, Tom," I said, brushing my bangs back off my face. "No, it's not the seat. I brought home a bag of glass milk bottles. I set it on the floor and now the darn thing's stuck. I don't want to pull too hard because I don't want to break them."

"May I take a look?" he asked. His voice still held a trace of his Scots accent even though he'd lived in Maine for more than fifty years now.

"Absolutely." I held up both hands and took a couple of steps backward. Tom was a particular, exacting man and I knew there was no chance that he'd break any of the bottles. The lawn around his gray-shingled, story-and-a-half house was the most perfectly manicured one in North Harbor, Maine, probably in the entire state. No weeds dared poke their heads up in the two planters that flanked the front door and ran the length of the house on either side.

Tom leaned into the truck, his head almost touching the floor mat as he peered under the seat. He slipped a hand beneath the canvas tote. "A-ha," I heard him say almost under his breath. Then he backed out of the truck and handed the bag of bottles to me.

"Thank you, Tom," I said. I gave a sigh of relief. "You're a lifesaver."

He smiled. "You're welcome. The strap had just gotten caught on a piece of metal on the frame of the seat." He reached over and tapped a bottle, which was half poking out of the bag. The newspaper I'd wrapped around it had come loose. Inside it, I could see a couple of dried-out, pointed-edged leaves and several deep red, wrinkled berries. I had no idea how long the bottles had been stored in the old chicken coop where I'd found them. I wondered how the leaves and berries had gotten inside. One of the chickens, maybe? "Make sure you dispose of those very carefully, Sarah," Tom said. "Those are holly berries, *Ilex opaca*. They're toxic to cats. And dogs, too."

I nodded. "I will." I realized then that Tom didn't have his Corgi, Matilda, with him. I glanced over at his little gray-shingled house. There was no sign of her. "Where's Matilda?" I asked. "Is she all right?"

He nodded. "She's over at the Burnses' house visiting Molly." He gestured toward the house diagonally across the street. "I'm on my way to get her."

"How is Molly?" I asked. Ten days earlier, the five-year-old had fallen out of the maple tree in her backyard and broken her right leg.

"When I left she had Matilda wearing a cowboy hat in preparation for painting her portrait," Tom said.

I grinned. "I look forward to seeing that."

He smiled back at me. "As do I."

I thanked Tom again for his help and he made his way across the street as I headed for the front door, where Elvis was waiting more or less patiently.

My big 1860s, two-story Victorian house was within walking distance of North Harbor's waterfront. The neighborhood, with its big trees and old houses, had felt like home from the first time I'd turned onto the street. My house had been divided into three apartments about thirty years earlier, and it had been let go over time, but both my dad and my brother, Liam, had agreed with my belief that it had good bones, and after a lot of work it had turned into the home I'd known it could be.

My grandmother and her new husband, John, lived in the top-floor apartment while Gram's friend—and mine—Rose Jackson, had the small main-floor unit. Elvis and I shared the other first-floor apartment. It was a living arrangement that, in theory, shouldn't have worked, but it did. Gram stayed out of my personal life—not that I exactly had one. And while Rose wasn't quite as hands off, she was very open-minded.

It also helped that they were all very busy. John was teaching a history course at University College at Rockland. Gram was working on a project for the Emmerson Foundation, which was run by her friend Liz. She was tracing the past of the charitable organization, rooting through dusty boxes of records and talking to past board members and employees. Eventually all of that information was going to be turned into a book on the history of the foundation. The idea of writing a book had begun as a bit of subterfuge on Liz's part, a way to ask questions about an incident in the charity's past, but after a recent scandal Liz had decided to turn the "fake" book project into a real one and had convinced Gram to organize everything.

Rose was probably busier than any of us. She worked for me part-time in the shop. She volunteered at the library and the elementary school. And she ran a detective agency, Charlotte's Angels, aka the Angels, with a couple of her friends. She kept us all in cookies and coffeecake *and* she had recently decided to play matchmaker for my brother. As she'd explained to Liam, "You haven't reached your expiry date yet but you need to be moved up to the front of the shelf." Since that meant Rose was no longer trying to play matchmaker for *me*, I thought it was a great idea.

I checked my watch as I unlocked the apartment door. I had just under an hour before I needed to collect Rose and Mr. P., her "gentleman friend." We had been invited to a reception to celebrate the rejuvenation of North Harbor's waterfront—a project that had taken years to get under way. For me, the highlight of the evening was going to be the chance to see the various items—mostly photographs and a collection of tin toys—that had been unearthed in several of the old buildings that had had to be demolished.

Liz was an investor in the project, although that wasn't common knowledge, and Liam was acting as a consultant, advising the builders on how to best incorporate all the materials that had been saved from the structures that had been torn down. Because of my brother's efforts, the new buildings would have some of the character of the ones they were replacing.

After a lot of back-and-forth, everyone involved with the harbor front project had agreed that any items that were found in the old buildings that couldn't easily be reunited with their owners would be sold, with the money going to the hot lunch program in the elementary school. I had a feeling that Liam had been the driving force behind that idea. The lunch program was one of our grandmother's pet projects.

I was looking forward to seeing some of the old photos. According to my brother, a box of class pictures from the elementary school had been found in one of the old warehouses. Neither Liam nor I had gone to school in North Harbor, but our friend Nick had and so had Gram and Rose and Liz. I was hoping for one or two slightly embarrassing pictures, considering that the latter three had more than a few photos like that of me.

I took the bag of milk bottles into the kitchen and lined them up in two rows next to the sink, making sure that the stray holly berries went into the garbage can. Then I washed my hands and took Charlotte's shepherd's pie out of the refrigerator. Elvis watched from a stool at the counter, whiskers twitching.

The shepherd's pie was as good as I'd expected it would be. Charlotte was an excellent cook, so good that she'd been able to help Rose teach *me* to cook, something no one else including my mom, dad, Gram, three teachers and two (small) kitchen fires had been able to get me to master.

After we'd eaten, Elvis made his way to the top of his cat tower, where he began meticulously washing his face. I decided on a shower. I was just pulling up the zipper of my black sweater dress when Elvis padded into the bedroom.

"What do you think?" I asked, doing a slow turn. The dress had three-quarter sleeves, a flared skirt and two rows of a delicate eyelet design at the neck. Rose had actually picked the dress out for me. It was a little shorter and a little tighter than I would have chosen. She had taken the dress off a rack in the store, handed it to me and made a shooing motion in the direction of the dressing rooms. I knew better than to argue.

Elvis cocked his head to one side and gave a soft "Mrr."

It sounded like approval to me. "Thank you," I said.

I finished my makeup, slipped a couple of gold bangles Gram had brought me back from her extended honeymoon trip onto my right arm and then set the timer on the TV so Elvis could watch *Jeopardy!* I'd never been able to figure out if the cat was an Alex Trebek fan or just liked trivia with the answers given in the form of a question. He was a quirky little guy. (Elvis, not Alex Trebek, although to be fair, I didn't actually know the game show host.)

Rose and Mr. P. were just coming out of her apartment when I stepped into the hallway. She smiled at me. "That's your new dress."

I nodded. "Yes, it is."

"Let me see," she said, making a circular motion with her right index finger.

I did a slow twirl.

She nodded her approval. "I knew that dress would look perfect on you."

"You do look lovely, Sarah," Mr. P. added.

"And you look very handsome," I said.

"Thank you. The credit goes to Rosie." He turned and smiled at her.

Alfred Peterson was a small man with just a few tufts of gray hair and warm brown eyes behind wire-framed glasses. He may have looked like the stereo-typical grandpa who showed up in life insurance ads, but he had a keen, curious mind and computer skills that rivaled hackers a fraction of his age. Most of the time he favored knit golf shirts and pants that tended to creep up to his armpits, but tonight he was dressed in a pair of charcoal gray trousers with a lighter gray turtleneck sweater and a black tweed blazer.

I shifted my attention to Rose. She was wearing a long-sleeved teal dress with a dove gray coat and gray shoes. "You look so pretty," I said. "I like that color on you."

Rose Jackson was just shy of five feet tall with short white hair and kind gray eyes. She had the type of skin that belonged in a face cream commercial and she could have lied about how old she was if she'd been willing to listen to Liz and color her hair the way Liz did. In theory, the two of us living next door to each other shouldn't have worked—she had changed my diapers, after all—but it did. We gave each other lots of space—and, in truth, Rose had way more of a personal life than I did.

She reached up to pat my cheek as she moved past me. "Thank you, my dear," she said. "I may be a senior citizen, but I've still got it." She squared her shoulders and gave her head a little toss as she headed out the door.

"That she does," Mr. P. said, one eyebrow rising slightly as he followed her.

I closed my eyes for a moment and gave my head a little shake as I brought up the rear. There were some things about Rose's personal life I was happier having stay personal.

* * *

The reception was being held in the Emmerson Foundation's former boardroom. After some recent financial misconduct had come to light, Liz had stepped up to once again take a more active role in the organization's day-to-day business.

"Why on earth do we need a boardroom?" she'd asked me as she walked around the huge space one Saturday morning.

"I don't know," I'd said. I'd been trying to estimate the cost of the gorgeous Oriental rug under my feet. I'd almost bid on one recently at an auction but in the end had decided it would be too easy to spend too much money. "How many board meetings do you have in a year?"

The meeting room was a beautiful space with a high ceiling, a wall of windows looking out toward the view of the bay and gleaming oak floors under that Oriental rug.

"Not enough to justify having this space sit empty most of the time," Liz had replied tartly, flicking a speck of lint off of the arm of her cream-colored sweater with an impeccably manicured nail. "And I happen to know that more foundation business gets done in Sam Newman's pub than is ever accomplished here." She'd tipped her head to one side then, narrowed her blue eyes, and tapped her chin with the same perfectly polished finger. "Would you have your wedding reception here, Sarah? Theoretically, I mean."

"Who am I marrying? Theoretically?"

Liz had made an exasperated sound. "I don't know. Hugh Jackman."

"I think he's already married," I'd said, "but yes, I can picture Hugh and I dancing our first dance as husband and wife in this room, toasting each other with champagne and sharing our first kiss as a married couple."

She'd rolled her eyes. "Given the speed at which your love life moves, it's about as likely as any other possibility."

I'd folded my arms over my chest. "Oh are we talking about our love lives now?" I'd asked.

"No, missy, we most decidedly are not," Liz had said. "We're talking about my plans to start renting out this space and using the money we raise to do some very needed work to the Sunshine Camp."

And it was as simple as that. Liz had worked out the details with her very capable assistant, Jane Evans, and the former boardroom became available for meetings, parties and receptions like tonight's event.

Jane had done a beautiful job with the space. Light gleamed from two teardrop capiz chandeliers. The photos, books and other items that had been found in the old buildings were in glass display cases that stretched across one long side of the room. There were small round tables with starched white cloths clustered by the tall windows and a makeshift bar had been set up in front of the exposed brick wall at the end of the room. There were easily fifty people already milling about and I knew from Liz that more were expected.

North Harbor sits on the midcoast of Maine, "where the hills touch the sea." The town stretches from the Swift Hills in the north to the Atlantic Ocean in the south. It's full of beautiful, old buildings and eclectic little businesses, as well as several award-winning restaurants. Our year-round population is just over thirteen thousand people, but that number more than triples in the summer with seasonal residents and tourists. Every business owner in North Harbor knows the value of good word of mouth from what we called the summer people.

The refurbishment of the harbor front had been talked about for years as a way of enticing visitors to stay in town longer, and more than one developer had submitted a proposal to the town. After several setbacks and delays the current development plan had been accepted. It included a new hotel, a row of shops and restaurants and a rebuilt boardwalk, all in the style and manner of the historic buildings that had been along the waterfront for decades, many for more than a century. Adding an apartment building or condominiums had been tabled for now. The idea was to offer visitors more of what they came to town for—the charm of a New England small town with the services they didn't want to be without.

I scanned the room for Liam. I spotted him standing near the bar talking with Joe Roswell, the developer in charge of the hotel and another man I didn't recognize.

"Rose, do you know who that is with Liam and Joe Roswell?" I asked.

"That's Robb Gorham," she said.

I studied the man. He was about average height with broad shoulders under his dark blue suit jacket. He had the stance of a confident person; feet planted firmly on the ground about shoulder width apart, shoulders back, body turned toward the other two men. "I feel as though I should know him," I said.

"He's related to Stella," Rose said. "A nephew or a cousin or something like that. He's a building contractor."

Stella Hall was a former client of the Angels detective agency.

"Do you remember the Starlight Inn?" Rose continued.

I nodded. "It was just outside of town where that ugly motel, the Knights Inn, is now."

Mr. P. cleared his throat. "Mr. Gorham built that motel."

"Gram started a petition to save the Starlight Inn," I said. "She threatened to chain herself to one of the newel posts on the verandah to stop it from being torn down."

Rose patted my arm. "If you're introduced it's probably better not to lead with that."

Liam had spotted us and was making his way in our direction. He caught one of Rose's hands in his and beamed at her. "Rose Jackson, you are a vision," he said.

"Flattery doesn't work on me," she said.

Mr. P. and I exchanged a look because we knew Rose had a soft spot for my brother.

Liam put his free hand over his heart. "But it's not flattery if it's the truth."

Rose shook her head, but she couldn't stop a smile from escaping.

He leaned over and kissed her cheek then straightened up and offered a hand to Mr. P. "Alfred, I'm glad you're here," he said. "We found a set of model train cars in the basement of the old hotel. Sarah told me you know a little bit about model trains."

Mr. P. knew a little bit about a lot of things. I'd discovered his interest in trains when we were clearing out Stella Hall's brother's house and Elvis unearthed a model steam engine and several cars that turned out to be a valuable Marklin train set.

"I'd be happy to take a look," Mr. P. said.

Liam turned to me then. "You look good, big brother," I said. He was wearing a dark suit that brought out his blonde hair and blue-gray eyes.

"You look pretty great yourself," he said as he hugged me.

Liam was older by just a few months and he liked to remind me that made him wiser as well. Technically we were stepsiblings, part of a blended family that had been created when his dad, Peter Kennelly, married my mom. To me, Liam was just my brother, the way Peter was just Dad. And I knew Liam felt the same way about Mom and me.

Liam took Mr. P. off to look at the model train while Rose and I made our way over to look at a collection of photos that were displayed on the wall to our right.

"Oh my goodness," Rose exclaimed no more than a couple of minutes after we'd started checking the images. "Sarah, look." She pointed at a black-and-white photo of an elementary school class. "The back row in the middle."

I leaned forward and squinted at the photograph.

The little girl Rose had indicated was tall with chin-length dark hair held back with some kind of clip, and a serious expression on her face. "Is that . . . ?" I took another look. "Is that Gram?" I turned to Rose, who nodded. "But she looks so serious."

"Having the class picture taken was serious business back then."

"Wait a minute," I said, gesturing at her with one finger. "You and Gram were in the same class. Where are you?"

"Far left in the front row."

I turned back to the photo. Then as now, Rose was a sprite. Like Gram, her hair was styled in a chin-length bob, only Rose had thick bangs, which cut across her forehead on a very unfortunate diagonal. Her hands were folded primly in her lap, but there was something in her body language that said there was nothing prim and proper about this little girl.

I put one arm around her shoulders and gave her a squeeze. "You were adorable. You look like you had spunk."

"I did have spunk," she said, a twinkle in her gray eyes. "So did your grandmother." She paused. "Our principal hated spunk."

I gave her another squeeze. "His loss."

Rose turned around and surveyed the room. "Where are Isabel and John?"

"Gram is at a meeting about the sunflower window. They'll be here later."

Rose linked her arm through mine and we moved on to the next collection of photos. "I hope they'll be able to keep the window in town."

"Me, too," I said. "With Gram and Liz and Judge Halloran involved, I don't think that window will be going anywhere."

The sunflower window was a round, stained-glass window that had been in the old library building. It dated back to the time the library had originally been built, in the late 1800s. The window had gotten its name from the different shades of yellow glass in the flower-like design. When the old library was torn down, the sunflower window had been removed and stored since it didn't "fit with the design" of the new structure, according to the library board. In the last couple of months, a businessman from Singapore had offered a significant amount of money to buy the window. Judge Neill Halloran was spearheading the fund-raising to match the offer already on the table and keep the window in North Harbor. He and my grandmother had been friends in school and she'd offered her help.

Rose and I spent the next fifteen minutes looking for people we knew in the collection of old school pictures, laughing at the way fashion and hairstyles seemed to run in cycles. Mr. P. and Liam rejoined us, with Liam looking like Elvis with a whole sardine to himself.

"So?" I asked. I knew that grin had to mean good news.

"They're Marx tin train cars," Mr. P. said. "In very good condition considering how long they could have spent in what was likely a damp basement."

"And worth several hundred dollars," Liam added.

"At least," Mr. P. agreed.

Rose beamed at him. "Wonderful!" she exclaimed.

"That's more money for the school's hot lunch program."

Someone touched my arm then and I turned to see Nick Elliot standing there. "Hi," he said. "What have I missed?" Nick was just over six feet tall, a big teddy bear of a man with broad shoulders and sandy hair. He was handsome and charming and funny and I couldn't imagine my life without him in it.

I smiled at him. "Hi yourself. You've missed a great school picture of Gram and Rose and you can settle an argument between Rose and me." I turned and gestured at a photo to my left and just at Nick's eye level. "Middle of the back row, guy who looks like a stockier Kurt Cobain. Is that Glenn McNamara?"

Nick leaned forward, studied the picture for a moment and then straightened up. "Yes."

Rose grinned like a little girl.

"C'mon, that's not Glenn," I said. "It can't be. Look at the hair." Glenn McNamara, who owned the local bakery and sandwich shop, kept his blonde hair in the same brush cut he'd had as a college football player. The young man in the photo that Rose kept insisting was Glenn had blonde hair parted in the middle that just brushed his shoulders and obscured part of his face.

"It's Glenn," Nick insisted. "He's a head taller than everyone else in that photograph and he told me once that he was always the biggest kid in his class. Besides, it looks like him."

"I told you it was Glenn, dear," Rose said. "All you have to do is look at his eyes."

"I can't see his eyes," I retorted. "Whoever that is has too much hair."

"Maybe that's the problem." Her expression turned thoughtful.

"That's exactly the problem. It's impossible to know whether that's Glenn because you can't see enough of the person's face."

Rose waved away my words. "No, no that's definitely Glenn. I mean, maybe the problem is with *your* eyes. When was the last time you had them examined?" She looked genuinely concerned.

"I . . . uh . . . not that long ago." I stumbled over my answer. It had to be less than a year since I'd had my eyes checked and I could see just fine.

A group of people had just come in. The noise level rose in the room and a man bumped my arm, mumbling an apology as he passed. He smelled of alcohol and a mix of rosemary and mint, aftershave maybe. I noticed as he moved away from me that he seemed to be making an effort not to look intoxicated, although I was pretty certain he was. He wasn't dressed for the occasion, either. He wore jeans with a white shirt and a tweedy wool sport coat over the top.

"You are over thirty now, Sarah," Rose said. "Are you getting enough antioxidants in your diet?"

"I eat carrots and green beans."

"Do you gets lots of leafy greens? Lots of spinach and kale . . . oh and sweet potatoes."

Liam was standing just behind her left shoulder not even trying to keep a straight face. I had no problem throwing him under the bus.

"How do you get your antioxidants, Liam?" I asked. "You're older than I am."

Rose laced her fingers over her midsection and shook her head. "Oh for heaven's sake. Really, is that the best you can do to distract me? I may have been born at night, but it wasn't last night."

Color flooded my cheeks. Liam was smirking now. At least Nick and Mr. P. looked a little sympathetic to my plight.

Rose smiled to let me know there were no hard feelings over my lame attempt to divert her attention away from me. "I know you're busy," she said. "So I'll get Avery to make you one of her smoothies. With extra kale."

Avery was Liz's teenage granddaughter. She had a repertoire of healthy breakfast drinks that all seemed to feature kale. Lots and lots of kale.

"Um . . . thank you," I said. I was going to need a big pot of coffee to wash down one of those smoothies.

Rose turned around and Liam immediately wiped the grin from his face. She gave him her sweetest little old lady smile, which I'd seen her use more than once to wheedle information out of someone. "Avery will make one for you, too," she said. "After all, as Sarah pointed out, you're not getting any younger, either."

Raised voices diverted our attention before Liam could reply. We all turned in the direction of the sound. The man who had just bumped into me was accosting Joe Roswell. He'd grabbed the contractor's arm with one hand and was gesturing with the other. Roswell was a shade less than six feet with a stocky build, and I was certain he could have shaken off the other man's grip if he'd wanted to.

"You're just a sore loser," the drunken man shouted. "But the judge is going to side with me. Me!"

Joe Roswell was somewhere in his fifties, I guessed, balding with a salt-and-pepper mustache and wire-framed glasses. His face was lined from years of working outside in the sun and wind and cold. My grandmother would have said he had nice eyes.

The man yelling at him was somewhere either side of thirty. He was a couple of inches shorter than Roswell and probably thirty pounds or so lighter, with sandy blonde hair that hung in his eyes.

"Back off," I heard Roswell say. Even twenty-five feet away I could see the warning in his eyes.

Liam and Nick exchanged a look and started for the two men.

Joe Roswell had clearly had enough. He rolled his forearm out and snapped it down on the other man's arm, breaking the man's grip. Then instead of moving away he took a step closer. "Walk away, Healy," Roswell said, his voice sharp with warning. "Otherwise I will call the police. This party is invitation only and you don't have one."

They glared at each other for a long moment, then Mr. Healy said something I didn't catch and made his way toward the bar. The argument was over.

People were already shifting their attention back to whatever they had been doing; in fact, I realized that not everyone had even noticed the brief altercation. Liam was talking to Roswell. Nick just stood there, hands stuffed in his pockets, listening. I saw the contractor shake his head. All three men looked in the direction of the bar and I did the same.

As I watched I saw the female bartender shake her head at Mr. Healy. I didn't think I was wrong about his state of intoxication and the last thing he needed was another drink. She set a cup and saucer on the bar in front of him, picked up a carafe that I assumed held coffee and poured a cup. He made a face at the coffee and said something. The bartender in turn pushed the cup at him. I had the sense from their interaction—the way he leaned in toward her, the way she seemed to snap back at her—that they knew each other.

And it was all none of my business. I turned my attention back to Rose and Mr. P. Rose was looking in the direction of the bar as well.

"Let's go take a look at some of the toys," I said.

Mr. P. nodded. "I'd like that. Liam tells me they found a View-Master and a box of reels in excellent condition. I'm thinking of making an offer on them."

"I'm guessing you had one when you were a boy." I remembered when Nick and I had found his mother's old View-Master in a box up in the attic one rainy summer afternoon. I was fascinated by the idea that we could see images in three dimensions.

Mr. P. smiled. "I did. I was quite the envy of my friends for a while." He touched Rose on the shoulder. "What do you think, Rosie?" he asked.

Rose still seemed to be distracted by what was happening at the bar. The bartender had moved on to serve someone else and Mr. Healy was drinking his coffee and surveying the crowd. She turned to look at us. "I'm sorry," she said. "I was just wondering if that poor man is okay."

I glanced around the room. Joe Roswell was standing by the windows now talking to Liam and Jane Evans. I tipped my head in their direction. "I think he's fine, Rose," I said.

She turned in the direction I'd indicated. "Oh I didn't mean him," she said.

"If you weren't referring to Joseph then who did you mean?" Mr. P. asked.

"The young man over by the bar, of course." She frowned as though she didn't understand why *we* didn't know that.

"Rose, he's drunk," I said.

"I can see that," she replied. "Maybe you should ask yourself why."

Conversations with Rose could very easily get off track. I knew she had a point to make but I had no clue what it was.

"I would assume he consumed more alcohol than his body could process," Mr. P. said.

Rose nodded approvingly. "Exactly." She shifted her attention to me. "Why?"

I was officially off in the bulrushes, as Liz would say. "You mean, why did he get drunk?"

"Yes. He got drunk, then he came to a party he hadn't been invited to and made a bit of a scene."

I glanced over at Mr. Healy again, who was now talking to Robb Gorham. It didn't look like a very happy conversation. Out of the corner of my eye I noticed that Joe Roswell was watching them, too.

Mr. P. was looking pensive. "Getting so intoxicated suggests the young man was upset about something."

Once again Rose smiled at him as though he were her best student.

"You're wondering what that something is," I said.

"I am," she said. "I hate to see anyone in such distress." Her eyes flicked to the back of the room again for a brief moment. "I guess that makes me a nosy old lady."

I slipped an arm around her shoulder and gave her a hug. "No. It makes you someone with a great big heart."

The three of us started working our way along the stretch of the glass-topped cabinets holding the toys. We were almost at the end of the row before we found the View-Master and its box of reels.

"It looks to be in very good shape," I said, leaning closer to the glass for a better look. The chocolate brown Bakelite viewer had no visible nicks or cracks.

"How many reels are there?" Rose asked.

I moved sideways so she could get a better look. Once again my attention was drawn back to the bar. Maybe now I was the one who was being nosy.

Healy was still standing there with his coffee. Joe Roswell was walking away shaking his head. Had they had another "conversation" I wondered?

Beside me Rose was counting the View-Master reels. Across the room Healy took a sip of his coffee. The hand holding his cup began to shake. He pressed his other hand against his upper chest. He made a guttural sound. The coffee cup fell and shattered and Healy fell to the floor.

I pushed past Rose and Mr. P. "Call 911," I said. I bolted to the man, reaching him at the same time that Nick did. He rolled Healy on his back, felt for a pulse at his neck and bent to listen for breathing. He shook his head. "Start chest compressions," he said. "I'll do the breathing."

I nodded, swallowed against the lump of fear that was lodged in my throat and pushed the man's sport coat open. I felt Healy's chest move under my hands. I hoped it would somehow be enough to keep him alive until help arrived. Under my breath I was humming the Bee Gees' "Stayin' Alive," something Nick had taught us all to do as a good way to maintain the proper number of compressions per minute. The irony wasn't lost on me.

Healy didn't move. His color was a pasty gray-green, his eyes almost closed. He had long eyelashes and a scrape on his chin that was probably the result of cutting himself shaving. I didn't know why my brain had noticed those things. Maybe because I didn't want to think that he might already be dead. I just continued to work in tandem with Nick as the wail of sirens got closer. I had no idea how long it took the ambulance to arrive. Probably not as long as it seemed to me.

Finally a paramedic in her blue uniform crouched beside me. "I've got this," she said. I moved out of the way and she took over.

I got to my feet. It was cold in the room. I wrapped my arms around my midsection for warmth. A suit jacket wrapped around my shoulders and Liam put his arm around me. We watched as Nick and the paramedics got Healy onto a stretcher. His color hadn't changed. He hadn't moved. I had the sickening feeling he was dead.

Chapter 2

Nick came back into the room. He'd tossed his sport coat over the back of a chair and he stopped to pick it up before walking over to Liam and me. Rose and Mr. P. had joined us.

"Nicolas, is that young man going to be all right?" Rose asked.

"The paramedics are doing their best," he said. He looked at me. "Thanks, Sarah." He looked back over his shoulder toward the entrance. "We gave him a chance, at least."

I nodded. I still had that lump in my throat and the sinking feeling that our efforts might not have made any difference in the end.

Michelle came in then.

Detective Michelle Andrews and I had been friends when we were kids. We'd reconnected recently and I was happy to have her in my life again. And while she wasn't really crazy about the cases Rose and Mr. P. and their friends got involved in, Michelle was willing to at least listen to what they had to say.

"Excuse me a minute," Nick said. He walked over and met Michelle in the middle of the room. I watched them talk, saw Nick gesture toward the bar where the pieces of the broken coffee cup were still on the floor. All around us people were getting restless, standing in small clusters, talking, bending their heads over their phones.

Finally Nick headed for the door while Michelle made her way over to us. She was dressed for work, not a party, in gray wool trousers with a plum-colored sweater under her vintage black leather jacket. Her red hair was pulled back in a ponytail.

"Hi," she said as she pulled a pen and a small notebook from the inside pocket of her jacket. She focused her attention on me. "Sarah, Nick told me what happened. I'd like to hear your version, please."

"Of course," I said. "I was over there with Rose and Alfred." I pointed over my shoulder with one hand. "We were looking at the toys, at an old View-Master. I just happened to glance over in the direction of the bar and I saw the man put a hand to his chest, and then he collapsed."

"And you went to help Nick do CPR."

"I didn't really think about it. I just reacted. I asked Mr. P. to call 911 and I ran to help."

"And I did," he said quietly.

"Did you know him?" Michelle asked me. She took notes in her own version of shorthand.

I shook my head. "No. The guy bumped into me when he first came in. I noticed him because . . . because he smelled like he'd been drinking. I think his last name is Healy."

"Christopher Healy," Liam said.

Michelle's attention immediately shifted. "So you *do* know him?"

Liam nodded. "Joe Roswell is the developer working on the new hotel. He and Healy were going to court over another piece of land."

"Why was Mr. Healy even here? It seems a little odd to invite someone you're battling in court with to a party."

Beside me, Liam shifted uncomfortably. "He wasn't invited. He got in somehow, he was drunk, he caused a bit of a scene with Joe. That was it."

"He wasn't asked to leave?"

Liam shook his head. "No. Joe didn't want any more trouble."

Michelle nodded as though she'd heard that reasoning before. "So what did Mr. Healy do? I take it he didn't cause any more trouble."

"He just stayed by the bar," I said. "He had a cup of coffee. He'd just taken a drink when he collapsed."

"Okay," Michelle said. "Is there anything else you think I need to know?"

"No," I said.

Liam shook his head again.

"You can go then." She turned to Liam. "I'd like to talk to Mr. Roswell. Could you point him out to me, please?"

Liam did a quick scan of the room. Joe Roswell was standing over by the windows in a group of half a dozen people next to a big easel that held an artist's rendering of the finished hotel. "I'll introduce you," he said. His gaze flicked back to me.

I slipped off Liam's jacket and handed it to him. "I'm okay," I said softly, in answer to his unspoken question.

He gave me a brief smile and turned to Michelle. "Joe's right over here," he said, gesturing toward the other side of the room.

Michelle reached out and touched my arm. "I'll probably have a few more questions in the morning, Sarah."

"I'll be at the shop."

She nodded and headed across the room with Liam.

I blew out a breath. "Let's get out of here," I said to Rose and Mr. P.

"An excellent idea," Mr. P. said.

We collected our coats, gave our names to the police officer at the door, and went out to the parking lot. Rose settled in the front seat and fastened her seatbelt. "Are you sure you're all right, Sarah?" she asked.

I shifted in my seat to look at her. I could see that she was worried about me. There was concern in her gray eyes and she wasn't smiling. "I am, really." I pulled a hand over the back of my neck. "I'm just worried about Mr. Healy."

Rose reached across the seat and laid her hand on top of mine. "I'm so sorry," she said. "Both you and Nicolas did your best, but Mr. Healy was dead when he hit the floor. There wasn't anything either of you could have done to save him."

I'd already come to the same conclusion, but I hated to admit that Nick and I hadn't been able to save the man. It made me feel profoundly sad and I hadn't even known him. I suddenly thought of John Donne's poem, "No Man Is an Island." I couldn't remember if it was Charlotte or my grandmother who had quoted it to me. "'Any man's death diminishes me,'

"'Because I am involved in mankind,'" I said, softly.

"'And therefore never send to know for whom the bell tolls; It tolls for thee,'" Mr. P. finished.

I started the SUV and pulled out of the lot.

"I wonder why anyone would have wanted to kill that young man," Rose said.

I shot her a quick look. "Hang on a minute," I said. "We don't know for sure that Mr. Healy is dead—and even if he is, why would you think someone killed him?"

"He was poisoned."

"Rosie, why do you think that?" Mr. P. asked from the backseat.

Rose turned to look over her shoulder at him. "He had a seizure right before he died. His body was twitching, shaking. He made some kind of strangled sound and he collapsed." Out of the corner of my eye I saw her look at me again. "You did see that, didn't you Sarah?"

I nodded and swallowed against the sudden tightness in my chest. "I did, but that doesn't mean the man was poisoned."

"It doesn't mean he wasn't," she replied.

I glanced over at her again. Her hands were folded in her lap and she didn't seem the slightest bit upset because I didn't agree with her.

This was not a good sign.

"Okay, let's assume Mr. Healy had a seizure," I said. "Other things can cause a seizure—a fever, a head injury. He may have epilepsy or be diabetic. He had been drinking. Too much alcohol can cause seizures."

"That's true. All of those things could have caused that young man to have collapsed the way he did," Rose said. "But I was watching him. He was fine. He drank some of his coffee and then he wasn't fine. He was poisoned, Sarah."

"Can we at least wait until we're sure the man is dead before we decide he was murdered?" I asked.

"Of course we can, dear," she said.

She was being very reasonable. That was also not a good sign.

Michelle called the next morning while Elvis and I were having breakfast. Actually, I was having breakfast. Elvis was sitting on the stool next to me at the counter washing his face after having mooched a bite of egg from my plate.

"I'm sorry to call so early," she said. "I just have a few follow-up questions from last night."

"Sure," I said. "Go ahead."

"Did you remember seeing Mr. Healy talk to anyone?"

"You mean after he had the altercation with Joe Roswell?" Elvis was watching me, paw paused in midair as though he were listening to my half of the conversation. Which, for all I knew, he was.

"Yes."

"I saw him have a conversation with the bartender," I said. "I was too far away to hear any of it but I did see her shake her head and then she poured him a cup of coffee. I assumed he wanted a drink and she refused to serve him, but I don't know that's the case.

After that, as far as I noticed, she pretty much ignored him."

"Anyone else?" Michelle asked.

"I saw Healy talking to one of the contractors who's working on the harbor front project. Robb Gorham. Rose says he's related to Stella Hall."

I thought about seeing Joe Roswell walking away from the bar. I hadn't actually seen him have a second confrontation with Christopher Healy, but I suspected that he had. "And I can't say for certain but it's possible Healy and Joe Roswell had a second . . . encounter."

"What makes you say that?" Her voice took on a bit of an edge.

I turned my coffee cup in a slow circle on the counter. "I didn't see them together, but right before Healy lost consciousness I saw Mr. Roswell walking away from that general area. He looked annoyed. He was shaking his head. Someone who was closer could probably tell you more."

"I do still have other people to talk to," she said. "One more question. Last night you said Mr. Healy smelled like he'd been drinking. Do you mean you smelled alcohol on his clothes?"

"No. As far as his person, he smelled like aftershave—something outdoorsy—I don't know what it was. I definitely smelled alcohol on his breath. Like I said, he bumped into me. He mumbled an apology. He was no more than six inches away from me."

"Okay," Michelle said. "Thanks. That's all I need to know, at least for now."

"He's dead, isn't he?" I said. "He never started breathing on his own. And he didn't have a pulse."

She cleared her throat. "I'm sorry, yes."

"I'm sorry, too," I said. We said good-bye with a promise that we'd have lunch together soon.

Elvis had given up eavesdropping and gone back to washing his face. I ate the last bite of toast on my plate and picked up my coffee. I remembered Rose's insistence that Christopher Healy had been poisoned. Was there a chance she was right?

Rose was just coming out of her apartment when I stepped out into the hallway. I was carrying the bag of milk bottles. Too restless to sleep when I'd gotten home I'd washed them all and left them in the dish drainer overnight. She was carrying one of her ubiquitous tote bags, the lid of a cake keeper peeking out of the top. She inclined her head at my bag. "Did you have trouble getting to sleep?" she asked.

"A little," I said.

She patted the top of her own bag. "So did I. Chocolate chip coffee cake."

We headed out to the SUV. "You were right," I said as I opened the passenger door for her. "Christopher Healy is dead."

She sighed. "I wish I'd been wrong."

I nodded. "Me, too."

Rose climbed in and set her bag between her feet. Elvis jumped up beside her, walked across her lap and settled himself in the middle of the bench seat. "*Back*seat," I said, motioning with one finger.

"Mrrr," he said without even looking in my direction.

"Elvis is all right here," Rose said.

"He's spoiled," I retorted.

She waved away my words with one hand. "Nonsense. Elvis is very intelligent and he has excellent people skills."

The cat turned and looked at me. If it were possible for a cat to look smug he did. Rose merely smiled.

"Fine," I said.

On the way to the shop we talked about what we were going to do with the milk bottles. "I was thinking I'd just get Avery to come up with a way to display them," I said. "On a table or something similar."

"Absolutely," Rose said. "I don't think you need to do anything fancy. The next group of leaf peepers and those bottles will be gone."

"You really think so?" I came to a stop at the corner and, as always, Elvis checked the traffic in both directions.

I saw her nod out of the corner of my eye. "Oh yes. Those kind of things are very popular with baby boomers." She smiled. "You know, I remember when the milkman used to come and leave the milk just outside the kitchen door. The bottles had a little cardboard top and in the winter sometimes the milk would start to freeze and it would push the cap up. Of course the cream would be at the top so my mother would just slice that with a knife right into my father's coffee." She shook her head. "Good gracious! Don't I sound like I'm a hundred years old?"

"No, you do not," I said. Elvis meowed loudly in agreement.

Rose laughed. "I think both of you may be biased, but luckily shameless flattery works on me."

Mac's truck was the only other vehicle in the parking lot when we pulled in, no surprise since he lived in a small apartment on the second floor. He'd bought the old truck fairly recently from Clayton McNamara—Glenn's uncle—when we'd decluttered the older man's house and it had been useful, more than once, for moving big pieces of furniture to the shop.

Mac Mackenzie was my second-in-command. He had been a financial planner in Boston, but he had walked away from all of that after some major changes in his personal life. He'd come to Maine because he loved to sail—his passion was to someday build a wooden boat. Since there were eight windjammer schooners based in North Harbor and dozens of other sailing vessels, Mac got lots of chances to sail, crewing for pretty much anyone who needed him. He worked at Second Chance because he liked working with his hands. He was a talented carpenter with a mechanical bent and when he'd spent several weeks back in Boston dealing with some personal issues we'd all missed him like crazy.

Rose headed for the back door of the shop carrying her bag in one hand and Elvis in the other. I scanned the parking lot for broken bottles and any other garbage before I followed. Second Chance was housed in a redbrick building that had been built in the late 1800s. We were located on Mill Street where it curved and began to climb uphill, about a fifteen- to twenty-minute walk from the harbor and easily accessed from the highway—the best of both worlds for tourists that made up a big chunk of our customers. Gram held the mortgage on the building and I was working to pay her back as quickly as I could.

Rose, and Nick's mother, Charlotte, worked for me part-time along with Liz's granddaughter, Avery. And the Angels ran their detective agency from my sun porch. That meant I tended to get pulled into their cases—but it was better than the alternative.

My father had been born in North Harbor, and after he died I'd spent every summer here with my grandmother. The rest of the year I'd lived first in upstate New York and then in New Hampshire. Both my father and mother had been only children, so I didn't have any cousins or aunts and uncles to hang out with during the summer. Charlotte, Rose and Liz were Gram's closest friends and they became my extended family, a trio of loving but very opinionated aunts. I likened them to Flora, Fauna and Merryweather, the three fairy godmothers from Disney's *Sleeping Beauty*.

When I'd moved to Maine and decided to open Second Chance, Rose, Charlotte and Liz had been almost as thrilled as my grandmother. They were my family even though they drove me crazy sometimes. There wasn't anything I wouldn't do for them.

I trailed Rose through the workroom into the store proper, flipping on lights as we went. Mac was just coming down the stairs carrying two coffee mugs, which meant one of them was for me. He smiled at Rose. "The kettle just boiled."

"You are a darling man," she said, smiling back at him. She set Elvis down on the bottom step and he led the way up the stairs.

Mac crossed to me and handed me a cup. He was all lean, strong muscle with light brown skin, black hair cropped close to his scalp and dark eyes.

I'd left the bag of bottles and my messenger bag by the cash desk. I wrapped both hands around the pottery mug, took a sip and sighed. The coffee was strong and hot, just the way I liked it. Mr. P. got the beans from a small specialty roaster in Boston and Mac ground them fresh every day. "Thank you," I said.

"I heard what happened last night," he said. "I'm sorry I wasn't there."

"There isn't anything you could have done." I took another sip of my coffee. Just standing here with him eased the tension in my body. "Nick used to be a paramedic so he knew what he was doing."

"It still had to be awful, having someone die right in front of you."

"His name was Christopher Healy," I said. "I didn't recognize him. Do you know the name?"

Mac shook his head. "It doesn't ring any bells."

"Liam said he was involved in some kind of lawsuit with Joe Roswell."

"The developer who's building the hotel?"

I nodded. "Some other deal that went bad maybe?"

His brown eyes narrowed. "You don't think that . . . ?" He let the end of the sentence trail off.

"I don't," I said. "But Rose is convinced that Healy was poisoned. He seemed to have some kind of seizure before he collapsed. Mr. P. and I pointed out that lots of things could cause a seizure."

Mac smoothed a hand over his hair. "But you didn't convince her?"

I smiled over the rim of my mug. "It's Rose. What do you think?" I gave my head a shake. "Could we talk about something else, please? How was the auction?"

Mac had gone to Ellsworth with two of our best customers who ran a bed-and-breakfast. They had bought the house next door to theirs and were looking for furniture for it.

"It was a bust," he said. "The dining room set and the bedroom furniture they were interested in both had woodworm."

I made a face.

"I said we'd watch for pieces for them. I'm going to call Cleveland to keep his eye out, too."

"Next time I see Teresa I'll mention it to her as well," I said.

Both Cleveland and Teresa were trash pickers. They made their living out of things the rest of us put out for garbage. I regularly bought items for the shop from the two of them, everything from dishes to furniture to old LPs. We always managed to make a deal both sides were happy with.

Mac nodded. "Is Liam still coming by with the toys?"

"After last night I don't know." I unzipped my jacket. "I hope so. I'd like to get Avery started taking photos of everything."

We were listing all of the toys that had been found in one section of our website along with a short write-up about the hot lunch program. It seemed like the best way to attract the attention of collectors and nostalgic baby boomers and I was hoping that learning where the money was going would encourage potential shoppers to make a purchase. Since Avery had a creative bent and was much better with a camera than I was, I'd asked her to handle the photographs. She'd readily agreed.

"We need the images to look good in thumbnail and when they're viewed on a phone," she'd said. Then she'd waved one hand in the air. "And you don't have to think about that stuff because you have me." I'd walked away from the conversation feeling a little bit like a dinosaur.

"What's your morning look like?" I asked Mac. He was wearing jeans and a denim shirt, both splattered with paint, which told me he was most likely going to tackle a project out in the work space we'd made in the former garage.

"I found four casters that I think are going to work on that metal sorting station that you bought when the old post office in Belfast closed. And at some point I have to pick up the glass for that metal table. What about you?"

I ran down the mental checklist I'd made while eating breakfast. "I'd like to start stripping that mantel you trash-picked last month and I need to bring in a couple of boxes of picture frames for Rose to go through. I'd like to frame at least some of the pictures that were found in the hotel. I think the old black-and-white photographs would look good that way."

"I can go get those frames for you right now," Mac said.

"Thank you," I said. I took his coffee cup out of his hand and he smiled at me. We stood there looking at each other for a long moment, like some scene in a romantic comedy. Then, just like in a movie, Rose came down the stairs and the moment was over.

Mac took a step back. He motioned in the general direction of the workroom. "I'll go look for the frames."

"Umm, sure," I said.

Rose was wearing her apron and carrying her tea. I looked at my watch. It was quarter to nine. "What would you like me to do first?" she asked.

"Mac's going to bring in some of our collection of picture frames. I'd like to see if we have enough to frame all the black-and-white photos or at least all of the ones that are of the downtown. I thought they might have a better chance of selling if they were framed. We probably need at least two dozen." Along with the toys, we were also selling some of the photos that had been unearthed. Those sales would benefit the hot lunch program as well.

"Are you thinking plain frames or more ornate?" She leaned her head thoughtfully to one side and at her feet Elvis did the same.

I shrugged. "Mostly I'm thinking I hope we have enough frames that are the right size."

Rose smiled. "Elvis and I will see what I can find."

"Thank you," I said. "I'm going to hang up my coat and get another cup of coffee."

Just then Mr. P. came in from the workroom. The strap of his messenger bag was over his shoulder and his cheeks were pink. It was clear that he'd walked to the shop.

"I didn't know you were coming in this morning," I said. "We could have stopped to pick you up."

"Thank you, Sarah," he said. "It was a last-minute decision."

Something was off with him. His smile didn't reach his eyes.

Rose had noticed as well. "Is everything all right, Alf?" she asked.

"I found out this morning that an old friend of mine—Elliot Casey—is back in town. He's been here for a few weeks." He slipped the messenger bag from his shoulder and set it at his feet. "Elliot has been gone from North Harbor for most of his adult life." He pressed his lips together for a moment. "Christopher Healy is—was—his stepson."

Rose closed her eyes for a moment and shook her head. "I'm sorry," she said. She laid a hand on his arm. Mr. P. covered it with his own hand for a moment.

"So am I," I said. "Is there anything we can do?"

He nodded. "Thank you, Sarah, yes. There is something you can do."

"What is it?" I asked.

"I haven't spoken to Elliot in a long time, but I'd like to go see him to at least pay my respects and maybe there will be something I can do to help. He and his wife are living at Legacy Place."

"I'd be happy to drive you," I said. The former chocolate factory—now a seniors' apartment building—was close to the downtown core. "When do you want to go?"

"Would the end of the day work for you?"

"It would."

"Thank you," he said.

"I'm coming with you, Alf," Rose said. "While you

see your old friend there are a couple of people I'd like to catch up with."

He smiled at her. "I'd like that." He picked up the messenger bag. "I have some work to do."

Rose patted his arm again. "I'll get you a cup of tea."

Mr. P. headed out to the Angels' sunporch office trailed by Elvis. Rose and I went upstairs. I dumped my things in my office and got another cup of coffee. When I came back and picked up my phone I discovered that I had a text from Nick.

Call me first chance you get, was all it said. No "Hi, how are you?" or even "Hey, it's me." Call me. Brief and to the point.

This was not good.

Chapter 3

I called Nick and, no surprise, got his voice mail instead. I left a message saying I'd gotten his text and that I'd be at Second Chance all morning. I was in the workroom about an hour later sitting on the floor, sorting through a box of candelabra when Nick returned my call.

"Hi," I said. "You wanted to talk to me?"

"I have some questions about last night."

I got to my feet and walked over to the back door for a little more privacy. Mr. P. was in the shop taking the glass out of a couple of picture frames for Rose. "Okay, what would you like to know?"

"First of all, you know that Christopher Healy is dead?"

I nodded even though he couldn't see me. "I talked to Michelle this morning. She told me."

"Were you looking in his direction before he collapsed?" Nick asked.

"Yes."

"What did you see, exactly?"

I pictured the room from the night before. "Healy was standing at the bar. He took a drink of his coffee, then his hand started shaking. He put his other hand to his chest, just below his throat. I thought maybe he was having trouble breathing. He made a noise."

"What kind of noise?" Nick said.

"It was almost like he was choking. The coffee cup hit the floor and then he collapsed."

There was silence for a moment and I wondered if Nick was making notes. "Sarah, was there anyone around Healy?" he asked.

"No." I looked across the parking lot. Mac had the big door to the former garage open and I could see him working on the mail-sorting table. "The bartender was at the other end of the bar and there was no one else around."

I heard Nick exhale on the other end of the phone. "When we started doing CPR, do you remember Healy smelling like anything in particular?"

"What do you mean?" I said. "He smelled like coffee because I think some got spilled on his jacket when he dropped the cup, and I could still smell alcohol. I'm pretty sure it was beer. And aftershave, something with rosemary I think."

"Did you catch the scent of anything else?"

I turned away from the window. "Like what?"

"I just want to know if you smelled anything besides coffee and beer." There was a bit of an annoyed edge to his voice.

I reminded myself that Nick was most likely just doing his job. He was an investigator for the medical examiner's office. He'd worked as an EMT to put himself through college and he'd been considering going to medical school before he took the investigator's job. Christopher Healy's death could be his case now.

I closed my eyes and pulled up the memory of bending over Healy's body. "All right. Like I said, the man was wearing aftershave. I caught the scent of that. Nothing else stands out."

"Okay, thanks," he said. I heard the squeak of a chair, which likely meant he was at the police station and not his office.

"Do you have any idea how Mr. Healy died?" I asked.

"The autopsy isn't scheduled until this afternoon." I heard voices in the background. "I have to go," he said. "And I probably won't make it to The Black Bear tonight." Both Nick and I were regulars at the Thursday-night jam at the downtown pub.

"Call me if there's anything else I can do."

He said he would, and ended the call. Nick hadn't answered my question about how Christopher Healy had died. He'd just put me off by saying the autopsy wasn't until that afternoon. And why had he asked me if I'd smelled anything?

A tight knot had formed at the back of my neck and I massaged it with two fingers. Rose had insisted that Mr. Healy had been poisoned. I knew certain poisons had distinctive aromas. Most people knew that cyanide has a bitter almond scent, although Nick had once told me that some people were genetically unable to smell it. Was it possible that Nick suspected the dead man had been poisoned, too? I hoped I was wrong about that supposition. I hoped the autopsy would prove that Christopher Healy had died of natural causes.

Liam showed up about half an hour later with several boxes filled with the toys that had been on display at the reception. No one was really sure where they'd come from or how they'd ended up in the basement of the old hotel. The best guess was that they were toys that had been kept for children who were guests. Most of them were in excellent shape, and they didn't look as though they'd been played with very much.

"These are just the toys," Liam said as he set the last carton on the workbench. "I'll bring the photographs by later this afternoon or tomorrow."

"That's fine," I said. "Avery is going to start taking pictures of everything when she gets here after lunch and Rose is already sorting through picture frames."

He nodded absently. His mind was somewhere else.

"Have you talked to Michelle today?" I asked.

"What?" He gave his head a shake. "I mean no."

"You know that Christopher Healy is dead?"

"Joe told me." His eyes narrowed. "Have *you* talked to Michelle?"

I glanced at the boxes, looking for the View-Master. I'd already decided I wanted to buy it as a surprise for Mr. P. "First thing this morning," I said. "But I don't know anything more than you do. I talked to Nick as well. He said the autopsy wouldn't be done until this afternoon."

Liam stuffed his hands in his pockets. "Healy seems kind of young to have had a heart attack."

"I don't think he had a heart attack," I said. "It looked like he might have had some kind of seizure."

"So maybe a stroke."

I shrugged. "I don't know." I didn't want to say that maybe, *maybe* he'd been poisoned when all it might be was speculation on my part—and Rose's. I straightened the box closest to me, lining it up with the edge of the bench. "What happens to the lawsuit now?" I asked.

"I'm guessing this will be the end of it and Joe will be able to buy the land just the way he'd originally planned to do."

"Liam, do you have any idea why Healy showed up last night?"

His expression changed. There was a wary look in his eyes. "What do you mean?" he said.

"I mean, what was he trying to achieve? Make a scene? Embarrass Joe Roswell? They were already going to court. How did him showing up drunk like that change anything?"

"Who knows?" Liam shifted restlessly from one foot to the other. "It wasn't about money, I know that much. Joe offered more than Healy paid for the land, but he wouldn't take it."

"Where is this piece of land, anyway?"

The question got a smile from Liam. "Remember when we used to go swimming at Gibson's Point when we were kids?"

I nodded.

"Remember that cove with that private beach that we used to sneak off to?"

I grinned at him and raised an eyebrow. "You mean that you used to ditch me and sneak off to with whichever girl you were dating that week." I made quotes in the air around the word "dating."

He grinned back at me. "That's what I said. It's the piece of land overlooking the water." His phone chimed then. He pulled it out of his pocket, took a quick look at the screen and then stashed it again. "I have to go," he said. "I'll try to get back this afternoon with those photos."

I nodded. "We'll get started with these boxes."

Liam started for the back door then turned around again. "Hey, Sarah, thanks for doing this. I owe you."

I crossed my arms over my midsection and smiled at him. "I know," I said.

He rolled his eyes and he was out the door.

I pulled the nearest box closer to me and started taking out the tin cars inside. I hoped that enough people had had the chance to see the toys that there'd be lots of bids on everything. I didn't want the hot lunch program to lose out because of what had happened. It struck me that based on what Liam had said, Joe Roswell *was* likely going to benefit. He might be the only person who would.

Joe Roswell was probably going to gain from Christopher Healy's death. I didn't want to think about what that could mean.

Chapter 4

By late morning I had found four wrought-iron candelabra that we could use for a spooky table setting on the mail-sorting table once Mac brought it inside. I'd sorted out all the toys and printed out the previous day's orders from the website. I had a kink in my neck, my stomach was already growling and I'd realized that I'd forgotten to bring any lunch.

I went downstairs. Rose had been sorting frames into two piles in between customers. "Can you hold down the fort for a while?" I asked.

"Of course," she said. "It's been quiet this morning." She held up a wooden picture frame painted black and silver. "What do you think of this?"

"I like it," I said.

"There are three of them. All they need are a little cleaning and I think they'll be perfect for those photos of the front of the old hotel."

I smiled at her. "I hope the photographs bring in some money. I know not everyone had a chance to look at them last night. I was hoping the reception would generate some interest in them and in the toys."

"Don't you worry," Rose said. "I have some ideas to get people talking."

"Do I want to know what these ideas are?" I asked. If Rose said don't worry, that usually meant I probably should.

She brushed some bits of paper off the front of her flowered apron. "It's been my experience that usually you're happier when you don't."

I thought about that for a minute. "Okay," I said, backing toward the door. "I have bail money if you need it."

"You're so funny," she said, giving me an indulgent smile.

I waved at Mr. P. as I went past the Angels' office. I found Mac in the old garage, one arm resting on the top of his head, a look of aggravation on his face as he contemplated the mail-sorting table. It had a noticeable list to one side.

"Problem?" I asked.

"Yes," he said, exhaling loudly. "Three of the casters slipped right on to the bottom of the table legs, but I can't get the fourth one to fit no matter what I do. I measured; it should fit, but it won't slide into place."

I leaned forward and studied the recalcitrant caster. For the moment the leg was balanced on top of it, which is what gave the table its cant to the left. I straightened up and ran my fingers around the corner of the table-top. Mac watched without saying anything. The metal was smooth under my fingers. I raised my arm in the air, pulled my fingers into a fist and brought the heel of my hand down hard on the corner of the table. The leg popped smoothly into the top of the caster.

I looked at Mac. He looked at me. Then he started to laugh. "That was luck," he said, pointing a finger at me.

I put a hand to my chest and tried to look chagrined. "No, it wasn't. It was physics. I estimated the tensile strength of the metal and found the best point to apply a downward strike without causing the leg to shear to the side."

"Tensile strength," Mac said.

I nodded solemnly. "Is there anything else I could do for you?" I asked. "Deadlift a bed frame? Leap a tall building in a single bound?"

He shook his head, still laughing. "No. I'm good."

I pointed over my shoulder. "I'm headed to Mc-Namara's. You want anything?"

"Nope," he said. "Still all good here."

I started for my SUV, walking backward across the parking lot so I could still see Mac's face. "You really should read up about tensile strength," I said.

He came and stood in the open garage doorway. "I should," he said. His eyes never left my face.

I glanced over my shoulder then shifted my gaze right back to Mac again. I held out both hands. "Physics is kind of my jam."

He laughed again. "That's good to know, in case I have any trouble when I'm reading up on tensile strength."

I'd reached the SUV and I pulled the keys out of my pocket. "If you have any problems with anything physics-ish, I'm your woman."

"You definitely are," he said.

Color flooded my face. I got behind the wheel and started the car. Mac and I had been dancing around each other for the last month, ever since he'd come back from settling his connections in Boston. I knew one of these days one of us was going to have to make a move.

It was quiet when I got to McNamara's. Glenn was behind the counter, setting a tray of crackle-top muffins into the glass display case. "Apple cinnamon?" I asked.

He nodded. "With brown sugar topping."

"I'm going to need one of those, for sure," I said.

He glanced back at the oversize round clock on the wall behind him then put two fingers to his temple. "And let me guess, a chicken salad sandwich with cheddar and extra tomato."

"Your psychic abilities are amazing," I said with a smile.

"I'm not done." Glenn put two fingers back to the side of his face. "And a large coffee."

"Am I that predictable?" I asked as I handed over my stainless steel travel mug.

He smiled. "I like to think of it as consistency." He relayed my sandwich order to the back and then poured my coffee, handing the cup over the counter to me.

"I have a question for you," I said.

"Yes, that was a picture of me. Yes, I had hair like Kurt Cobain."

I stared at him and I think my mouth hung open a little. "How did you know I was going to ask that?"

Glenn brushed flour off the front of his apron. "Because Nick was in earlier and told me that you and Rose had been debating whether you'd found my class photo last night. I actually appreciate your insistence that there was no way that I ever had a grunge phase."

"Hey, I went through a phase where I wore embroidered jeans and a newsboy cap everywhere and I'm very grateful there is no photographic evidence out there."

Glenn laughed.

I gave him an appraising look as I sipped my coffee. "You know, you could buy that photo and no one would ever have to see it again."

"When are you going to start taking bids?" he asked.

"Sunday, if all goes well. Just check the store's website."

"Don't worry, I will," he said. He hesitated for a moment. "Nick told me what happened last night. I'm sorry."

"Me, too," I said.

Glenn grabbed a set of metal tongs and picked up one of the apple muffins. He put it in a small waxed paper bag and set it on the counter. "Healy had been in here a few times. You heard he bought that piece of land down by Gibson's Point?"

I nodded. Clayton McNamara lived close to the point. "Liam told me."

"So you know Joe Roswell was suing him over that?"

"I know about the lawsuit, but Liam didn't really fill in the details. Why was Roswell suing?"

One of the kitchen staff came out and handed Glenn my sandwich. He put it in a paper bag along with the apple muffin.

"Joe had been trying to buy that piece of property to develop some kind of a private getaway for affluent city people," he said.

"Wait a minute. I thought that whole stretch of shoreline was washing into the bay. That beach was closed years ago." I handed Glenn the money for my lunch.

"You're not wrong," he said, giving me back my change. "It seemed the land wasn't stable enough to support any kind of building. But do you know who Robb Gorham is?"

I nodded, wondering how the building contractor was connected to the story.

"It seems that he's developed some type of system they use in parts of Asia to build support into terrain like that. It's a new type of geo-textile fabric with fibers that penetrate the soil, like the roots of native grasses, and hold it in place."

"Do you think it could work?" I asked. I knew soil erosion was a big problem in several areas along the coastline.

"Honestly, I don't know," Glenn said. "The supposed advantage of this fabric is that it's made from soy pulp left over from the tofu-making process, if you can believe it. No chemicals seeping into the ground or the water. And the important thing is that Joe is convinced it would work."

I was having a bit of trouble seeing how a fabric made out of what were essentially tofu leftovers could shore up an unstable piece of ground. On the other hand, silk fiber was stronger than steel and had been used in early bullet-resistant vests. Maybe soy fiber was just as durable. "So where did the lawsuit come from?"

"Healy swept in and bought the land out from under Joe. He said he was going to turn it into a nature preserve. Joe filed a lawsuit claiming he had a purchase agreement in principal, which Healy knew." Glenn shrugged. "You know what they say about verbal agreements. They're not worth the paper they're not written on."

I picked up the bag with my lunch. "What about the original owner of the property? How does he or she connect to the lawsuit?"

"She. Elderly woman well into her nineties. There's some indication she really wasn't clear on who she was selling to."

I made a face. "Messy."

"Maybe a little less so now that Healy is dead," Glenn said.

The door behind me opened and three women came in. I thanked Glenn for the food and left. I thought about what he'd said: That Christopher Healy's death had made life a little less messy for both Joe Roswell and Robb Gorham. I hoped that neither one of them had done anything to nudge things in that direction.

Chapter 5

When I got back to the shop Charlotte had arrived for her shift. Nick's mom was a former school principal. It was from her that he got his stubborn streak and his kind heart. She wrapped me in a hug. "I heard that you and Nicolas tried to save that man last night."

"I just wish we'd succeeded," I said.

"You tried," she said as she tied her apron. "That will matter to his family."

At four thirty I drove Mr. P. and Rose over to Legacy Place so Mr. P. could visit his old friend. Mac had finished cleaning the old table from the post office and we'd carried it into the shop. Avery had set the table with a plain white tablecloth and heavy white china plates and bowls that had been in the store for at least six months. She used plum-colored napkins and crystal goblets at each place. Down the center of the table she'd arranged small white pumpkins around a mismatched collection of silver candlesticks holding plum-colored tapers that coordinated with the napkins. Scattered around them were bright orange seed pods from a Chinese lantern plant. The effect was fall-like without being too traditional.

"That's beautiful, Avery," I said. "You have a wonderful eye for color. Orange and plum don't sound like they would work together, but they do."

"Thanks," she said, brushing her hair back behind one ear. "I'm going to start working on the photos of those old toys. Do you care if I get a little creative with them?"

I shook my head. "I trust you," I said.

More often than not Avery was the one who came up with the idea for the front window display. She had decorated the shop's window for Halloween with her version of a romantic dinner, which included a cozy round table set for two with a stark white tablecloth, black and pewter placemats, pewter plates and black glass wine goblets. The centerpiece was made with branches she'd spray-painted black and festooned with black crystals, along with white feathers and tiny black and white butterflies all arranged in two flower vases she had spray-painted black. The romantic couple holding hands and gazing into each other's eyes were two full-size skeletons—plastic, not real. And because it was Avery, they both looked very dashing in black silk top hats.

I parked the SUV in one of the visitor spots in the parking lot at Legacy Place. The brick building was the former Gardner Chocolate factory—"A little bite of bliss in a little gold box." Back in the early 1990s, the company had built a state-of-the-art manufacturing facility just on the outskirts of North Harbor. In the following twenty years the old building had had a number of incarnations. About four years ago the Gardners had turned the space into an apartment complex for senior citizens. At one time Rose had lived at Legacy Place, which she still referred to as "Shady Pines."

Mr. P. had spoken to his old friend on the phone so Elliot was expecting us. He was waiting when we got off the elevators. "It's so good to see you, Alfred," he said. "It's been too many years." The two men shook hands, leaning in and clapping each other on the back.

Elliot Casey was of average height, which made him a bit taller than Mr. P. He had thinning white hair, a lived-in face and pale blue eyes behind wire-rimmed glasses. I tried to picture the two of them as teenaged football players and couldn't quite get there.

"I'm sorry this visit isn't under better circumstances," Mr. P. said. "But I am very glad to see you after all these years." He turned toward Rose and me. "Elliot these are my friends Rose Jackson and Sarah Grayson."

"Hello," he said, smiling at both of us.

Rose took Mr. Casey's hand in both of hers. "I'm sorry about your stepson," she said.

He nodded. "Thank you so much."

I touched Mr. P.'s arm. "Rose and I are going to visit a couple of her friends. We'll be back to get you in about an hour, if that's all right."

He nodded. "That will be fine, my dear."

"We're in 206," his old friend said. "Down this hall and turn right. And you don't need to rush. Alfred and I have a lot of catching up to do."

Rose had pushed the down button for the elevator. We got on and once the doors closed I turned to her.

"Where do we start?" I said. I didn't believe for a moment that she was looking to catch up with anyone. When Rose had lived at Legacy Place her main complaint was that all everyone did was complain about what had stopped working and what had started sprouting hair. I knew this was a fact-finding mission.

To her credit Rose didn't even try to deny it. "When you're looking for information in this place, you want it straight from the horse's mouth, as it were. That means Tabitha Gray."

We got off the elevator on the main floor and I followed Rose down a long hallway to the back section of the building. Rose stopped in front of an apartment door and rummaged in her bag.

"We're not breaking in, are we?" I asked.

She shot me a look. "Of course not! You've been spending too much time with Liz. She's a bad influence. You're getting very suspicious." She eyed the space between my eyebrows. "And that kind of thing will give you wrinkles." She pulled a small white cardboard box tied with twine from her purse.

"What's that?"

"Brown sugar fudge. You don't come on fact-finding missions empty-handed."

She smoothed the front of her cranberry red sweater. I smoothed the space between my eyebrows with one finger while she wasn't looking.

Tabitha Gray turned out to be a tiny, round woman in an oversize white T-shirt and cropped black yoga pants. Her hair, styled in a bob with bangs, was dyed a vibrant shade of magenta. Avery would have loved it.

"Rose Jackson, what on earth are you doing here!" she said when she answered the door.

"I brought you some fudge," Rose said, holding out the cardboard box.

"Peanut butter or brown sugar?"

"Brown sugar."

"The good stuff," Tabitha said. "Well, whatever it is you're looking to find out you might as well come in for a cup. Lucky for you I just put the kettle on." She looked pointedly at me.

I wondered if I was going to be sent to sit in the lobby. I wondered if I'd at least get a piece of fudge. The answer turned out to be no on both counts.

"Tabitha, this is Sarah Grayson," Rose said.

"Hello, Mrs. Gray," I said, hoping I'd addressed her properly.

She looked me over not even trying to hide her curiosity. "You're Isabel's granddaughter."

I nodded. "Yes, I am."

"How is your grandmother?"

"She's well, thank you," I said.

"She's still married to that young piece of arm candy."

John Scott was a young piece of arm candy? "Umm, yes, ma'am."

"Well, good for her!" Tabitha said with a hoot of laughter. "Why get stuck with an old one when you can have a newer model with all the options." I heard the whistle of a teakettle from inside the apartment. She turned and disappeared inside. "Come in, the both of you," she called. "None of us are getting any younger."

Tabitha Gray's apartment was impeccably clean, filled with lots of light and lots of furniture. She led us through the living room into the small kitchen and gestured at the chrome table and chairs. "Have a seat."

Rose pulled out a chair at one end of the table and I took a seat at the other, assuming—since there was a teacup in front of the center chair—that the third place was Tabitha's.

While she busied herself with the teapot, I surreptitiously looked over the chrome dining room set. It was a 1950s vintage blue cracked-ice table with four chairs. The chrome shone, there were no marks or stains on the deep blue Formica top and no rips or cuts in the matching vinyl-covered chairs. I would have loved to have had the set in the store. I would have loved to have had it in my own kitchen.

Turns out I wasn't quite as furtive as I thought. Tabitha set a cup on the table in front of Rose and one at my place. I got to my feet and brought over a small lacquered black tray that held a cream pitcher, sugar bowl and three spoons. Tabitha eyed me as she poured my tea. "You like my furniture."

"Yes, I do," I said, running my hand over the smooth Formica tabletop.

"Sears Roebuck catalog, nineteen fifty-three," she said.

"You've taken beautiful care of it."

"No point in having nice things if you don't take care of them." She took the teapot over to the stove and came back to the table.

Rose added milk and a little sugar to her tea. She took a sip and smiled with pleasure. "Tabitha, is that—"

"—the good stuff? Damn straight it is. Canadian Red Rose tea. Last month I brought fourteen boxes back across the lines." She grinned like she'd perpetrated a great ruse.

Rose insisted that the Canadian version of Red Rose tea was better than what was sold in our stores. She'd been tickled when I'd inadvertently bought a casket filled with boxes of the Canadian product several weeks ago. I'd given it all to her because I was a coffee drinker. All tea tasted the same to me.

Tabitha took a sip from her own cup then turned to look at Rose. "You didn't come down here with a box of fudge just for a cup of tea and the pleasure of my company. What are you looking to find out?"

"The new people on the second floor, Elliot Casey and his wife, Nora. What can you tell me about them?"

Tabitha gave a snort of laughter. "If you're looking for information about them you wasted a trip and that fudge. They haven't been here a month, and they pretty much keep to themselves." She made a face as though she disapproved.

"What do you know about Nora Casey's son?"

I tried my own tea. It was hot and strong and, as tea went, pretty good.

A sly smile spread across Tabitha's face. "Christopher," she said. "Not exactly work brittle."

I'd heard that expression before. It was a way of saying that Christopher Healy was a bit lazy.

"What makes you say that?" Rose asked.

"Well this is all secondhand, you have to understand."

Rose nodded.

"You remember Cora Haining?" Tabitha said.

"Corner apartment. Third floor."

"Her oldest went to college with young Mr. Healy." Tabitha gave a slight shrug as she took another drink of her tea. "He owns three restaurants now. Vegan. Cora's daddy must be rolling in his grave." She shot me a sideways glance. "He was a pig farmer."

I nodded, which was all that seemed to be required.

"And Christopher Healy?" Rose prompted.

"The boy—well, I should say man because he wasn't a child anymore—seemed to go from one all-consuming idea to the next. The latest thing was some kind of nature park out by Gibson's Point. Cora was pretty certain that would have gone the same as him going to law school, getting his PhD in art history and running a coffee roaster. He didn't have any stick-to-it-ness, it seemed."

Rose's gaze flicked across the table at me for a moment. "What did he do for a living?"

"There's the rub," Tabitha said. "His father died about two years ago and the young man inherited a good chunk of money, from what I was told. Takes away the incentive to get up in the morning and put in a day's work if you ask me, although it didn't seem to affect his sister in the same way."

"Christopher Healy has a sister?" Rose said.

"Half sister. Chloe. From a brief relationship the father had before he married Nora. Nora was like a mother to that girl. But Christopher and his sister had some kind of falling-out. It seems Chloe wanted to use some of the money from the estate for a scholarship in her father's name. Christopher wasn't interested and Nora sided with him." Tabitha shook her head in disapproval.

If she was right—and I had no reason to think she wasn't—that inheritance explained where Healy had gotten the money to buy that piece of land out from under Joe Roswell. And to defend himself in the subsequent lawsuit. If she was also right about Healy's lack of stick-to-it-ness, I wondered if the nature preserve would have ever become a reality.

We spent the next few minutes getting all the news from the building. I found myself amazed by how many things there were that could be cut out of or off of the human body.

I checked my watch and then caught Rose's eye. "We have to get going, Tabitha," she said. "Thank you for everything."

I got to my feet and carried the cups over to the sink.

Tabitha walked us to the door.

"It was a pleasure to meet you, Mrs. Gray," I said.

"I hear when people get too feeble or too dotty to stay in their own home you'll come in and clear the place out," she said.

I nodded. "We do."

Tabitha looked around the living room. There was a vintage brass dolphin clock on a side table that I would have loved to get a better look at. "Do you get good money for everything?" she asked.

"As much as we can."

"I might call you someday," she said.

"We'd be happy to help."

"That's good to know. But don't go holding your breath."

"Yes, ma'am," I said.

Rose and I walked back to the elevator. "Well, that was interesting," I said. "Do you think she was right about Christopher Healy?"

"Yes, dear, I do," she said. "Tabitha Gray may be the biggest gossip in this place but her information is above reproach." She reached over and pushed the up arrow. "I'm not sure I learned anything that suggests who poisoned that young man, though."

I'd wondered earlier what this fishing expedition was for. Now I knew. I opened my mouth to say something and shut it again. Until she had unarguable proof to the contrary, Rose was going to believe that Christopher Healy had been poisoned.

The elevator arrived, we both got in and I pressed the button for the second floor.

"Go ahead," Rose said.

"Go ahead where?" I said, turning my head to look at her. "The elevator just got started."

She pursed her lips for a moment. "I mean, go ahead and say whatever it was that you wanted to say. I can take it."

I sighed. "All I was going to say is that you don't know that Christopher Healy was poisoned."

"Fair enough," she said. "But you don't know that he wasn't."

It was impossible to win against Rose's logic. It was a lesson I could never seem to learn.

"I will concede that," I said. "Where do we go from here?"

The elevator dinged and the doors opened on the second floor of the building. "We go get Alfred," Rose said.

"Hello again," Elliot Casey said when he opened the apartment door. He looked at me, smiling just a little. "Sarah, I apologize. I didn't recognize your name when Alfred introduced us. Please, could you come in for a minute? My wife, Nora, would like to meet you."

I glanced at Rose who nodded encouragingly. "All right," I said.

Nora Healy-Casey was sitting next to Mr. P. on the living room sofa. She stood up when Rose and I came into the room. She was tall and slender in black pants and an ice blue sweater. Her dark hair, streaked with silver, was pulled into a smooth French twist and she was pale but composed. She offered her hand to Rose.

"I'm very sorry about your son," Rose said.

"Thank you," Nora said. She turned to me. "Sarah, I wanted to thank you for trying to save Christopher." Her eyes shone with unshed tears.

I had to swallow before I could speak. "It wasn't just me. Nick . . . Nick Elliot . . . it was the two of us . . . he's trained as a paramedic. I promise you he did everything he could. I'm sorry . . . we weren't successful."

She caught one of my hands in both of hers. They were very cold. "So am I, but at least I know someone tried to help him."

Mr. P. had gotten to his feet. Elliot Casey smiled at his friend. "Alfred, I can't tell you how good it's been to see you."

"For me as well," Mr. P. said. He turned to Nora. "If there's anything you need, please ask."

"I will, Alfred," she said. "Please, come back for another visit."

"You have my promise on that," he said.

We said our good-byes and headed for the elevator. Mr. P. was quiet, seemingly lost in thought. Rose looked worried, lines pulling at the corner of her eyes.

"Mr. P., do you mind me asking how long you and Elliot have been friends?" I said as we rode down to the lobby. I was genuinely curious and I hoped the question would help lighten the mood a little.

"Of course not, Sarah," he said. "It's longer than you've been alive. We actually met in Scouts."

"You were a Boy Scout?"

"Alfred was an Eagle Scout," Rose said with a note of pride in her voice.

"Elliot was as well," Mr. P. added.

"I had no idea," I said. I probably shouldn't have been surprised. Mr. P. was very resourceful.

The elevator doors opened and he gestured that Rose and I should step out ahead of him. "It's not really the kind of thing that comes up in day-to-day conversation," he said.

"Neil Armstrong was an Eagle Scout," I said. "It's a big deal."

Mr. P. smiled then. "I'm flattered that you're impressed, my dear."

"Did you and Elliot go to school together?" I asked.

"Yes and no," he said as we started across the parking lot toward the car. "We were never in the same class. Elliot is actually a year and a half younger. But we did play football together. He was one of my wide receivers."

"One of your wide receivers?" I stopped walking. "Mr. P., did you play quarterback?"

"I did," he said. "We went ten and oh in my senior year."

I stared at him. Just when I thought I knew the man, I discovered I didn't. "How can I not know this?" I exclaimed.

Rose studied me over the top of her glasses. "Perhaps you need to start paying a little more attention," she said with just a touch of reproach in her voice.

I nodded slowly. "Perhaps I do," I said.

Mr. P. told me more about his high school football career as we drove home.

"Did you play in college?" I asked.

"No," he said from the backseat. "I could see the writing on the wall. I wasn't big enough to succeed at that level."

"I don't know about that." I looked at him in the rearview mirror. "I have a feeling you could succeed at pretty much anything you set your mind to."

"I appreciate the vote of confidence," he said. "What I'd like to succeed at right now is to find a way to help Elliot and Nora. I feel helpless."

"Losing a child is about the worst thing that can happen to you," Rose said in a quiet voice. We exchanged a look.

I knew she was thinking about Gram. I'd sometimes wondered how my grandmother had managed to get up in the morning after my dad died. He had been her only child. I was just five years old when it happened and it had been devastating for me. Finally, a couple of years ago, I'd asked her how she'd done it.

"It was the hardest thing I've ever done," she'd said. "I felt like I was drowning. But I wouldn't have been honoring your father's life if I'd given up. And then, of course, there was you. If I needed a reason to go on with my life, all I needed to do was look at you." She'd folded me into a hug.

I felt a pang of sadness for Nora Casey.

Silence settled in the car and I glanced at Mr. P. in the rearview mirror again. "I think you are helping," I said. "It was pretty obvious that seeing you again today meant a lot to Elliot."

"I hope so," Mr. P. said. "It meant a lot to me."

I waited for Rose to agree with me but she didn't say anything and when I looked over at her I could see that she was lost in thought, staring out the windshield seemingly at nothing. I knew exactly what that look meant.

Chapter 6

When we got to the house Mr. P. thanked me once again for driving. "Anytime," I said. "I mean it."

I'd left Elvis in the apartment when I'd come to pick up Rose and Alfred. When I unlocked the front door I found him sitting on one of the stools at the counter. He looked over at his empty food dish and then looked pointedly at me with a loud meow thrown in for good measure in case I didn't get his point.

"Yes, I know you're hungry," I said, stopping to scratch the top of his head. "Just let me wash my hands and I'll get your supper."

"Mrrr," he said and it sounded like a question to me.

"Everything went fine," I said. "Although I did learn way more about warts and cysts and carbuncles and where on the human body they turn up than I ever wanted to know."

The cat made a face.

"That's exactly how I felt," I said.

I washed my hands, fed Elvis and went to have a shower while he ate. When I got back to the bedroom he was sitting on the chair by the bedroom window washing his face. "Does this mean we've given up the pretense that's my chair and not yours?" I asked.

He lifted his head for a moment, stared unblinkingly at me and then went back to cleaning behind his left ear.

I pulled on my favorite Aerosmith T-shirt and wiggled into my black skinny jeans. Elvis watched me hop around the room with what seemed to be a glint of amusement in his green eyes as I pulled them up.

"They shrank in the dryer," I said, wondering why I felt I had to justify myself to a cat.

I brushed my hair and left it down, fished my red Converse out of the closet and set the timer on the TV so Elvis could get his *Jeopardy!* fix. I sat on the footstool to put on my shoes and reached over to stroke his soft black fur. He nuzzled my hand and I thought for probably the one-millionth time how lucky I was that Sam had conned me into taking the battle-scarred cat.

Sam Newman owned The Black Bear pub. He had also been my father's closest friend and he'd made a point of staying in my life after my dad died. Elvis—named for his apparent love of the King of Rock and Roll's music—had just appeared one day around the harbor front, depending, as it were, on the kindness of strangers, Sam, of course, being the kindest. The next thing I knew, I had a Jeopardy-loving, backseat driving roommate with an uncanny ability to tell when people were lying.

I kissed the top of Elvis's head and stood up. "No wild parties," I said. "I won't be late."

He murped a good-bye and focused his attention on the TV.

Jess and Liam already had a table when I got to The Black Bear. The place was always packed for Thursday-night jam. The jam as everyone called it, had started off as just something to do in the off-season once most of the tourists were gone, but it had proved so popular Sam had caved to the pressure and kept the gathering going year-round. It was always Sam and his band, but anyone with a guitar or a bass who wanted to sit in for a song and a set was welcome. Nick had played with them more than once. He always downplayed his skills, but he'd been playing guitar since he was a teenager and he was good.

I slid onto the chair Jess had saved for me. The two of us had been friends since she answered the ad for a college roommate that I'd stuck on a bulletin board. She'd actually taken down the ad so no one else would answer it before she could. In our last year of university we'd lived in a tiny one-room cabin and were still friends at the end of the year. I'd always taken that as a sign that we'd be friends forever.

"Hi," she said with a smile. She was wearing jeans, chunky-heeled brown boots and a caramel-colored cowl-neck sweater. Her long dark hair was pulled into a braid over one shoulder. She leaned behind me, scanned the room and caught the eye of a waiter who started for us. "I'm guessing you haven't eaten," she said.

"Thank you," I said. "No, I haven't."

When the waiter got to the table I ordered the turkey chili. Once she was on her way back to the kitchen

I grabbed the last two tortilla chips from the basket Jess and Liam had been sharing.

"Are you really okay?" Jess asked. I'd talked to her briefly on the phone before I'd left to pick up Rose and Mr. P. for the visit to Legacy Place.

"I am," I said. "I feel a bit sad, but I don't think there's anything else Nick and I could have done. So let's talk about something else. Tell me how your day was."

"Better than the last couple of days," she said. "I was beginning to think I've been hexed. Tuesday my sewing machine jammed and I had to pretty much promise Lee Leigh my firstborn to get her to fix it on short notice."

Lee Leigh—her first and last names really were the same—could fix anything that had a motor and even some things that didn't. She was somewhere between forty and sixty; town scuttlebutt wasn't exactly clear on that. However, she worked when she felt like it and no amount of begging, wheedling or outright bribery would change her mind.

"Then I dropped a container of tiny, tiny crystals I was using on a wedding veil. I didn't get them all up off the floor. They're still crunching under our feet. It's like walking on Rice Krispies. And then yesterday right after lunch this couple—or maybe they weren't a couple, I don't know—got into an argument out in front of the store. I don't know what they were fighting about, but I was about to call the police when she suddenly shoved him, yelled something like, 'Eat dirt and die!' and stalked away. I hope she's okay."

"Eat dirt and die?" Liam said. He looked at me.

"I'm pretty sure you said that to Nick a couple of times, but you were about eight."

"Did you recognize them?" I asked

She shook her head. "No. But he was wearing a really great 1970s vintage tan-colored car coat with a wide black plush notched lapel collar. I had one of those coats. I got it in a thrift store in Bangor. And she had a pair of hand-painted high-tops. Ladybugs, I think."

"Wait a minute. You could tell the design on someone's shoes from inside your store?" Liam said. He looked skeptical.

Jess eyed him as though he'd just suggested Tom Brady couldn't throw a touchdown pass.

I leaned forward into Liam's line of sight. "Jess. Shoes," I said, holding up both hands as though the connection was obvious because it should have been. "It's her superpower, Liam. She probably knows what size those high-tops were."

"Six, maybe six and a half," Jess immediately said. "Whoever she was, she had tiny feet."

The waiter came back then with a big bowl of chili and a wedge of corn bread, butter melting on the top. She set the food in front of me and smiled. "Could I get you anything else?" she asked.

"No, thank you, this is wonderful," I said. My stomach growled, loudly, as if to emphasize my words.

"Actually, you could bring another order of tortilla chips and salsa, please," Liam said. He made a circular motion over the table with his index finger. "And this is all my check," he said.

The waiter nodded. "I'll be right back."

"Thank you," I mumbled around a mouthful of corn bread.

"Yes, thank you," Jess said. "Not that this lets you out of the whole sweeping thing."

Liam smiled at her. "I wasn't trying to get out of anything."

I looked sideways at Jess and held up one hand. "Number one, what is the 'sweeping thing'? And number two, for future reference my brother rubs his left eyebrow when he lies."

"I do not," Liam said hotly, but I noticed he immediately dropped his hand over the top of his beer glass.

"Yes, you do," I said. "You've been doing that since *you* were eight." I turned back to Jess again. "The sweeping thing?"

"The boardwalk is a mess," she said. "It's mostly dust and bits of construction debris from the work site and it's getting tracked all the way down to the end. First of all, it looks awful; and second, that mess gets tracked into my store and everyone else's."

"I thought the boardwalk was supposed to be swept twice a week during construction?" I dunked a chunk of corn bread in my chili.

"Three times a week, actually," Jess said. "I complained, but I've been getting the runaround."

"And I'm sorry about that," Liam said. "I promise it *will* be swept tomorrow, even if I have to do it myself."

Jess grinned and leaned sideways, bumping him with her shoulder. "Nice to know there are real-world perks to being your pretend girlfriend."

The waiter returned then with the chips and salsa.

"Thank you," Jess said, scooping up what seemed to be a third of the bowl of salsa with one chip.

"Are you two still carrying on with that ruse?" I said.

Rose, Liz and Charlotte had spent the better part of a year trying to get Nick and I together. To them it seemed like the perfect happy ending. They'd tried just about everything short of wrapping me in a big red bow and depositing me on Nick's doorstep, and they probably would have done that if they could have figured out how to get me to stand still long enough to tie the ribbon.

Nick and I had come to realize that there just wasn't any romance between us. He'd been in my life as far back as I could remember and I had had a crush on him when we were teenagers, but that had flamed out long ago. I would have done anything for him: climbed the proverbial mountain, given him a kidney, punched anyone who hurt him in the throat, but as Jess had so eloquently put it, he didn't melt the elastic in my underwear.

So Rose and her cronies had given up on my love life and turned their meddling instincts instead to Liam's romantic life. It had sounded like great fun to me, but Liam had done an end run around them and convinced Jess to go along with the pretense that the two of them were dating.

"Oh c'mon, Sarah," Liam said. "You know what they're like. They've decided I'm getting close to my 'best before' date."

I laughed. "Okay, that had to have come from Liz."

He nodded.

"All three of them are smart," I said. "They're going to figure out what you're up to."

"All I need is to get through the next month. After that I won't be here full-time and Jess and I can 'break up.'"

I looked at Jess. "I know why he's doing this. I still don't get why you are."

She shrugged. "I don't know. It's just that he's so cute when he begs." She smiled at Liam and he smiled back.

People started to clap then and I looked over to see Vince Kennedy, carrying his guitar, headed for the small stage, followed by Sam and the rest of The Hairy Bananas. Sam caught my eye and smiled and I waved at him. Vince started playing the first few notes of Eric Clapton's "Wonderful Tonight" and the place got very quiet. It was probably my favorite of all the songs the band did, perfectly suited to Sam's voice. I leaned against Jess and let the music wrap around me.

By the time the band's first set was over my throat was dry and the back of my neck was damp with sweat.

"We're gonna take a little break, but we'll be back," Sam said. He got to his feet and looked in my direction, raising his eyebrows.

"I'm just going to talk to Sam for a minute," I said to Jess. "I'll be right back."

She nodded. Liam was already two tables away, talking to Glenn McNamara. I raised a hand in hello to Glenn and then made my way over to Sam.

Sam Newman was tall and lean in jeans and a dark blue henley. His shaggy hair was a mix of blonde and white, more white these days, and he had a close-cropped beard.

I hugged him. "You sounded so good," I said.

"I think the credit goes to the instrument, not the musician," he said, indicating the guitar leaning against the stool he'd just gotten up from. The guitar was a handmade Bourgeois Slope D steel string with a spruce top and mahogany sides, neck and back. The fingerboard and bridge were ebony. It was a beautiful instrument. Sam had bought it from me a little over a month ago and had been playing it pretty much steadily since them.

"You're way too modest."

Sam smiled. "And you're biased." He studied me for a moment. "I heard about last night," he said, his smile fading.

"I think everyone has by now. You didn't know Christopher Healy by any chance, did you?" I asked.

He shook his head. "I didn't. I knew Joe Roswell was suing him over a piece of land, but that's all."

"That piece of land out by Gibson's Point; do you really think Joe—or anyone for that matter—could build some kind of inn or hotel there?"

"I don't think anyone could build an outhouse on that piece of land," Sam said. "At least not one that I'd want to set foot inside. The bay has been wearing away that stretch of shoreline since I was a boy."

Vince Kennedy moved past us carrying a cup of coffee. "Hey, Sarah," he said with a smile.

I smiled back at him. "Hi, Vince."

"Liam's not getting involved in that whole thing, is he?" Sam asked.

"Not as far as I know," I said. "Why?"

"You know about this whole idea that the land can be anchored with some kind of fiber network?"

I nodded. "Uh-huh."

"Look," he said. "I've had some tofu that's been a little chewy, but I don't see how you can make a substrate from what's essentially fermented bean curd that will support a three-story building."

Put that way, it did make the whole project seem a little unrealistic.

"Apparently Mr. Roswell does," I said.

Sam shrugged. "Well, Robb Gorham is involved in this and I wouldn't trust him as far as I could throw him. His whole family can stretch the truth so thin you can see through it."

I had chip crumbs on the front of my T-shirt. I brushed them off. "As far as I know, the only project Liam is involved in is this whole waterfront development. But I appreciate the warning." I smiled at him. "I'll let you get back to your adoring fans."

"From your mouth to the big guy's ear, kiddo," he said.

I made my way back to the table, dropped onto my chair and pulled one leg up underneath me.

"My pretend boyfriend is flirting with another woman," Jess said. She pointed across the room to where Liam was talking to Jane Evans. Whatever Liam was saying to her seemed to be good. Jane was smiling and nodding her head.

"I think your pretend romance is safe," I said. "Gram and Liz roped both Jane and Liam into their project to save the sunflower window from the old library. That's probably what they're talking about."

"Do you think they can raise enough money to keep the window from going to Singapore?" she asked.

"Gram and Liz," I said holding up two fingers. "Neither one of them takes no for an answer very well."

"They're both pretty kick-ass," Jess said. Something caught her attention then. She leaned forward, then smiled and nodded her head. "Six and a half, definitely."

I had no idea what she was talking about. "Six and a half what?" I felt like I was having a conversation with Rose.

"Those ladybug high-tops. They're definitely a size six and a half."

I stared at her. "Wait a second, is the 'eat dirt and die' woman here?"

Jess nodded. "Uh-huh. She's on her way to the bar. Right over there." She gestured to a spot left of Liam and Jane Evans. "See? Black pants, white shirt, dark hair, ladybug high-tops."

I leaned forward, scanned the crowd and caught sight of the woman. Black pants, white shirt, dark hair, ladybug high-tops. "Wait a minute. That's the woman?" I said. "You're sure?"

Jess nodded, frowning at my questions. "I'm sure. Why?"

I slumped against the back of my chair. "Jess, that's the bartender from last night."

"Seriously?"

"Seriously."

"It's a small place." She shrugged. "You were at that reception last night and now you're here."

"I know," I said. I watched the woman move behind the bar.

"What's going on?" Jess asked. Her head was propped on her hand, elbow on the chair back.

"She knew him."

"You mean the man who died."

I nodded. "Yes. I saw them argue before she brought him a cup of coffee. It wasn't the type of polite refusal you see when a bartender cuts someone off who's had too much to drink. She was angry."

"So why does it matter? Do you think there was something suspicious about the guy's death?"

When I didn't immediately answer her eyes widened. "That is what you think, isn't it?"

I blew out a breath. "It's what Rose thinks."

"Is it what you think?"

I remembered how Nick had evaded my question about the cause of Christopher Healy's death. "I'm not sure," I hedged.

Vince Kennedy was passing close to our table. Jess caught his eye, smiled and beckoned him over. "Who's the woman over there behind the bar?" she asked. "Dark hair, red lipstick." She pointed with one finger. "Right there at the end."

"That's Cassie," he said. "I don't know her last name. Why do you want to know?"

"I saw some guy arguing with her out in front of my shop a couple of days ago. He seemed pretty mad. I just wanted to make sure she's okay."

"From what I hear, Cassie's pretty good at taking

care of herself. She was working demolition at the old hotel and hoping to get on with a crew to learn dry-wall and crack-filling on another of Joe Roswell's projects, but it doesn't look like that one's going to get off the ground—at least not this year."

"I haven't seen her around here before," I said.

Vince glanced over at the bar. "Sam just hired her for a few shifts." One hand tapped against the side of his leg. Vince's hands or feet were always moving. It was as if he was so full of music it just kept spilling out. "He knew her dad. You know he's kind of a soft touch. Cassie has a little kid and a husband who was in a pretty bad car accident. Money's kind of tight for them, especially since that chance to learn a trade fell through for her."

He had to be talking about the project connected with the lawsuit.

"Thanks," Jess said.

Vince smiled. "Hey, no problem. Most of the time the boardwalk is pretty safe, but there are a few people half a bubble off plumb hanging around sometimes."

Jess laughed. "Tell me about it."

Over on the small stage Sam had picked up his guitar.

"Showtime," Vince said, heading over to join him.

Liam came back to his seat, swinging one leg over the back of his chair, just as Sam and Vince were starting to play. The second set was just as good as the first and I found myself wishing Nick were with us.

By the time Sam thanked everyone for coming and said good night I was pulling at the front of my

T-shirt, trying to cool off. I dropped sideways onto my chair.

"Man, I'm going to miss this," Liam said. He was still on his feet, still buzzing with energy.

"So don't go," I said. My foot couldn't seem to stop keeping time to the last song.

Liam picked up his beer glass and when he saw it was empty put it back down again. "What do you mean, 'Don't go'?"

"Come live here." I didn't know why the idea hadn't occurred to me before. "Buy a house. Rent an apartment. Move in with Nick. Move in with *me*."

Jess gave him a sly smile and raised one eyebrow. "Or move in with me."

"Okay, obviously there was something in the salsa because you've both lost your minds."

I rested my right forearm on the top of my head. It was warm in the pub. "I'm serious, Liam," I said. "Hear me out."

He held up both hands in a gesture of surrender. "Fine. Make your case."

"You've done some projects in passive solar design."

He nodded.

"You got involved in the small-house movement and you used a lot of solar design ideas with that."

"I did."

"But your passion is old things, old buildings, saving parts of the past, reusing things the way you did with the windows and the trim when you renovated the sunporch for me." I started tapping my fingers against the side of my head. "I'm the same way. Look how we grew up. We never lived in a new house. Remember how Mom and Dad would take us to a flea market and give us each five dollars to spend?" I couldn't help smiling at the memories.

Liam grinned. "Remember the time we pooled our money and bought that wagon?"

"The Pepsi Flyer!" we both said at the same time.

Jess held up a hand. "Hang on a second," she said. "The Pepsi Flyer? Don't you mean the Radio Flyer?"

I shook my head. "No. It was the Pepsi Flyer. It was made from a wooden Pepsi crate, the kind they used to stack bottles in."

"That was a good wagon," Liam said. "I mean, at least until we hit the tree."

"Is there a short version of this story?" Jess asked.

I thought for a minute. "Yes. Little wagon, little kids. Big hill. Big tree."

She started to laugh. "You know the two of you were crazy hooligans, don't you?"

Liam gave her his best wide-eyed look of innocence. "You say that like it's a bad thing."

Jess got to her feet. She gave him a playful poke in the chest with one finger. "I'm starting to rethink this whole fake romance," she said. "I think you're too much of a wild man for me. I don't want to get my heart broken."

I gave a snort of laughter. Generally it was Jess who did the heart breaking, not the other way around. That was another reason—aside from the deception itself—that I wasn't crazy about their pretend relationship. Even though it was pretend, I didn't want my brother to somehow get hurt.

Jess turned to look at me. "I see someone I need to talk to. Do I have time before we leave?"

I was giving her a ride home. I nodded. "Go ahead."

She smiled at Liam. "Don't miss me too much," she said. She headed across the room. Liam watched her go and shook his head.

I stood up as well. "Do you need a ride back to Nick's?" I asked.

"What? No," he said. "I think I'll walk."

"Gram mentioned having supper with her and John sometime soon," I said. "Maybe this weekend?"

"Yeah, let me check my schedule. I'll text or call you."

"Sounds good." I gave him a hug. "Think about what I said. It would be great to have you here all the time."

"I will," he said. He pulled on his jacket and headed for the door.

I glanced over at the bar. I saw Cassie the bartender speak to someone and gesture at the overhead rack of wineglasses. She was about to take a break, I realized. Before I could decide whether it was a good idea, I was on my way across the room. She'd just come around the bar and I touched her arm to catch her attention. "Cassie?" I said.

She turned to look at me and I saw a flash of recognition in her dark eyes.

"I'm Sarah Grayson," I said. "I was at the party last night."

"I remember you," she said. Her expression was guarded.

Suddenly I didn't know what to say. *Did you see anyone poison Christopher Healy? Did you poison him?* I should have thought it through. "I . . . uh . . . I saw you talking to Mr. Healy. I just wanted to make sure you were okay."

"I'm fine," she said. "I'm on my break right now. Excuse me." She was gone through the door to the kitchen before I could say anything else. I stood there feeling stupid. I wasn't sure exactly what I'd been trying to accomplish, but I hadn't learned anything.

Rose was much better at this kind of thing than I was.

Chapter 7

The next morning when Elvis and I came out of the apartment Rose was waiting in the hall, her blue and gray tote bag over her arm, hands folded in front of her, fingers laced together.

I jumped at the sight of her. I'd made myself get up early and go for a run and my thoughts were all on the breakfast sandwich I'd made that was tucked in my messenger bag.

"I'm sorry, dear," she said. "I didn't mean to scare you." She smiled down at Elvis.

"It's all right," I said. "I just didn't expect to see you. I didn't think it was your morning to work."

"Oh, it's not. I have a couple of things to do at the office." I knew she meant the Angels' office. "You don't mind if I ride in with you, do you?"

"Merow," Elvis interjected. It seemed he didn't mind.

I smiled. "As my friend says, we're happy to have you."

Elvis led the way out to the SUV and hopped up to sit in the middle of the seat as soon as I opened the passenger door for Rose.

"How was the music last night?" she asked as I pulled onto the street. We both waved at Tom Harris, who was out in his front yard with Matilda. Elvis pointedly studied his feet.

"It was great," I said. "Sam and the guys just keep getting better." I glanced over at her. "You should come sometime." Rose had been at the jam once when we were celebrating the end of a case, but that was quite a while ago.

Her eyes narrowed as she considered the idea and her head tipped from side to side. She reminded me, as she often had, of a tiny, inquisitive bird. "Maybe I will," she finally said.

We drove for another minute or so in silence, then Rose said, "I want the Angels to take on Christopher Healy's murder."

"Okay," I said. Her head snapped in my direction. Elvis was staring at me as well.

"Okay?"

I nodded. "Yes."

"You're not going to tell me that we don't even know yet whether Christopher Healy was murdered?" she asked.

"I am not," I said. I kept my eyes fixed on the road in front of me.

"You're not going to point out that we wouldn't have a client, which means we'd be doing this pro bono?"

"I'm not doing that, either."

"Well my stars, this is not the response I was expecting," she said.

I came to a stop at the corner and looked over at

her. "I like to mix it up once in a while to keep you on your toes." I raised one eyebrow at her a la Spock from *Star Trek*.

She smiled then. "As Avery would say, are you messing with me?"

I tried to stifle a smile of my own but didn't succeed. "No, Rose, I'm not." I exhaled slowly. "I think you might be right."

"So none of this sits well with you, either?"

I shook my head. "It doesn't. Christopher Healy was a young man and I don't believe he had a heart attack or a stroke. When Nick and I were working on him, it was already too late. Something else killed him."

"You think he was poisoned, too?"

"That I don't know." We turned up the hill. "You're doing this because of Mr. P., aren't you?" I said.

"Yes, I am," she said. "They may not have seen each other in a long time, but Elliot Casey is important to Alfred and Alfred is important to me."

"Mr. P. is important to me, too."

"Mrrr," Elvis said. Alfred Peterson was important to all of us.

"Have you talked to Charlotte and Liz?" I asked.

"Last night," Rose said.

"I take it they're in agreement."

"Everyone's in agreement."

"So where do we start?" I turned into the shop's parking lot.

"I don't exactly know. I thought you were going to take a lot more convincing."

"I'm sorry to disappoint you," I said, smiling at her.

"As for where to start, you know what the king said in *Alice in Wonderland*: Begin at the beginning and go on till you come to the end: then stop."

Rose smiled back at me. "You do like that quote, dear, don't you?"

"*Alice in Wonderland* is one of my favorite books and that happens to be very good advice."

"So we start at the beginning," she said. "Who wanted Christopher Healy dead?"

"Exactly," I said.

Mac had made coffee as usual. He brought a cup to my office. "How was the jam last night?" he asked.

"Fantastic, as always," I said. That reminded me that I hadn't told Rose what I'd learned about Cassie, the bartender. I made a mental note to go down later to the Angels' office and bring her up to date on what little I'd found out. "Tell me what the boat was like."

Mac had gone to look at a sailboat with one of the guys he crewed with fairly regularly.

He made a face. "The expression 'needs a little TLC' wasn't exactly accurate."

"That bad?"

"Two words: carpenter ants. They were everywhere belowdecks. The guy who owns the boat tries to tell us that a little bug spray will fix the problem. He actually grabs a can and starts spraying it and we realize it's not bug spray at all."

"Air freshener?"

"Cooking oil spray."

I laughed. "You're making that up."

"I'm not," Mac said, laughing himself. "I wish I were, but I swear I'm not."

I fished the sandwich I'd made out of my bag. "I'm going to warm this up and I need more coffee."

"I could use a refill, too," he said. We headed for the stairs.

"So the Angels have a new case and I need you to tell me if I've lost my mind," I said as I leaned against the counter in the staff room with my breakfast.

Mac smiled. "Are the two connected?"

I nodded. "They are."

"All right, first, tell me about the case."

"It's Christopher Healy. Rose thinks someone poisoned him. She wants to investigate because he's the stepson of Mr. P.'s old friend. When we were driving home Mr. P. said he wished there was something he could do for Elliot. I think taking this on as a case is her way of doing that."

Mac didn't seem the slightest bit surprised. "What do you think?" he asked.

"That's where the 'have I lost my mind' part comes in," I said. "I think she might be right—at least that Healy didn't die of natural causes."

"What makes you say that?" He leaned against the counter beside me and took a sip of his coffee.

I explained why I didn't think Healy had had a heart attack, how evasive Nick had been and the questions he'd asked, even how I'd gotten nowhere trying to talk to Cassie. "Usually I'm the voice of reason, trying to reel Rose in. This time I'm actually encouraging her. Am I crazy?"

He shook his head. "No, you're not. Just the fact that Nick didn't answer your question makes me think you might be on to something. He was a paramedic. He knows when someone is having a heart attack."

I licked a bit of mayo off my thumb. "That's what I thought. When we were doing CPR I don't remember Nick ever saying Healy was having a heart attack or even a stroke."

"But none of that matters in the end," Mac said. "This is about Alfred. We're going to find out who killed Christopher Healy for him."

I turned to look at him. "We?"

He smiled. "Yes, we. Why should you get to have all the fun every time Rose and her cohorts have a new case?"

"I'm going to remind you that you said that," I told him, gesturing at him with the last bite of my sandwich before I ate it. Then I pushed away from the counter and started for my office.

After I'd checked the store's website and taken a second look at the photos of the toys Avery had taken—they were even better than I'd expected—I pulled out my phone and called Nick. "I just called to warn you that Charlotte's Angels have a new case," I said.

"Christopher Healy's death. I know."

"You know? How?"

"Rose called me about half an hour ago. She thought I should know."

I rocked back in my chair. "That's because you're part of the team now."

"I am *not* part of the team." He sounded a little huffy.

I closed my eyes for a second and pictured the canvas tote Rose had been carrying when I stepped into the hallway. There had been a plaid cookie tin at the top. "Did she or did she not tell you she made oatmeal cookies and you should stop by around ten thirty and have a couple?"

"I'm part of the team," Nick said. He sounded . . . resigned.

I didn't even try to hide my laughter.

"It's not funny, Sarah."

"From my perspective, it's hilarious," I said. "All that time you spent trying to convince Rose and your mother that they shouldn't be in the private investigation business and now you're Team Rose."

Nick made an exasperated sound in my ear. "How did I get into this mess?" he asked.

"You stopped being pigheaded and admitted that they're actually pretty good detectives."

He laughed. "That was my mistake. I was just trying to be reasonable. See what I get for listening to you?"

"This case is important to Rose," I said. "Christopher Healy is—was—the stepson of one of Mr. P.'s old friends."

"Elliot Casey."

"Yes."

He muttered a word his mother would have raised an eyebrow at.

"Look, Nick," I said. "I'm not asking you to reveal any private information or do anything that will compromise your job. And I'm not going to give you the speech about how good Rose has always been to you."

"You're just asking me to be reasonable."

I smiled even though he couldn't see me, picturing him making a face when he said the word "reasonable." "Yeah, I am."

"Okay," he said. "I'll help *if* I can." It was impossible to miss the emphasis on the word "if."

"So is the autopsy done?" I asked.

"It is."

"Healy didn't die of a heart attack, or a stroke or anything like that, did he?"

For a long moment there was nothing but silence. "No, he didn't," Nick finally said.

"So what did kill him?" I knew I was pushing it.

"I don't know, Sarah. Honestly, I don't. Toxicology results take time. When I know something *that I can share*, I will."

"Fair enough," I said.

"And the next time I see you, you better have at least three of those cookies."

I promised I would and we said good-bye.

I set my cell phone on the desk. Nick had told me more than he'd realized. Or maybe he hadn't. *Toxicology results take time.* Was that something he felt he could share? His words suggested Christopher Healy might have been poisoned.

Which meant Rose could have been right from the very beginning.

Chapter 8

I headed downstairs just before ten o'clock. Charlotte was packing a set of encyclopedias into three card-board boxes. She looked up and smiled at me.

"Don't tell me that you sold those old encyclopedias?" I said.

She nudged her glasses up her nose with her arm. "Yes, I did," she said.

"I can't believe these books finally have a home." The entire set of books, from A to Z, had been packed in an old tea chest we'd discovered in the garage when I'd bought the property. We'd used them in a couple of window displays and filled more than one bookcase with them, but no one had been interested in buying even one of the books, which were early 1960s vintage.

I picked up one of the volumes and turned it over in my hands. It was bound in red leatherette with the lettering stamped in gold. There was very little wear on it or any of the other twenty in the set. "Book collector?" I asked. There wasn't much market for old sets of encyclopedias.

Charlotte shook her head. "A collage artist. She's heading back to Rhode Island tomorrow morning. She'll be back to pick these up this afternoon." She closed the flaps of the box and pushed it to one side.

I looked down at the text I was still holding. "These encyclopedias have been here since the store opened. I think I'm going to miss them."

"I can cancel the sale," Charlotte said, giving me a teasing smile.

I immediately set the book on the counter and stuffed my hands in my pockets. "I'm not going to miss them that much," I said.

She laughed. "When I was a girl—back when dinosaurs roamed the earth—I think every second house had a set of encyclopedias just like these." She tapped the cover of the book lying on the counter. "I'm not sure how many kids ever read a page—well, other than my brother, who was looking for bad words."

Behind me I heard the front door open. I turned around as Liz walked into the store. "I'm here," she said. "Let's get this show on the road."

Elizabeth Emmerson Kiley French had presence, that indefinable quality that drew people to her. She was confident, smart and beautiful but it was more than that. You had the sense that whatever was happening or going to happen, Liz would be at the center of things.

I walked over to join her. She was holding a small gift bag, which she handed to me. "You brought me a present?" I said.

"Elspeth sent it to you," Liz said. "They're samples from a line of foot care products that she's thinking of carrying." Elspeth was Liz's niece. She ran a high-end spa called Phantasy here in North Harbor. "She was looking for testers and I thought of your knobby feet."

I took a tube of foot cream from the bag and unscrewed the cap. It smelled like vanilla. "My knobby feet say thank you." I leaned over and kissed her cheek.

"How are you?" she asked.

"I'm fine," I said. I knew she meant after what had happened Wednesday night.

"That was a good thing you did—helping Nicolas try to save that man's life."

I swiped a hand over the back of my neck. "I wish we had saved him."

"You did your best," Liz said.

"That's what I told her," Charlotte said, looking over the top of her glasses at us.

"I'm sorry the reception was ruined."

Liz waved away my words. "Nonsense. Nothing was ruined. And I happen to know that the hot lunch program has received four checks in the last couple of days." She smiled. "And we aren't done yet."

"I have no doubt about that," I said.

"Is the tea on yet?" she asked.

I looked at Charlotte, who shrugged.

"I'm not sure," I said.

"The tea is made," a voice said from the vicinity of the stairs. Rose was standing there carrying a tray that held the teapot in its knitted cozy, along with a tiny pitcher of milk and a bowl of sugar cubes.

"Let me take that," I said, hurrying over to her.

"Thank you, dear," she said, handing over the tray.

"I didn't know you were making the tea. I could

have brought this downstairs." I eyed her suspiciously. "You were very quiet."

"I'm little and stealthy. Just think of me as a geriatric ninja." She pointed at the gift bag hanging from my left arm. "What's in the bag?"

"Foot stuff. Liz brought me some samples from Elspeth."

"What a good idea," Rose said. "You can borrow my foot bath. And Mr. P. gives an excellent foot massage."

"The foot bath will be just fine," I said, heading for the workroom with the teapot before Rose got any more good ideas.

My brother, with a lot of help from Nick, had renovated the Angels' office space back in September. The walls were painted a creamy shade of off-white and there was lots of insulation now behind the new drywall. Liam had replaced the drafty windows with new ones that had thermal shades to keep the heat out in the summer and in during the winter. The guys had put down vinyl plank flooring and an electrician had installed a baseboard electric heater for extra warmth during the coldest months.

Mr. P. had a small desk against the inside wall with a chalkboard on the wall above it and two wall sconces on either side. The long, farm-style table we had always seemed to gather around in the workroom was at the far end of the sunporch, surrounded by a collection of mismatched chairs.

Alfred was at his desk, head bent over his laptop. "Knock knock," I said since my hands were full.

He looked up and smiled. "You brought the tea, my dear," he said. "Thank you."

I set the tray in the middle of the table. Rose had already brought down the cups and the plaid cookie tin.

I turned around just as Mac poked his head around the doorframe. "I'll hold down the fort," he said, tipping his head in the direction of the shop.

"Thanks," I said.

"Would you like a cookie?" Mr. P. asked.

Mac nodded.

I handed Mr. P. the plaid tin. He took off the lid and offered it to Mac, who took a cookie and immediately took a bite. "So good!" he said.

Rose had come out from the shop. "You can have another," she said with a smile. She reached into the can and handed him two cookies. It occurred to me that I might not be able to keep my promise to Nick.

Mac thanked Rose and headed for the front. Liz and Charlotte joined us and we all got settled around the table. Rose poured and once we all had a cup of tea she looked at me. "Is Nicolas joining us?" she asked.

"No," I said as I added milk and sugar to my cup.

"Yes," Nick said from the doorway.

I looked up, surprised to see him after our earlier conversation. He took the chair beside me and Rose got him a cup of tea.

Liz raised an eyebrow at me but didn't say anything.

Rose looked around the table. "You all know that we have a new case," she said.

"But we don't have a client," Liz said.

"Actually we do," Mr. P. said. "Me."

Everyone looked surprised. Even Rose. "Alfred, are you sure?" she asked.

"Yes," he said. It was his turn to look around the table. "Christopher Healy was the stepson of my old friend Elliot Casey. His death is suspicious. I want to find answers for Elliot and his wife."

Liz rapped on the table with her beautifully manicured fingernails. "Before we get started on what could turn out to be a wild-goose chase are we sure Mr. Healy was murdered?" She looked across the table. "Nicolas?"

"I can't answer that," he said. He held up a hand before she could object. "I don't know the cause of death yet. The autopsy has been done but the medical examiner hasn't finished her report."

"Did he die of natural causes?" Rose asked.

Nick's mouth worked for a moment before any words came out. "It doesn't look that way."

Liz reached for her tea. "That's good enough for me."

"The first thing we need to do is make a list of possible suspects," Rose said.

"Robbie Gorham," Charlotte said. "Since Joe Roswell's land deal fell through he's had to lay people off. Robbie always was one to take the easy way out."

Rose wrote the name on the blackboard. Underneath she printed Joe Roswell's name. "He has the most to gain from Christopher Healy's death."

"The bartender," I said. "Her name is Cassie. I don't know her last name."

"Why do you suspect her, Sarah?" Mr. P. asked.

Nick was looking at me and he nodded in agreement.

"My reasoning is pretty flimsy," I said. "I watched the two of them when Healy first went over to the bar. I can't put my finger on anything specific, but I got the sense from seeing her talk to him that they knew each other. She wouldn't serve him a drink and she seemed angry."

"Healy had just disrupted the reception," Nick said. "Maybe she saw her tips going out the window."

So he was going to be the voice of reason.

"I tried to talk to her, last night. She's working some shifts at The Black Bear. I didn't get anywhere."

"What did you say to her?" Liz asked.

"I introduced myself and told her I just wanted to make sure she was all right. She said she was and then she walked away."

"You did just fine," Rose said.

I felt like I was five and had just made a very rudimentary attempt to tie my shoes.

She put "Cassie" followed by "bartender" on the list.

"Do you know who owned that piece of land before Healy bought it?" Nick asked. He broke a cookie in half. One of the pieces disappeared in two bites.

Rose looked at Liz and Charlotte who both shook their heads.

"All I can tell you is that Liam said the woman was elderly," I said.

"I could find out," Mr. P. said. "Do you think it matters?"

Nick shrugged. "It might. I'm thinking the lawsuit probably means that the property is in limbo. And the original owner could get dragged in even deeper. My understanding is that Joe Roswell thought he had a deal, a handshake one at least."

He must have talked to Liam about the case I realized. That made sense given that Liam was staying with Nick.

"Courts have been known to uphold verbal agreements in this type of circumstance," he continued. "If the previous owner felt that she'd been misled by Healy and that Joe Roswell was going to come after her next, well, people have been killed for lesser reasons."

"Nick, the woman is old," I said.

He reached for another cookie. "Okay, so maybe a son or daughter."

Rose nodded and wrote "original landowner/ family" on her list. "We have somewhere to start."

"I'll find out the name of the woman who owned that piece of property and see what I can dig up on Mr. Roswell's lawsuit," Mr. P. said.

Rose looked across the table at Liz. "You know Mr. Roswell, don't you?" she asked.

"From the Chamber of Commerce among other things," Liz said. "I'll ask around about him."

"I'm guessing you'd like me to see what I can find out about Robbie Gorham," Charlotte said.

"I would," Rose said. "And I'll talk to Stella Hall as well since they're family." She put a hand on Mr. P.'s shoulder. "Let's get started."

Charlotte leaned sideways to speak to Liz. Mr. P. reached up and gave Rose's hand a squeeze. Then he got to his feet and made his way over to his desk while Rose joined Nick and me.

She put a hand on his arm. "I don't expect you to tell tales out of school, but will you at least be able to share when you find out how that young man died?"

He nodded. "That I can do."

"Did you have a cookie?" she asked.

"He had three," I said.

Rose gave me the look that had struck fear into the heart of more than one middle-schooler when she was still teaching. "Did someone ask you to keep track, Sarah?"

"No, ma'am," I said ducking my head contritely.

There were two cookies left in the open can. Rose reached over and put the top back on. Then she handed the container to Nick. "One for you and one for Liam," she said.

He kissed the top of her head. "Thank you, Rose," he said. He looked at me. "See you later, Sarah." The smile he gave me as he went out the door was decidedly smug.

"I didn't get a cookie," I said. "I didn't even get a crumb of a cookie."

Rose reached up and patted my cheek. "Don't sulk. It will give you wrinkles."

Charlotte had gone back out front. Liz waved her fingers at us and headed for the parking lot. I gathered the teapot and the milk and sugar onto the tray. Rose brought the teapot.

"Do you have a minute?" she asked when we reached the staff room.

"For you, always," I said.

"Avery and I have come up with an idea to promote some interest in those old photographs. We thought we'd post a new picture every few days from our school days on the store's website and encourage people to look through the old photos to find themselves from *their* school days."

"And then buy the pictures so no one else sees them."

Rose's face turned a little pink. "Or as a reminder of a happy memory."

"By the way, what do you mean by 'our'?" I asked as I rinsed out the teapot.

"Charlotte, Liz, Alfred, me, you."

"I look horrible in every single one of my high school photos and in the ones from middle school."

"Nonsense," she said. "I've seen all of those pictures and there's nothing wrong with them. But if it will make you feel better, my mother cut my bangs until I was in the tenth grade and I'm willing to put up one of my photos."

"All right, I'll do it," I said. "Just try to find one where my eyes aren't half closed." I turned the teapot upside down in the dish rack to drain. "You know, Liam tried to cut my hair when we were about eight. I yelled for Mom and she stopped him. He gave Barbie a Mohawk in retaliation."

Rose smiled. "That boy always did have a creative side."

Mac was just coming in the front door when we came back downstairs. "I sold the rocking chair that came from Clayton McNamara's place," he said. "What would you like me to put in its place?"

I thought for a moment. "How about the oak one with the slat back? I think it says cozy nights by the fire."

Mac nodded. "I'll get it." He set the coffee cup he'd been holding on top of the bookcase.

I turned to Charlotte. "There was a big patchwork pillow in the ones Jess dropped off the other day."

"You mean the one she made from that old quilt that was beyond repair," she said. "I was thinking the same thing. I'll go get it. I know where it is."

"Thank you," I said.

Charlotte headed for the storeroom, holding the door open for Mac, who was bringing the rocking chair.

"What do you think?" I asked Rose. "By the window or at an angle next to the bookcase?"

"Next to the bookcase," she said at once. "There's more room."

I realized she was right. If the rocking chair was next to the bookcase there was enough space for customers to sit down and try it. I knew that once a customer had sat on a chair or played a few chords on a guitar they were a lot more likely to buy them.

Mac set the chair in place. Charlotte added the cushion.

"Perfect," I said.

"I'm going out to the office to try Stella Hall," Rose said.

"Before you go, would you like me to try talking to the bartender again?" I asked. "Maybe if I caught her when it's not so busy she'd be more likely to talk to me."

Rose smiled. "I appreciate the offer, but I think she'd be more receptive to Mac's questions and charms."

Mac had picked up his coffee cup. He almost choked on her words. "Me?" he said. "You want *me* to question someone?"

I bit the inside of my cheek. This was not a good time to laugh.

"All you have to do is talk to the woman. Steer the conversation around to the night of the reception. See if you can find out what she and Christopher Healy talked about," Rose said. "Just be yourself. I would have asked Nicolas, but I didn't want it to turn into an actual interrogation."

"All right. I'll see what I can find out," Mac said.

Rose clasped her hands together. "Splendid!" she said.

"Is there anything I can do?" I asked.

She nodded. "Talk to Liam. We need to know more about the land deal and the inn."

"I can do that," I said.

Mac went back out to the old garage. Rose headed to the Angels' office. I checked my phone and discovered that I'd missed a call from Gram. Since there were no customers in the store I stood by the front door and looked out over the street as I called her back instead of going up to my office.

"Hi, sweetie," she said. "I was just calling to see if you're free for supper tonight. I decided if I wanted to get us all together I was going to have to take the bull by the horns, so to speak. I talked to your brother and his plans for tonight have fallen through so he's available and I'm fully prepared to guilt you into coming as well."

Since my father had been Gram's only child, technically I was her only grandchild, but Gram didn't get caught up in biology. When Mom and Dad had gotten married Gram had embraced Liam as another grandchild. "There's no such thing as too many people to love," she'd told me more than once.

I laughed. "You don't have to guilt me. I don't have any plans and I'd love to come to dinner."

"We're having chicken stew. Bring Elvis. And before you say it, yes I know he's a cat and not a person. Bring him anyway."

"Okay," I said. "Is there anything else I can bring?"

"Having you and Liam here together is more than enough."

She told me to come upstairs as soon as I got home, and we said good-bye.

I tucked the phone back in my pocket. Tonight would be the perfect time to get information from Liam.

I went up to my office to change into an old shirt and pair of jeans so I could go out and do some work on the fireplace mantel I was stripping. Elvis was stretched out on his back on the dark gray button-tufted settee.

"Shouldn't you be downstairs, charming customers?" I asked.

The cat's response was a huge yawn, which showed off his very sharp teeth.

"Yes, I'm aware that it's very tiring work." I leaned down and gave him a scratch under his chin. He started to purr.

When I straightened I noticed a small plate was sitting on my desk, a bowl turned upside down on top of it like a lid.

"Where did that come from?" I said.

Elvis sat up and craned his neck for a better view. "Mrrr," he said. Cat for *I don't know.*

I lifted up the dish. There were two oatmeal cookies on the plate.

Rose.

I sat down next to the cat. "We have to figure out

what happened to Christopher Healy," I told him. "Not just for Mr. P., for Rose, too. I didn't believe her when she said Healy had been murdered. I should have."

Elvis reached over and put a paw on my hand. He was in.

Chapter 9

Just after lunch, I was on my hands and knees, head stuck in the under-the-stairs storage space, looking for two blue cornflower CorningWare teapots when I heard Mr. P. clear his throat behind me. I reached one arm back, holding up a finger to let him know I needed a minute. I stretched out my other arm and snagged the box I was looking for. Pulling it along with me, I crawled backward out of the space and got to my feet.

"I'm sorry to disturb you, Sarah," he said.

"You didn't," I said. I shook my head and a dust bunny floated to the floor. "I was just trying to find a couple of teapots. Charlotte has a customer who was looking for these particular ones." I gave the box a nudge with the toe of my shoe. "What's up?"

Mr. P. smiled. I knew that particular smile. He'd discovered something. "I've located young Mr. Healy's former girlfriend," he said. "Her name is Annika Nilsson." He looked at his watch. "We're going to talk via Skype in about fifteen minutes. I'm wondering if you'd like to sit in."

"I would," I said. "What are you hoping to find out?"

He smoothed one hand over his few wisps of gray hair. "Nothing specific. I'm actually hoping to get a better sense of what he was like as a person. At the moment Christopher Healy is a bit of a cipher."

I nodded. "I'll give the teapots to Charlotte and wash my hands and I'll be right there."

Annika Nilsson was tiny, with delicate features, blonde hair pulled into a messy bun, and blue eyes behind red-framed glasses. "I'm not really sure what I can tell you about Chris," she said, pushing a stray strand of hair away from her face.

I was sitting to Mr. P.'s left, out of the range of his computer's camera, although I could easily see Annika on the screen.

"We just wanted to get a sense of who he was as a person," Mr. P. said. "Anything you can tell me will help."

"He was smart." She smiled. "We met in grad school. Chris was the smartest person in every class. I loved to listen to him talk. When he was into something it just consumed him."

"He didn't finish his degree."

She shook her head. "You know that his father died?"

Mr. P. nodded. "Yes."

"I think Chris only started working on the degree because of his father. He loved books and storytelling, but I never got the sense that he really cared about doing research, writing papers, actually being an English professor." I could see a large whiteboard behind her and I wondered if she was at the university. As he was setting up the call Mr. P. had mentioned that Annika was finishing her PhD in English.

Mr. P. made a note on the pad beside him. "What was Christopher into?" he asked.

Annika shrugged. "He loved books and old movies, but other than that he wasn't really into anything, not for very long. He was smart and he was good at everything he tried without having to try very hard. I think he got bored easily. Does that make sense?"

"It does," Mr. P. said, smiling at the computer screen.

"I saw Chris about three weeks ago. He was in town and we had dinner. He seemed happy." The smile returned to her face. "He'd had some kind of argument with his sister after their dad died and they weren't speaking, but he said he was going to see her soon—she lives in Arizona—and try to work things out. And he told me about his nature preserve project. He was so enthusiastic about it. I was hoping that he'd finally found his passion."

Mr. P. thanked Annika for her help and they ended the call. He closed his laptop and looked at me. "I'm not sure we learned anything we didn't already know."

I got to my feet. "Everything seems to lead to that piece of land."

Mr. P. raised one eyebrow. "Then perhaps it's time we followed that lead."

The rest of the day was busy. I spent some time working on the fireplace mantel. It was covered in several layers of paint. The top one was a particularly bilious shade of pea soup green. Underneath it I discovered the top of the mantel had been covered with some kind of faux brick self-adhesive wallpaper that seemed welded to the wood.

I was using a hair dryer and a plastic scraper to remove the wallpaper when Mac came out to the work space. I turned off the dryer and pushed my dust mask up onto my forehead.

"I just wanted to double-check and make sure it's okay for Avery to start taking pictures of the photos she and Rose framed," he said.

"How do they look?" I asked.

"Good. Especially the old black-and-white ones of the street in front of the old hotel."

"I trust your judgment," I said. "Tell her to go ahead. I'll be in soon anyway."

He nodded. "Okay." I picked up the hair dryer again. Mac paused in the doorway. "I know it's short notice, but do you have plans for dinner?"

I brushed a stray piece of hair that had come loose from my ponytail off of my face with the back of my hand. "Actually, I do. I'm having dinner with Gram and John—and Liam. But how about tomorrow night?"

"I'm going to Bangor with Glenn to bring back that truck he bought."

"And Sunday aren't you helping a couple of the guys get their boats in?" This was crazy. How long were Mac and I going to keep dancing around each other?

"Monday's no good, either," he said. "Mr. P. is doing another seminar for seniors at the library about online scams. I'm his guest speaker."

"And you still have to use your charms on the bartender." I smiled and shook my head.

Mac looked at me for a long moment. "When this case is over," he said.

I nodded. "When it's over." I turned back to the fireplace mantel.

"I missed you," Mac said.

I glanced over my shoulder at him. "We missed you, too."

"I mean I missed *you*." He gestured in the direction of the shop. "I missed them as well, I did. Rose, Alfred, Avery—all of them—they make life interesting. But I missed you the most."

I turned to face him again. "When you were gone I felt as though one of my arms was gone. I don't know how many times I started out here to ask you something before I remembered you weren't here."

Mac smiled. "We make a good team."

"It's more than that," I said. "You're always the voice of reason. Whenever I get involved in one of their cases"—I pointed across the parking lot—"which seems to be all the time, you're the one who reminds me that Rose and Mr. P. and the rest of their merry band do actually know what they're doing."

"And you see the best in people," he said.

I shook my head. "I don't know about that. Getting mixed up in the Angels' cases has shown me the worst of some people."

Mac tipped his head to one side and studied me. "I know you convinced Liz to push for extending the harbor front plan to include that old warehouse Vince Kennedy's father owned because he needed the money."

I looked away for a moment. How did he know

that? I hadn't even admitted my motivation to Liz, although I had a feeling she'd suspected.

"He broke into the shop and you still did that for him."

I shrugged. "That was a bad time for Vince. He's not a bad person."

"Like I said, you see the best in people." Mac smiled and for probably the hundredth time I thought how that smile could turn my day around and how much I'd missed seeing it while he was in Boston. "Without you in my life, I think I'd probably be a cranky old hermit living in a shack in the woods building a boat in my basement."

I laughed at the mental image his words created. "You couldn't be cranky if you tried," I said. "And I don't think shacks in the woods actually have basements. As for being a hermit"—I made a sweeping gesture at the shop with one hand—"there's no way they would leave you alone. Charlotte would be organizing your hovel, Avery would be picking some kind of wild plants to make you a healthy smoothie and Rose would be trying to set you up with every female hermit within a five-mile radius."

Mac laughed, too. "Yeah, you're probably right." He ran a hand over the top of the mantel. "I'll let you get back to work and I'll let Avery know she can start taking photos."

"Thanks," I said, reaching for the plastic scraper.

"Coming to work here is one of the best things that ever happened to me," he said. He was gone before I could say that him coming to work at Second Chance was one of the best things that had ever happened to me, too.

* * *

When we got home Elvis immediately headed for the stairs to Gram's upstairs apartment. "Come back here," I said. "We're not going up yet. I need to take a shower."

He looked back over his shoulder at me and meowed his displeasure.

I took a deep breath and let it out. "Fine then. Go ahead. But you'll just end up sitting in the hall outside the door." I pulled out my keys and unlocked the apartment door. Elvis came back down the hall and followed me inside. He didn't say anything and neither did I.

I kicked off my shoes, hung up my sock-monkey sweater and went into the kitchen for a glass of water. I put fresh water in Elvis's dish in case he was thirsty, too.

He wasn't. He was impatient, though. He trailed me to the bedroom, making annoyed little grumbling sounds in the back of his throat. I threw a sock at him, or maybe a better way of putting it would be to say I threw a sock in his general direction since it didn't land anywhere close to him. He gave me a green-eyed stare that was equal parts pity and disdain.

I had a quick shower and pulled on my softest and oldest pair of jeans along with a red-and-navy-striped V-neck sweater over a plain T-shirt. I left my hair down and slipped into my favorite pair of red Keds. I was ready.

Elvis took a couple of passes at his face with his paw. He was ready as well.

Gram folded me in a hug when she answered the door. "I'm glad we could do this on such short notice."

She smiled down at the cat. "Hello, Elvis," she said. "I'm so glad you could come."

He murped a "hello" back at her and went inside. He was always on his best behavior when he visited.

Isabel Grayson Scott was taller than average—about five feet seven or so. She had beautiful smooth skin, deep blue eyes and wavy white hair cropped short to show off her long neck and gorgeous cheekbones. She was one of those people who truly was beautiful inside and out.

I stepped into the kitchen and the aroma of rosemary and buttery biscuits wrapped around me. John came in from the living room. I gave him a hug.

John Scott was tall and strong with brown hair streaked with gray waving back from his angular face. He was thirteen years younger than Gram. That had generated some whispers when they had first started seeing each other—not that Gram "cared a fig" what people thought, as she put it.

"I started listening to some of the albums in that box you scavenged," John said to me.

I'd found a box of vinyl records on the side of the road a week earlier when Jess and I were heading home from a weekend flea market. She'd laughed when I put on the pair of rubber boots I kept in the back of my SUV and waded through a muddy ditch to get it.

"So was I wasting my time when I forded that ditch?" I asked. John was the only person I knew with a working turntable and I knew how much he loved the sound of vinyl over digital, so I'd had no trouble saying yes when he'd offered to check out the albums.

He smiled. "Well, I haven't unearthed a mint copy of the Beatles' *White Album* so you aren't going to get rich, but so far what I've listened to is in very good shape. The box couldn't have been by the side of the road very long. I think you should be able to sell all of them just for the nostalgia value."

"Assuming John doesn't buy them from you first," Gram said.

"If you're interested in any of them, they're yours," I said. The napkins were sitting on the counter. I took them over to the table and put one at each place.

"There are a couple of albums I think I'd like to have," John said. "But—" He held up one hand. "I want to pay for them."

"I found them in a cardboard box by the side of the road. I'm not out any money."

"You find things by the side of the road all the time. And in recycling piles and garbage cans."

I laughed. "You're making me sound like a raccoon."

"Only in the sense that you're very resourceful," John said with a smile.

"How about this?" I said. "You can buy the albums you'd like to keep, but I'll give you the friends and family discount."

He nodded. "That's fair."

There was a knock on the door then. I was closest so I went to let Liam in.

"You beat me here," he said as he gave me a hug.

"I had a very short commute." I took his jacket. He'd shaved and the ends of his hair were damp from the shower.

I hung up his jacket while Liam hugged Gram. He

shook hands with John. Elvis poked his head in from the living room.

"Hey, furball," Liam said.

The cat murped "hey" in return and went back to whatever he'd been doing, most likely a kitty version of casing the place.

Liam leaned against the counter. "How was your day?" he asked.

"Good," I said. "Charlotte sold a set of encyclopedias we've had since the shop opened."

"Do you mean those ones in the old tea chest?" Gram asked. She was peeking in the oven again.

"Those are the ones."

"Why would someone want a set of old encyclopedias?" Liam said.

I shook my head. "You'd be surprised by the things people collect. But in this case it was a collage artist who bought them." I poked him with my elbow. "How was your day?"

"Good," he said. "And before you ask, yes, the boardwalk has been swept and Jess is happy."

Gram lifted four heavy stoneware bowls from the cupboard. She made a face. "I'm sorry, Liam," she said. "I should have invited Jess to join us."

"It's okay," he said.

She shook her head. "No, it's not. Jess is your girlfriend. I should have included her."

"Next time, Gram," I said.

Liam shot me a daggers look.

Gram waved a large metal spoon in our direction. "I know it's early, but do you know if she has any plans for Thanksgiving?"

"Umm, I don't know," Liam said as the color rose in his cheeks.

She smiled at him. "Don't worry. I'll call her and ask her myself."

Liam glanced in the direction of the living room. "Sarah, is that the box of those record albums you found in the ditch?"

I nodded. "John's listening to them to make sure they're not scratched or damaged."

He turned to John. "May I take a look?" he asked.

"Sure," John said.

As soon as they were out of earshot in the next room I sidled up to Gram and put an arm around her shoulders. "You know, don't you?" I asked in a low voice.

She gave me a look of wide-eyed innocence. "Know what, sweetie?"

I just stared at her without speaking and after a moment the innocent act dissolved into a smile. "That Jess isn't your brother's girlfriend? Of course I know. He thinks he's great at subterfuge, but everything shows on his face."

I glanced toward the living room. Liam was reading the back of an album cover. "How *long* have you known?" I asked.

"From the beginning," Gram said. "The whole sudden romance thing was just a bit too sudden, if you know what I mean." She raised an eyebrow.

"Does everyone else know? Rose? Liz?"

"Well, of course they do," she said.

I leaned sideway against the counter while she reached for her oven mitts. "How long are you going to let this thing go on?"

She gave me a mischievous smile. "I don't know. Thanksgiving, maybe?" She narrowed her eyes. "Are you going to out us?"

I grinned and shook my head. "Absolutely not. This is way too much fun."

Gram dished out the food and I carried the bowls to the table. "I forgot to tell you," she said, gesturing with her spoon again. "I had tea with Stella Hall last week. They have an offer on her brother's house. Unless there's a problem with the financing it will be sold by the end of the month."

"I'm glad to hear that," I said. When Rose had called she'd learned that Stella was out of town for a few days so we hadn't been able to talk to her yet, otherwise I probably would have heard about the pending house sale.

We had taken on the job of clearing out Edison Hall's house after he died, mostly as a favor for Gram. The old man had been a bit of a packrat, albeit a packrat who turned out to be pretty well organized. The job had taken an unanticipated turn when Elvis discovered a body on our first day in the house. I was happy to hear that it was finally going to be sold. That had been a horrible time for Stella.

Gram also had made a small dish for Elvis with some shredded chicken and mashed carrots. He licked his whiskers and smiled at her as she set it in front of him.

Liam talked in general terms about the work on the new hotel as we ate. "What's going to happen to the lawsuit now that Christopher Healy is dead?" I finally asked. "Will it be dismissed?"

He shrugged. "I don't know. It could continue with Healy's executor—whoever that turns out to be—representing the estate."

"Or the court could decide that Mr. Healy would have provided testimony that was crucial to deciding the case," John said. "In that case it could be dismissed."

"Exactly," Liam said. "At this point no one knows."

"Wouldn't it make more sense financially to offer to buy the land from the man's estate?" Gram asked.

"Maybe. But it could take months to settle the estate—a year or more, if Healy didn't leave a will."

"Could the executor make an offer to settle the lawsuit?" I asked. "Maybe give Joe Roswell the chance to buy the property for something close to what Healy paid?" I broke off part of a biscuit and ate it. No one made biscuits like Gram.

"I think Joe's hoping that's what will happen," Liam said as he reached for his glass. "But even that will take time."

"So what's the rush?"

"The inn was going to be Joe's next project. His work on the hotel is almost finished. He's already started to lay people off."

"So he really thinks this system Robb Gorham is pushing to stabilize the ground is going to work?" I said as I speared a chunk of carrot with my fork.

"Yes, he thinks it's going to work," Liam said. I saw a flash of annoyance in his eyes. "The entire project is based on it working."

"It's untested technology. It seems like Joe is betting *everything* on it working."

"And you're suddenly an engineer?"

"No. But neither is Robb Gorham, as far as I know."

"But he has consulted a geologist and she thinks it's a viable process."

"Take a breath, both of you," Gram said sharply.

Liam looked away.

I set my fork down, took a deep breath and slowly let it out. "I'm sorry," I said. And I was. This wasn't going to work. Liam and I may not have been biological siblings but one trait we had in common was our intense loyalty to the people we cared about. I wasn't going to find out anything useful about the lawsuit or Joe Roswell. In similar circumstances I'd be reacting the same way. "I wasn't criticizing. I just didn't want to see you end up working on this inn project and then have the whole thing fall apart because you bought a pig in a poke."

His lips twitched. "A pig in a poke?" he said.

"I spend a lot of time with Rose," I said, feeling my face get red. "I pick up expressions."

Gram and John exchanged a smile.

Liam put a hand to his chest. "I hereby promise you that I will not get involved in any projects that feature pigs in bonnets."

I made a face at him then turned toward Gram. "Tell me what's happening with the sunflower window. Please." We needed a change of subject and I was interested in the window.

"I'd like to hear about that, too," Liam said, breaking a biscuit in half.

She smiled. "We have enough money raised to meet the Singapore offer. In fact, we have a cushion of about ten percent."

"Aww, Gram, that's great," I said. I high-fived her across the table.

"Most of the credit should go to Liz and Neill Halloran. The two of them make a formidable fund-raising team. I don't think anyone they approached turned them down."

John put a hand on Gram's shoulder. "And who got the project so much publicity?" he said.

Liam nodded, "John's right. Without you getting so much of the town's—so much of the state's—attention focused on the window, the library board would have quietly sold it and a part of the town's history would have ended up in another country."

"So what will happen to the window? Will it stay in storage?" I asked, picking up my fork again.

"Do you remember the original plan for the harbor front development project?" Gram said.

"North Landing."

She nodded. "One of the parts of that project was some kind of residential living space."

"Condos," John said.

"Yes," Gram said. "The idea is being tossed around again. Apartments this time."

"And the window would be part of this somehow?" I said.

"The centerpiece of a two-story entrance."

"I like that idea," I said. I looked at Liam.

He held up one hand. "I've heard the rumors. It's just in the talking stage right now, but it is a possibility."

"I hope it works out," Gram said. She got to her feet and went over to check Elvis's bowl. "Would you like a little more?" she asked.

"Merow," he said. His whiskers twitched.

"Gram, is there any point in me asking you not to spoil my cat?" I said.

She paused, a thoughtful expression on her face, her mouth twisted to one side. "No," she said after a moment. She picked up the cat's dish and took it over to the stove. "You know, when the condos were being proposed, Liz talked about buying one."

I nodded. "I remember that. Do you think she'd really be interested in an apartment?"

Gram frowned. "I guess that depends on how much longer Avery stays with her." She added one more piece of chicken to the cat's bowl and carried it back to the spot it had been before, on a folded dish towel close to the table. Elvis murped his thank-you and Gram came back to the table. "I know this is a little gossipy of me," she said. "But what's happening with her and Channing Caulfield?"

Channing Caulfield was a former bank manager and financial adviser who had worked with Liz on Emmerson Foundation business. He'd also helped the Angels more than once. He was smitten with Liz, who claimed not to return his feelings.

I dipped the last bit of biscuit into the gravy in my bowl. "I don't know," I said. "She's insistent that she's not interested in him, but I don't know if I believe her."

"The lady doth protest too much, methinks," John said with a smile.

I stabbed the air with my fork. "Methinks, too."

"I wouldn't be surprised to find out there's been a little something going on with those two," Gram said, wiggling her eyebrows.

Liam almost choked on his water. He sputtered and coughed.

I reached over and patted him on the back.

"Are you all right, sweetie?" she asked.

He waved off her concern, coughed again and wiped his mouth with his napkin before he spoke. "I'm fine but do we have to talk about people's . . ." He made a circular gesture in the air with one hand.

"Love lives?" Gram said. There was a mischievous glint in her eyes.

Liam rubbed the space between his eyebrows. "Yes."

"Older people have romantic lives, Liam," she said. "We're old. Not dead."

Liam shifted uncomfortably in his seat. Given all the times he'd had no problem whatsoever talking about *my* love life—or, more accurately, the fact that I didn't have one—including repeatedly urging me to "lay a big ol' wet one on Nick," it was hard not to see the humor in his discomfort.

"We could always talk about *your* love life," Gram said. "How serious are things with Jess?"

"We're not serious," he said. "Well, not that serious. I'm too busy working for anything like that."

"You work too much."

"And you sound like Mom," Liam said.

She smiled. "Doesn't mean either one of us is wrong."

He looked at me. "You could help me, you know."

I leaned back in my seat and folded my arms. "Nope. I'm pretty sure I can't."

"I'm not going to nag you about your personal life," Gram said. "But I am going to remind you that life is short. And Jess is a lovely person." She turned to me. "The same reminder applies to you, Miss Work-All-The-Time. There aren't nearly as many chances to be happy as you might think. When one comes along, grab it with both hands."

"Or at least whack it over the head with a book," I said. I tried to keep a straight face but couldn't.

John laughed. "You walked into that one, Isabel," he said. He and Gram had met when she knocked a library book off a shelf and it hit him in the head.

Two spots of color appeared on her cheeks. "That was not my fault." She squared her shoulders and her chin came up. "The book was not set on the shelf properly and the shelf itself was crooked."

I leaned toward Liam, keeping my eyes on Gram. "Turns out it wasn't the first time she tried something like that," I stage-whispered.

"Really?" He looked across the table at Gram. "And when did this caveman-like behavior start?"

"I thought we weren't going to talk about people's love lives," she said.

"I didn't agree to that at all," I said. I turned my attention back to Liam. "It started when she was six. She brained Clayton McNamara with her book bag."

"That was totally Clayton's fault," Gram said indignantly. "He just stood there grinning at me. He should have gotten out of the way. Or at least ducked."

John got to his feet and picked up his plate. "Maybe he liked assertive women." He kissed the top of her head. "I know I do."

Gram swatted his arm. "Stop trying to charm me," she said. She was pretending to be annoyed, but I knew she wasn't. I could see the gleam in her eye when she looked at John.

He kissed her again. "Never," he said.

"I want that," I said softly to Liam.

"Me, too," he said.

We finished the meal with Gram's apple crisp and talked about some of the school photos that had been unearthed. I told Gram and John about Glenn McNamara's class photo.

"I'd like to see that." She laughed.

Liam and I cleared the table and loaded the dishwasher. Gram sent us both out with leftovers.

"Love you," I said as I hugged her good night.

"Love you, sweetie," she said. Then she wrapped her arms around Liam. "Love you, too."

"To infinity and beyond," he said, referencing Buzz Lightyear from the movie *Toy Story*. He and Gram both loved that movie. They'd seen it and the various sequels more times than I could count.

We both said good night to John and headed down the stairs, trailed by Elvis.

"I'm glad we did this," I said as I fished out my keys.

"Yeah, me, too," Liam said.

"Do you have plans for the weekend? Maybe with Jess?" I teased.

"Ha, ha. Very funny." He raked a hand back through his hair. "How am I going to get out of this Thanksgiving thing?"

"I don't know." I gave him my best faux innocent look. "Maybe you could just tell the truth."

"Yeah, there's a good idea. Tell Gram and the rest

of the matchmaking crew that I don't really have a girlfriend and have another very awkward conversation with Rose about how I should be wearing boxers instead of briefs."

I started to laugh.

"It's not funny."

"Oh yes, it is. You didn't have the slightest bit of sympathy when they told Nick I had all my own teeth."

Liam started to laugh as well. "They aren't going to give up, are they?" he said.

"No." I brushed a stray hair back off my face. "You know what they're like."

His expression grew serious. "Speaking of not giving up, I know they have a new case."

"Nick told you."

"Yeah, he told me." He shifted from one foot to the other as though the subject made him a bit antsy. "Look, I know how the lawsuit makes things look, but Joe had nothing to do with Healy's death."

"No one is saying he did." Elvis butted my leg with his head. His way of saying he was getting tired of waiting for me to let him inside.

"So then maybe they don't need to dig around in the man's life."

"If you're asking me to tell Rose and the others not to investigate Joe, there's no point. They don't listen to me." Rose had been hit over the head and almost killed doing something I'd asked her not to do and she *still* didn't listen to me.

"Joe's a good guy, Sarah."

"You keep saying that," I said. "If it's true, then he doesn't have anything to worry about."

"I gotta go," Liam said abruptly. "Let me know when you get everything for the auction up on the website."

He was gone before I had a chance to reply.

I looked down at Elvis. "If Joe Roswell is such a good guy, why doesn't Liam want anyone checking him out?"

The cat's green eyes narrowed. It seemed he didn't know why, either.

Chapter 10

Elvis and I picked up Avery on Saturday morning. Her and Rose's plan for using our school pictures to catch people's attention on the website seemed to be working. I'd noticed an increase in the bids on the old school photographs. Glenn had already offered a hundred dollars to get the photo of him with long hair.

Avery climbed into the SUV carrying her own glass smoothie bottle and a second one. "Hey, Sarah; hey, Elvis," she said. Avery belied every stereotype about teenagers who won't get up in the morning. She liked to be up early and often sat up in the branches of one of the big trees in Liz's front yard with a green concoction and watched the world go by. Not that much of it was going by before six AM.

She offered the second smoothie bottle to me. The contents were a deep green and made me think of seaweed. "This is for you."

"Thank you," I said. I saw Rose's hand in this, which Avery quickly confirmed.

"And Rose said yes you have to drink it. She said you need more greens." She looked expectantly at me. Elvis cocked his head to one side and did the same. The furball had a sense of humor.

I was going to have to at least take one taste right now. I unscrewed the top. It smelled like . . . bananas. I took a drink. "That's not bad," I said. The smoothie tasted like blueberries and banana.

Avery nodded. Elvis had nudged her hand and she was scratching behind his left ear. "People always say that." Her dark hair was cut in shaggy layers with long bangs. Like a lot of teens, she dressed mostly in black. The colorful collection of bracelets on her left arm—I counted five today—were the only color she wore.

I took a second drink and screwed the cap back on the bottle. "So what's in it?"

"Blueberries, banana, orange juice, vegan protein powder and spinach," she said. "The spinach is what makes it kinda look like pond slime." She looked at me and shrugged. "I probably shouldn't have told you the last part."

I nodded. "Probably."

We started for the shop.

"So where are Rose and Charlotte going this morning?" Avery asked. "It's something to do with the new case, right?"

"Yes, it is," I said, slowing down as the car in front of me turned. "They're going to interview someone."

"A suspect?"

"More like a person of interest."

She laughed. "Like I've never watched *Dateline*.

Person of interest is another way of saying 'person we think might have murdered the guy.'"

She had a way of cutting away all the fluff in a conversation. I figured it came from spending so much time with her grandmother.

"Person of interest is also another way of saying someone who may have information," I said.

"Right." She didn't roll her eyes, but she came close.

It seemed like a good time to change the subject. We spent the rest of the ride to the shop talking about options for displaying the rest of the photos.

Mac had the door to the old garage space open when we pulled into the parking lot, but it was what was sitting in front of the doors that caught my eye. And Avery's. "Oh man, what did he do?" she said.

I shook my head. "I don't know." I parked and we got out of the SUV. We walked over to Mac, Elvis leading the way.

Mac smiled. "Good morning."

"Good morning," I said.

There were two wooden garden benches sitting on a tarp in front of the open door. At least, I thought they were wooden. It was hard to tell because both of them were painted a glow-in-the-dark shade of Pepto-Bismol pink.

Elvis hopped up onto the closest bench. The pink did set off his black fur.

"Anything you want to share?" I asked.

Avery had made a wide circle around both benches. She looked at Mac now. "What did you do? Raid Barbie's Dreamhouse?"

Mac laughed. "No. I was out here and Cleveland pulled in. He had these in the back of his truck. I asked him what he wanted for them and the price was just too good to let them go. They're teak."

"They're pink," I said.

"Well, that, too, but we can fix that. They're sturdy and well-built."

I ran a hand along the back of the bench closest to me. The pink finish was glossy and rock hard. "It's going to take an awful lot of sanding to get these down to the original wood. That's enamel paint."

"We've done it before," he said.

Avery immediately took a step backward and held up her hands. "I have photos to sort. I'm going to the shop." I handed over the keys and she headed across the parking lot taking long strides. Elvis jumped down and followed her. He wasn't interested in sanding, either.

I looked at the benches again. "They're really pink."

Mac smiled. "Trust me. You won't recognize them when I'm done."

"Then I'll just leave them in your capable hands," I said.

"In other words, you're with Avery and Elvis."

I smiled back at him. "In just one word, yes." I started for the back door.

"I made coffee," Mac called after me.

"Doesn't change anything." I kept walking.

"It's strong, just the way you like it."

"Thank you." I waved over my shoulder at him. "I'm still not sanding those benches."

Mac did not give up easily. "I know where the left-over cookies are."

"And I know where the leftover cake is." I turned around, held up my right index finger, and drew an imaginary one in the air. He was still laughing when I went inside.

Avery was already at the cash desk looking through a box of photographs with a furry helper. "Want me to open?" she asked.

I checked my watch. "We have a few minutes yet."

"Okay," she said. She narrowed her eyes at me. "Do you really know where the leftover cake is?"

So she'd heard Mac and me.

"Would I joke about cake?" I said.

She actually considered the question for a moment. Then she shook her head.

"It's Charlotte's banana chocolate chip cake. Do you want a slice?"

"Please," she said with a smile.

No spinach smoothie, no matter how good it might taste, was ever going to top a slice of Charlotte's banana chocolate chip cake—not as far as I was concerned. I did, however, find out that spinach smoothies taste even better when you have them with cake.

Rose and Charlotte came in about quarter to eleven. Avery and I had handled a steady stream of custom-ers all morning. I'd sold a guitar, a lace tablecloth and two mason jars full of salad forks. Avery had man-aged to sell everything that made up her autumn ta-ble setting, including the china plates and bowls, the white pumpkins and the mismatched collection of silver candlesticks. The customer had even asked for the orange seedpods from the Chinese lantern plant. Since I'd noticed the woman take a couple of photos of the table with her phone, I felt confident that she was going to replicate the entire look when she got home.

"How did it go?" I asked them once the man who had bought the forks left the store. Avery had gone back to sorting photos, but she wasn't even pretending not to listen.

"Robbie Gorham hasn't changed since he was a teenager," Charlotte said with a shake of her head. "He's all charm but not a lot of depth."

Rose was wearing her fisherman-knit sweater and she undid the round wooden buttons. "He's the kind of man who calls women our age 'girls' and thinks that's a compliment."

"So, you didn't find out anything."

"Heavens, no," Charlotte said. "Unless you count that I don't look a day older than when I retired."

"And you're just as nice as you ever were," Rose added with a smile.

"Robbie claims he didn't have any problem with Christopher Healy." Charlotte smoothed the back of her hair with one hand. "He said he figured the lawyers would work it all out."

"So he didn't admit to talking to Healy at the reception?" I said.

Rose shook her head. "In fact, he made a point of telling us that he didn't speak to the man, without us asking."

"Maybe he didn't," I said, picking a bit of cat fur off the front of my pants. "I didn't actually see him talking to Healy at the bar. I only saw him walking away."

"No, he was lying," Rose stated matter-of-factly. "He spun quite a tale about all the people he talked to instead of Mr. Healy."

Charlotte nodded. "I agree with Rose. As I told you before, Robbie always was one to take the easy way out. I was hoping he'd grow out of that." She sighed softly.

"I had dinner with Liam last night and I didn't find out anything useful, either," I said, "other than it looks like the lawsuit will continue even though Healy is dead."

"That's not surprising," Charlotte said.

"I didn't really get anywhere when I tried to talk to Liam about Joe Roswell. Liam just got . . . well, defensive. He doesn't believe Roswell could have had anything to do with what happened."

"He's very loyal," Rose said. She put a hand on my arm. "Why don't you let me talk to him instead?"

"I think that's a good idea," I said. "What are you going to do about Robb Gorham?"

"Talk to Stella as soon as she gets back," Charlotte said. "They're related somehow and you know whatever Stella has to say, she won't sugarcoat it."

"What else can I do?" I asked. That was a change, I realized. In the past I'd tried not to get involved. Now I was looking for ways to help.

"I think Alfred would like to see Elliot again," Rose said.

"I'd be happy to take him anytime."

Rose smiled. "Thank you. I appreciate that and I know Alfred does, too."

Mr. P. showed up just before lunch. He had a satisfied smile on his face. I was just coming back from the garage workshop and we walked in together.

"You look like you had a productive morning," I said.

He nodded. "I did."

"Would I be butting in if I came and listened while you update Charlotte and Rose?"

"Of course not," he said, hiking his already high-water pants up a little more. "You're part of the team."

We gathered in the Angels' office, Charlotte in her flowered apron because she was about to start her shift and Rose with several pages she'd printed that seemed to be part of the Chamber of Commerce member directory. Mr. P. sat at his desk.

"I had breakfast with Sammy this morning," he began. Sam and Mr. P. had been friends for years despite their age difference. They were both well-read and insightful and I'd often thought I'd like to be a fly on the wall when they talked. "I learned quite a bit about Cassie the bartender. For one, her last name is Gibson."

I held up one hand. "Wait a minute, Gibson as in Gibson's Point?"

Mr. P. smiled approvingly. "Ironically, yes, although Cassie Gibson is a Gibson by marriage only. Her husband is a descendant of Oliver Gibson, a crewmember on a British ship that explored the New England coast back in the early 1600s. Several of the crew stayed behind. Oliver Gibson was one of them. Gibson's Point belonged to that family a long, long time ago."

"So she was angry because Christopher Healy bought a piece of land that used to be in her husband's family?" Charlotte asked.

Mr. P. shook his head. "No. That property hasn't been in the Gibson family for several generations."

"But Cassie Gibson did have a reason to dislike Mr. Healy," Rose said.

"Yes, she did." Mr. P. looked over at me again. "You said that Vincent told you Cassie had been hoping to get hired with a crew to learn drywall and crack-filling on another one of Joe Roswell's construction projects."

I nodded. "That's right."

"Well, according to Sammy she had been hired, but then the project was put on hold—no paycheck and no health insurance."

I blew out a breath. "The inn project."

"Exactly," Mr. P. said. "When Christopher Healy bought that piece of land, Cassie Gibson lost a salary and the health insurance her husband needs to get back on his feet. Sammy says she didn't have a good word to say about young Mr. Healy." A cloud seemed to pass over Mr. P.'s face.

Rose gave his shoulder a squeeze.

"It's a long way from hating someone to killing them," I said.

Charlotte nodded. "Assuming she poisoned him— and we don't know for sure that's even how he died— what did she use and how did she obtain it? And how did she know Healy was going to crash the reception?"

"All very good questions, Charlotte," Mr. P. said. "I have a possible answer to one of them. Cassie Gibson's sister works at the holistic health center in the building next to Legacy Place. One of the practitioners is a homeopath."

"You think Cassie could have stolen something from the health center and poisoned Christopher Healy," Charlotte said.

Mr. P. nudged his glasses up his nose. "It's possible."

"Maybe all Cassie wanted to do was make Healy sick, not kill him," I said.

"The same thought occurred to me," he said.

Rose hadn't said a word. She looked a little disconcerted.

"Rose, is everything all right?" I asked.

She nodded. "I talked to Mabel last night. To see if she'd heard anything. She knows what's wrong with everyone."

I frowned. "Mabel?"

"My next-door neighbor when I lived at Shady—I mean Legacy Place." She shook her head. "You'd think a woman with so many ailments would be dead by now, but she's still with us."

I stifled a smile.

She waved one hand in the air. "Anyway, Mabel mentioned that there had been a break-in at the health center about a week or so ago."

We looked at one another.

"That's too coincidental to be a coincidence," she said, quoting the New York Yankees late catcher Yogi Berra.

Mr. P. adjusted his glasses. "So let's find out if it is," he said.

Chapter 11

Mr. P. turned to the internet to look for information about the break-in. Rose and Charlotte turned to their version of the information superhighway—town scuttlebutt, specifically all the gossip around town that their various friends and contacts were privy to. Since this wasn't a task I had the skills for, I went out to the garage to do some work on my mantel.

Mac had gotten the glass for what I had started calling the ice cream table and was working on attaching it to the top of the metal frame when Rose came across the parking lot. She stopped by the door and looked over the two pink garden benches. "Well. They would certainly get your attention," she said. She smiled at Mac. "I just came to let you know that you're having lunch on Monday."

He looked at her a little uncertainly. "I have lunch every day," he said.

"I know that," Rose said with just a touch of irritation in her voice. "I mean you're having lunch at Sam's."

"I am?" Mac still looked clueless.

Rose looked at me and gave her head the slightest of shakes.

I pushed my dust mask off of my face. "What time does Cassie Gibson's shift start?" I asked. I had a lot more experience than Mac did with the conversation veering off on a tangent.

"Eleven thirty," she said.

"Are you sure I should be doing this?" he asked, twisting the screwdriver he was holding between his fingers.

"Of course," Rose said. "All you have to do is talk to her. I've never seen you have any trouble talking to women here in the shop."

Rose was right. Mac was personable and friendly without being smarmy.

"You can do this," I said.

He blew out a breath. "Okay, I'll take a shot at it."

"Splendid!" Rose said. "If you need any tips, just talk to Alfred." She gave us a sly smile. "He's got game." She turned and made her way back to the shop.

Mac was struggling not to laugh. "He's got game?" he said once Rose was out of earshot.

I sat back on my heels. "One Saturday morning I came back from a run to see Mr. P. getting the newspaper wearing Rose's bathrobe and slippers and when he opened the door to her apartment I could hear her singing 'Sweet Emotion.'"

Mac shook his head. "That did not happen. "You're making it up."

"It happened and I'm scarred for life," I said. I wasn't sure which had been more traumatizing: seeing Mr. P. in a pink ruffled bathrobe and quite possibly nothing else or hearing Rose sing "Cause the backstage boogie sets your pants on fire."

Mac couldn't stop laughing. I pointed a finger at him. "Alfred Peterson's got the computer skills of a teenager hacker, he quotes Shakespeare like an English professor, and he's a pretty good dancer. I promise you, he's got game."

Although Mr. P. and I both wanted to see the piece of property that Christopher Healy owned, getting there seemed to take as much planning as Hannibal crossing the Alps. We were both in agreement that the terrain might be a bit too much for Rose—although neither one of us would have dared say so to her. I was secretly concerned it might be too much for Mr. P., too. In the end, we enlisted Nick's help and decided not to tell anyone else about our little field trip.

Nick picked me up right after supper, Mr. P. riding shotgun in the SUV.

"I feel a little guilty deceiving Rosie," Mr. P. said as Nick backed out of the driveway.

"I can stop at Mom's and you can tell her what you're doing and why you think she should stay home," Nick offered. He was obviously enjoying someone else potentially being in the hot seat with Rose since it was often him getting the third degree.

I smacked the back of his head. "Alfred said he feels a little guilty, not a little crazy," I said.

Nick just laughed.

The sky was low, heavy with dark clouds and the water was rough and angry, crashing against the shore below when we reached Christopher Healy's land. I could smell the salt in the air. The wind pulled at my hair. I pushed it back from my face and pulled the sleeves of my sock-monkey sweater down over my hands as I folded them across my chest.

"It's so beautiful," I said to Nick. It was, even with the clouds and the wind and the rain not that far away. There were some patches of grass and low stunted bushes on the sand and rocks, but much of the area was bare.

Nick picked up a smooth, flat rock and turned it over in his fingers. "Don't tell Liam, but I hate the thought that this place could end up as some kind of a hotel. Do you remember when we used to sneak down there to swim?" He pointed at the shore below.

I smiled and leaned against his arm for a moment. "I remember." They were good memories. I looked around. "And I think Christopher Healy was right. This place should be left alone."

Mr. P. was standing between us, one hand on the top of his head to keep his hat from blowing away. He had made his way carefully across the windy, uneven terrain and I mentally chastised myself for wondering if he would be up to it. I should have known better than to underestimate him. "I agree," he said. "There are some places that just need to be."

I nodded. There was a wildness to the stretch of land that made me think of huge sailing ships and adventures.

"I understand why Healy was fighting so hard to protect this piece of land," I said. I glanced down at my feet and then looked up again to see Nick watching me. "What?" I asked.

"You're thinking what I'm thinking, aren't you?" he said, stuffing his hands in his jacket pockets. "This land is the reason Healy is dead."

I pushed my hair behind one ear, but the wind tugged it free again. "I can't come up with any other reason."

Mr. P. nodded in agreement. "Neither can I."

"So what now?" Nick asked.

"You know what Rosie would say."

"Time for a cup of tea?" I said.

Mr. P. smiled. "She probably would say that, although that wasn't exactly what I was thinking of."

Nick tossed the rock he'd been holding out over the water. "Rose would say follow the money."

"'For the love of money is the root of evil,'" Mr. P. said softly. Most people misquoted the line as *Money is the root of all evil*—something Rose always gently corrected. Whether the line was stated exactly right or not, I knew she believed in the sentiment.

"So where do we start?" Nick said.

"McNamara's," I replied.

He frowned. "What does Glenn have to do with any of this?"

I pulled a strand of hair away from my face. "Nothing. But he does have hot chocolate. And if I'm going to follow the money, or the people with the money, *or* the people without the money I'm going to need a cup of hot chocolate. A big cup."

"Splendid idea, my dear," Mr. P. said, patting my arm. He and Nick started back to Nick's SUV. I took one last look around before I followed. Now that we understood Christopher Healy's passion for this piece of land maybe we'd be able to figure out who killed him.

Mac was helping a couple of his friends bring in their boats on Sunday. Jess was having brunch with Liam to continue the dating subterfuge. And Elvis had disappeared into the backyard. I called Michelle and invited her to lunch.

"I'm sorry for the late notice."

"Don't be," she said. "Believe it or not, I was just about to call you and suggest the same thing." She hesitated for a moment. "Can we declare a moratorium on talking about the Healy case? At least for today."

"Absolutely," I said.

We ended up going to McNamara's. Most of the lunch crowd had cleared out so we lingered over our coffee and dessert—tiny chocolate lava cakes—regaling Glenn with stories about our not-exactly-misspent youth. I laughed until my stomach ached. I hugged Michelle when she dropped me off and we both agreed we needed to do it again soon.

Rose was working Monday morning so we drove in together as usual. Mac had the coffee made and came down the stairs with a cup for me when we walked into the shop. Rose stopped, put her hands on her hips and eyed him. "You're not wearing that shirt to Sam's, are you?" she said. He was dressed in jeans and a green-and-blue-plaid shirt. He looked good to me. Then again, he always looked good to me.

"I'm guessing the right answer is no?" he said, somewhat uncertainly.

She pressed her lips together. "Well, it's not that there's anything wrong with your shirt." Her tone of voice said there definitely *was* something wrong with the shirt. "It's just that it doesn't showcase your assets." She thought for a moment. "Where's that long-sleeved black T-shirt?"

Mac held up a hand. "Wait a minute. What do you mean, 'showcase my assets'? Why does what shirt I wear to lunch matter?"

"Why does it matter?" Rose said, making a dismissive gesture with one hand. "If you were pounding in a nail, would you use the end of a screwdriver when you had a perfectly good hammer in your toolbox?" She didn't wait for his answer. "Of course you wouldn't. You'd use all the tools in your toolbox. That's what we're doing here." She started for the stairs. "You don't have to change until it's time to leave." She stopped on the second step from the bottom. "And put on your black jeans." She disappeared up the stairs.

Mac turned to me. "I'm already starting to regret this."

"I'm not," I said. "It'll work out. They know what they're doing. Don't panic. Rose won't do anything stupid." I counted off on my fingers all the things he'd said to me about the Angels' other cases.

He gave me a sheepish smile. "Okay, I deserved that. Anything else you need to say?"

I gave him the same kind of appraising look he'd gotten from Rose. "Nope. Just that she's right about the black jeans."

*   *   *

Mac came downstairs about eleven thirty, trailed by Rose, who wore a self-congratulatory smile. He was wearing the long-sleeved T-shirt and black jeans and he looked great. I was waiting on a customer interested in Mac's refurbished postal sorting table and it was hard not to get distracted—just to be absolutely certain he looked great from all sides. By the time the customer had decided that he wanted the table and I'd helped him wedge it in the back of his hybrid SUV, Mac had left in his old truck. Charlotte was just coming up the sidewalk. I waited for her and we walked inside together.

"We're going to have to wait a bit longer to talk to Stella," she said. "She's staying an extra day."

"I don't think that'll be a problem," I said. "She's a bit of a long shot anyway. I'm still not clear on how she and Robb Gorham are related."

"Second cousins once removed," Charlotte said. She frowned. "Or maybe it was first cousins twice removed."

I laughed. "Let's just say cousins and go with that."

"I saw Mac go by," she said.

"Are you sure this whole sending him to charm Cassie Gibson thing is a good idea?" I asked.

"Well," she hedged for a moment. "I won't say it's a good idea, but it's not a terrible one, either."

I sighed. "That doesn't exactly fill me with confidence."

Charlotte gave my arm a squeeze. "Mac will be fine. He's a smart man and what's the worst that can happen?"

"Oh I don't know," I said. "Maybe she'll hold Mac at knifepoint and I'll have to rush her while Mr. P. hits her over the head with a mixing bowl." I was referring to a previous case that had gone a little off the rails.

She smiled. She had obviously caught the reference. "Well, lucky for Mac, if that happens, both you and Alfred have already had some practice."

We stepped into the shop, where Rose was circling a wire mannequin torso that was taller than she was. A long striped scarf was wrapped around its neck. Charlotte walked over to join her.

I went upstairs thinking I'd get another cup of coffee, but instead I detoured into my office. Elvis was stretched out in the middle of my desk. He looked like he was doing a yoga corpse pose.

I caught sight of the guitar case beside my desk. It held a Seagull S6 that I'd bought a week ago from Cleveland, who had scavenged it from the contents of an old basement he'd been hired to lug to the landfill. I knew the Canadian company made good instruments—it had a cedar top and maple neck—but the guitar had only had three strings so I couldn't judge its tone. Still, it had seemed like a good buy and so I'd said yes to Cleveland's price. I needed to get to the music store and buy a new set of strings so I could be sure, as Liam had said when we were talking about Joe Roswell, that I hadn't bought a pig in a bonnet.

"I should just run down to the music store now and get the strings," I said to Elvis.

"Mrrr," he said. It could have meant "yes, you should" or it could have meant "whatever." I decided to go with the former.

I went back downstairs. It was quiet in the shop. Charlotte was watering the teacup gardens, a perennial favorite with tourists. Rose was nowhere to be seen.

"I'm going down to Herbie's to get a set of strings for that guitar up in my office," I said to Charlotte.

"So you think it's in good shape?" she said.

"I don't think it spent very long in that basement." I reached down to turn one of the teacups a half circle so all the handles were pointing in the same direction. "The neck is straight and the body is in very good shape. There's no sign of mold or warping."

"Do you think Nick would like it?"

I tucked my hair behind one ear. "Maybe," I said. Nick was a very talented musician although he tended to downplay his ability. "Why? Did he say something about it?" Nick had stopped by the day I'd bought the guitar from Cleveland. He'd tuned the three strings and told me I'd gotten a good deal.

"No." Charlotte shook her head. "I just noticed how completely focused he was when he was playing with that guitar. I thought maybe I'd surprise him with it for Christmas. What do you think?"

I remembered watching Nick with his head bent over the instrument. "I think it's a great idea," I said.

"Are we going to argue about the price?" she asked.

"Probably," I said.

She smiled. "Good to know."

I drove down to the music store and bought the guitar strings. Sam had offered to restring the guitar for me and I thought that I should probably stop by the pub and make sure the offer was still open. The fact that Mac was there trying to get information out of Cassie Gibson was just a happy coincidence. At least that's what I told myself.

I stepped inside The Black Bear hoping that there were enough people around that Mac wouldn't spot me. He was seated at the bar, back to the door, waiting for his lunch, I was guessing. Cassie Gibson was hanging wineglasses on the rack above her head. There was no indication they were having any kind of a conversation. Maybe he'd already gotten all the information Rose needed. Maybe he was waiting for the right moment to start talking to her. Maybe she wasn't going to tell him any more than she'd told me.

I heard an insistent sound, like air coming out of a punctured tire. I looked around. Liz was at a table across the room, where she could watch what was happening at the bar, but for the most part stay out of Mac's line of sight. She jerked her head to one side. I knew that meant "get over here." I went.

I slid onto the chair to her left.

"What are you doing here?" I asked.

"The same thing you're doing here," she said. "Spying on Mac."

"I'm not spying on Mac." I self-righteously squared my shoulders and sat up very straight in my seat. "I came to see Sam."

"Oh please!" Liz pointed a pink-tipped nail at me. "The way you came skulking in the door, all you needed was a cape and a mask covering half your face and you could have passed for the Phantom of the Opera."

"I wasn't skulking," I said. "I was being discreet."

"Well, whatever it was you were doing I don't think he saw you."

I leaned to the right a little so I could see the bar. "Has he talked to her yet?" I asked.

"Other than to order, no."

We watched for a couple of minutes. Mac tried more than once to start a conversation with Cassie Gibson, but it wasn't working.

"He's going down in flames," Liz muttered. "Enough of this foolishness." She got to her feet and headed across the pub. I scrambled after her.

Liz stopped next to Mac at the bar. His eyes widened in surprise. I stayed back a little. Cassie Gibson turned around, gave Liz a polite smile and said, "Can I help you?"

"Yes, I believe you can," Liz said. "My name is Elizabeth French. You were tending bar at a reception Thursday night in my boardroom."

Cassie nodded. "Yes. I was there." She swallowed as though her mouth was suddenly dry. Liz could be intimidating without even trying.

"Did you poison Christopher Healy?"

I winced. So much for subtlety.

"No, I didn't." The bartender stood her ground and her gaze stayed fixed on Liz's face.

I believe her, I thought.

"You broke into the clinic at the health center," Liz said. She tapped her nails on the bar. She was getting impatient.

"No, ma'am, I did not," Cassie said. Something flashed in her dark eyes.

"But you did take something from it, from the office where your sister works."

Cassie didn't answer. Her eyes darted away from Liz for a moment. We were getting somewhere.

"I'm a pretty good judge of people, young lady," Liz said. "I do believe that you didn't kill Mr. Healy. But you planned to do something."

"I didn't do anything," Cassie blurted. "I just wanted to make him miss court on Friday, that's all. I swiped something that I knew would make him sick to his stomach." She swallowed again like there was a lump in her throat that wouldn't go away. "The day after I took it, I saw him just down along the boardwalk and I couldn't help it. I told him what he'd done by messing up Joe's deal. I wasn't the only one who was out of work. He didn't care. I yelled something stupid and I walked away before I punched him and got in real trouble." She was sliding her plain gold wedding ring up and down her ring finger. "I was ashamed of myself. I went home and dumped the stuff I'd swiped down the sink and I took my husband to his physiotherapy appointment. I didn't want to be the kind of person who was out for revenge. The only thing I gave Christopher Healy that night was coffee, ma'am. I swear. That's all."

Liz took a card out of her purse and handed it across the bar. "Come to my office tomorrow."

Cassie picked up the card and looked at it before looking at Liz. "Why?" she asked.

"You're looking for a job, aren't you?"

The younger woman nodded.

"That's why," Liz said. She turned around, elbowing Mac as she did. "You're done, bucko," she said.

He turned halfway around, realizing for the first time that I was behind him. "Sarah, what are you doing here?" he asked.

"Long and embarrassing story," I said.

He smiled, gesturing at the bar. "I have a short and embarrassing story. I'll tell you mine if you tell me yours."

I nodded. "Deal."

He looked at Cassie. "Could I get my check, please?"

She was still watching Liz. She gave her head a shake. "Uh, yeah, no problem." She hesitated for a moment. "Do you know her?" she asked.

"Yes," I said.

"Is she legit?"

"She is."

Cassie looked a little shell-shocked. "So I might have a job?"

"As long as you're willing to work hard, yes."

She smiled, a genuine smile that lit up her face and I smiled back because what the heck, I like a happy ending as much as the next guy and this looked like a happy ending for Cassie Gibson and her family.

Mac paid his bill and I grabbed part of his sandwich because I hate to see food go to waste and because I had a feeling this was the only lunch I was going to get.

Liz was already gone. Mac and I stepped outside.

"Well, that went well," he said.

I started to laugh.

"Liz was spying on me, wasn't she?" he asked.

"Well . . ." I couldn't think of any other way to put it. "Yes, she was."

We started walking. "And so were you."

I shook my head. "No. I came to buy strings for the guitar that's up in my office."

Mac gave a long look. "And you ended up at Sam's because?"

"I needed to double-check that Sam was going to be able to put the new strings on." I could see Mac struggling not to smile out of the corner of my eye.

"And is he?"

"I didn't exactly get to ask him. Liz sidetracked me." I pressed my lips together and tried to look serious. I was pretty sure it wasn't working. We were walking past Cooks, which was a kitchen products store, owned by Marleigh Cook, who had been a chef in San Francisco for years before coming back to Maine. I loved the layers of meaning in the shop's name. I pointed at a red stand mixer in the front window. "I'm thinking of buying a mixer," I said, mostly to change the subject.

"I'm thinking of buying a house," Mac replied.

"Oh," was the only response I could come up with. We walked in awkward silence for maybe a minute.

"Why do you want a mixer?" Mac finally said. I gave him a sideways glance. He seemed genuinely curious.

"I want to make cakes the way Rose does." I felt my cheeks get warm at the admission. Now that Rose had taught me how to cook without a visit from the fire department, I'd discovered I actually enjoyed it.

"I like the sound of that," he said.

"Why do you want a house?" I asked. "I'm assuming it's not because you want to build a boat in the basement."

Mac grinned at the reference to our previous conversation. "I do want to build a boat, just not in my basement. I'm thinking about a house because I want to put down some roots."

I smiled at him. "*I* like the sound of that."

We walked for another few feet without talking.

"Do you believe her?" Mac suddenly asked. I knew he meant Cassie.

"I do," I said. "I watched her body language. She looked Liz in the eye. She didn't shuffle her feet or play with her hair. I think she was telling the truth."

He nodded. "So do I." He kicked a rock and sent it skittering along the boardwalk. "So now what?"

I shrugged. "So now there are two."

Chapter 12

Tuesday morning I got up early for a run. I did the hills route, pushing myself hard, hoping that somehow the exertion might lead to some kind of insight into Christopher Healy's death. It didn't.

My cell rang while I was getting dressed. Elvis immediately jumped up onto the bed and put a paw on the screen. "Excuse me, that's mine," I said. I grabbed the phone. He wrinkled his nose at me in annoyance.

It was Michelle. "Look, I know that Alfred Peterson is friends with Christopher Healy's stepfather so you're going to find this out anyway. Christopher Healy's death is being ruled a homicide."

I sat down on the edge of the bed. Elvis climbed onto my lap. "He was poisoned, wasn't he?"

For a moment there was silence. "Yes."

Rose had been right from the very beginning. I decided to go out on a limb. "Whatever killed him wasn't in the coffee."

"What makes you say that?" Michelle asked.

Elvis bumped my hand with his head and I started

to stroke his fur. "Liz talked to Cassie Gibson, the bartender. If the poison had been in the coffee she would have been the most likely person to have put it there."

"And she managed to convince Liz that she hadn't."

"Yes." Something occurred to me then. "If Christopher Healy wasn't poisoned at the party then the poison wasn't fast-acting," I said. "He could have ingested it hours before that."

"He could have," Michelle said, her tone noncommittal.

"It couldn't have been antifreeze or rat poison. The symptoms were wrong." I was thinking out loud as much as talking to her. I'd done a little reading online the night before about poisons.

Michelle sighed. "It will be impossible to keep something like this quiet for long. It was aconite."

"Aconite?"

"It comes from a plant. Several hours can pass between ingestion and death."

"I don't understand," I said. "Could Healy have been poisoned by accident? Did he come in contact with the plant in someone's garden or maybe on one of the hiking trails?"

"I can't tell you anything else, Sarah," Michelle said. "I know that Rose and Alfred and the rest of them aren't going to keep their noses out of this case, but if they come across anything, no matter how inconsequential it might seem, please call me."

I promised I would and we said good-bye.

I finished getting ready for work, collected my messenger bag and packed my lunch into a retro *Wonder*

Woman lunchbox I'd found at a yard sale back in the summer. I was unlocking the SUV when I noticed Tom Harris out in his driveway with Matilda. I knew botany was a hobby of his.

"I'm going to talk to Tom for a minute," I said to Elvis. The cat was already sitting on the front seat, but he started over to the door. "Matilda's with him."

Elvis made a sound like a disgruntled sigh and sat down again.

I gave him a scratch behind his left ear. "I won't be long."

Tom smiled when he caught sight of me. "Good morning, Sarah," he said. "Isn't it a beautiful morning?"

I looked up at the blue sky overhead and the red and gold leaves in his yard and mine. "Yes it is," I said. Matilda was quivering with happiness and I crouched down to talk to her. I knew Elvis was likely looking daggers at me from the car.

Once I'd given the little dog some attention I stood up again, brushing off my hands. "Tom, I need to pick your brain," I said.

He tapped his temple with one hand. "You're welcome to whatever is in there," he said.

"What can you tell me about aconite?"

"Tiny amounts are used in Chinese and homeopathic medicine, but larger amounts are poisonous."

"Where does it come from?"

"Monkshood. *Aconitum napellus*," he said. "It's a pretty plant, little purple-blue flowers. You've probably seen it." He pushed his glasses up his nose. "It grows wild in New England, but you can find it in a lot of gardens as well. It's also known as wolfsbane. Folklore holds that it's an effective way to defeat a werewolf."

"I'll try to remember that in case I ever come across a werewolf," I said with a smile.

"May I ask why you're interested in aconitum?"

"The Angels have a new case."

Two furrows formed between his bushy white eyebrows. "And you think someone may have been poisoned with aconite?"

"Is it possible to poison a person with the plant?" I asked. Matilda had leaned her warm, furry body against my leg. I reached down and patted her side.

"It certainly is," Tom said. "All parts of the plant are poisonous and aconite has a long history of being used to commit murder. Back in 1882 in England Dr. George Lamson was hanged for putting it in a Dundee cake—a Scottish fruitcake—and giving it to his brother-in-law. He was after the man's inheritance. I think you'll find the poison would most likely have been ingested between two and four hours before death occurred. Anyone with basic chemistry skills could have concocted it."

Two to four hours. That meant Cassie Gibson was likely in the clear assuming she'd been telling the truth about taking her husband to his physiotherapy appointment. Mr. P. had probably confirmed that by now.

Tom narrowed his gaze again. "Have I been of any help at all?"

"You've been a great deal of help," I said. "Thank you."

He smiled. "You're most welcome. If you have any more questions, please come and ask."

I nodded. "I will."

I said good-bye to Matilda and walked back to my SUV. I had a lot of information to relay to Rose and the others. Problem was, I had no idea how it was going to help.

Chapter 13

I spent the first part of the morning working on the mantel out in the garage workspace. Elvis lounged on a footstool that needed a repair to one of the legs, eyeing my work and making little murps every so often like a furry peanut gallery. A busload of Canadian tourists on their way home from a model train convention in Portland stopped in midmorning. They cleaned us out of all the teacup planters, half of the glass milk bottles, several Halloween-themed flowerpots and a box of glass test tubes.

"I am no longer surprised by the things people buy," I said to Charlotte as the bus headed down the street.

She smiled. "You know that old saying, 'There's a cover for every pot'?"

"Rose might have quoted it to me a few . . . dozen times," I said.

"Well, I think a variation of that might be there's a collector for everything."

"Which helps—at least in part—to keep us in business," I said. "So it's okay by me." I looked around the store. "Are there any more of the clay flowerpots left under the stairs? I think I should get Avery to paint a few more."

Charlotte shook her head. "No. The ones we just sold were from the last box we had under there."

"I think there's a box left out in the garage. I'll go out and get it." I looked at my watch. "Rose and Mr. P. should be here soon."

"Alfred was supposed to have coffee with his friend last night. He may have learned a little more about our victim—assuming, of course, that Christopher was murdered."

"He was," I said quietly.

"So you have some things to share as well," Charlotte said.

I nodded. "Yes, I do."

I found the box of clay flowerpots on the shelf at the back of the garage work space. Mac had one of his pink benches lying on its back. Even the underside was pink.

"Not saying a word," I said as I passed him.

"I appreciate that," he called after me.

I was halfway across the parking lot when Nick's SUV pulled in. Rose was in the front seat and Mr. P. was in the back. I waited while they parked and got out.

"Thank you, Nicolas," Mr. P. said.

Rose reached up and patted Nick's cheek. "Yes thank you," she said. "And remember what I told you— coconut oil."

"I will," he said.

"I'll be in in just a second," I said to Rose. "I have a couple of things to tell you."

"Take your time," she said. "I'm going to put the kettle on."

Nick walked over to join me. "What would happen if we ran out of tea?" I said.

He shook his head. "It's too ugly. I don't want to think about it." He glanced in the box I was holding. "Can I carry your pots?"

"You can," I said, handing over the box. "Coconut oil?"

"For my dry hands." We started for the back door. "You talked to Michelle this morning," he said.

I nodded. "She told me Healy was poisoned, murdered."

Nick nodded. "He was. We retraced his steps for the entire day. He wasn't anywhere that he could have encountered the poison by accident. This was deliberate."

"Michelle told me it was aconite."

Nick looked surprised at that information, but he made no comment.

"Did Rose tell you about Cassie Gibson?" I asked.

"The bartender? Yes. And Jess told me about seeing her and Healy arguing earlier on the day he was killed."

"Cassie's not the killer," I said. I hadn't bothered to pull on a jacket, but the sun was surprisingly warm on my back.

"I know. Alfred told me that he'd confirmed her alibi." Nick shrugged. "It would have been so simple if it had been her or any of the other half-dozen workers who got laid off because of the lawsuit."

"When have the Angels ever had a case that was simple?"

He shook his head. "They do seem to get involved in investigations that are kind of complicated."

"Rose sort of has a knack for that," I said.

"She would have made a good investigator and don't you dare tell her I said that." He pointed a finger at me in warning.

"Or what?" I teased.

"Or I'll tell Sam that you want to sit in on a song at the next jam and you're too shy to tell him."

"Sam won't believe the too-shy part."

"I can sell it." There was a challenge in his gaze. "Maybe I should try."

"No. No. No." I shook my head as I said the words. "You know I can't sing and I haven't touched my guitar in months." I punched his left arm. "You play dirty."

"First of all, you can sing and second, you know playing is like riding a bike."

I laughed. "You've seen me ride a bike. It's not exactly one of my strengths."

We'd reached the back door. I took the box back from Nick. "Get your guitar out," he said.

"I don't exactly have a lot of time at the moment," I said. "There's the shop and—"

"And the Angels latest case," he finished.

"Yes." I sounded a little self-righteous.

"So the sooner this case is solved the sooner you can get up on the stage at the pub." He nodded his head. He looked like a bobbleheaded dashboard doll.

"A little extra incentive is good on any case." He gave me a gentle punch in the shoulder. "I gotta go catch me a bad guy."

I took the box of flowerpots inside and set it on the workbench. Charlotte was in the store showing a lace tablecloth to two young women. Rose was coming down the stairs. "Alfred is making the tea," she said.

"I'll be out in a couple of minutes," I said. I headed for the storage cupboard under the stairs. Charlotte had sold two of the five cut-glass decanters that had been arranged on a small side table. I knew there was one more I could put out.

Charlotte had the tablecloth draped over two chairs when I came back, and the two women were studying it. The shorter of the pair frowned as she fingered a corner of the lace.

"Sarah, do you by any chance know anything about the history of this piece?" Charlotte asked. I walked over to join them and to get a closer look at the lace design.

"This one I do," I said, smiling at the women. "It belonged to Mary Kenney. It was a wedding present when she married her husband, Jack. She was eighteen and he was twenty. She used it on the table the first time she made Sunday dinner for the two of them. The roast was still frozen in the middle. She burned the potatoes and the gravy was more lumps than liquid."

The taller of the two women smiled. She was wearing a pile-lined denim jacket that Jess would have loved. "But he didn't care, because they were in love," she said.

"Not quite," I replied. "Jack told her that her cooking couldn't hold a candle to his mother's. Mary dumped the gravy on his head."

The two women exchanged a look. They didn't seem to know whether to laugh or be disappointed.

"But they worked it out in the end," I said. "They had seven kids."

The women exchanged a smile. "You have to buy it now," the woman in the denim jacket said to her friend.

The other woman nodded. "I'll take it," she said.

I helped Charlotte refold the cloth and wrapped it carefully in tissue paper while she rang up the sale. Mr. P. came down with the tea just as the two women were leaving.

"I won't be very long," I said to Charlotte. "Yell if you need me."

"I will," she said.

"I brought a cup for you," Mr. P. said as we headed to the office.

"Thank you," I said.

"I noticed the rest of Charlotte's banana chocolate chip cake seems to have disappeared." He studied my face for a moment. "Perhaps we have a ghost."

I nodded in agreement. "Perhaps we do."

"May I go first?" I said once we all had a cup of tea.

"Of course," Rose said.

"First of all, you were right. Christopher Healy was poisoned. And not by accident."

Mr. P. nodded as though that's what he'd suspected all along.

"Did Nicolas tell you?" Rose asked.

I took a sip of my tea. "No. I talked to Michelle."

"Does she know what the poison was?" Mr. P. said.

"Aconite."

"Monkshood?" Rose looked taken aback.

"Yes," I said.

"My grandmother used to have it in her side garden," she said. "We were all given strict orders not to go near it."

Mr. P. took off his glasses and reached for the little cloth he kept on his desk to clean them. "Where would Christopher have come in contact with monkshood?" he asked. "Especially at this time of year."

"He wouldn't have, which means he had to have ingested the poison without realizing it—anywhere between two and four hours before he died. The police went over his entire day. So did you. There's no way it could have happened accidentally." I told them what I'd learned from Tom about the poison.

"So whoever killed that young man most likely stole the aconite or made it themselves," Rose said. "And they would have had to have gotten close enough to him to put the poison in whatever he was drinking."

I nodded. "It looks that way."

"That suggests it was someone he knew, someone who could get close to his food in a way that wouldn't look suspicious. A colleague. A friend."

"Well, we know it wasn't Cassie Gibson. For most of that window of time she was at her husband's physiotherapy session," Mr. P. said. "I checked with the clinic. As for friends, from what I can see of Christopher Healy's social media, he didn't really have any."

"What about the other people on the crew with Cassie who got laid off?" Rose asked. She was holding her teacup but hadn't taken a drink yet. "Maybe it was one of them."

I sighed. "I don't think so. When I was talking to Nick out in the parking lot just now, he let it slip that all of them have been ruled out."

"We haven't eliminated Mr. Roswell or Mr. Gorham," Mr. P. pointed out.

"And I think that's where we should concentrate our efforts," Rose said. I recognized that determined look in her eye.

"I think you're right," I said.

Mr. P. nodded in agreement. "As do I."

"Do you mind if I ask if you've learned anything more about Christopher Healy?" I said. "Even after talking to his old girlfriend, I still think it would help to know more about him."

"Of course I don't mind," Mr. P. said. He turned in his chair so we were facing each other. "I spent some time with Elliot last night and we talked about Christopher and the lawsuit and the land at Gibson's Point." He hesitated. "It's complicated. Christopher is Nora's son, of course, not Elliot's, but he did tell me that if it were up to him, he would settle the lawsuit and sell Joe Roswell the land."

"But Nora doesn't agree."

"No, she doesn't. She wants to continue with Christopher's plan to turn the property into a nature preserve." He picked up the gray cloth he had used to clean his glasses and folded it into a neat square. "The problem is, Nora isn't well. She had skin cancer and now it's spread to her bones. Elliot would like to take her to Europe for an experimental stem cell treatment."

"And if they settle the lawsuit the money would pay for the treatment."

He nodded. "Sadly, it seems that Rosie's friend was right. Young Mr. Healy had some trouble finding his place in life. He tried a number of things but he didn't stick with anything. He lacked . . ."

"Strength of purpose," Rose said quietly.

"Yes," Mr. P. said. "It seems this nature preserve was the first thing to hold his interest for any length of time. Elliot didn't say so directly, but I suspect Nora has paid the bills for quite a few of her son's . . . dalliances despite the inheritance he received from his father."

"So there was a good chance that he would have seen the lawsuit through."

He nodded again. "Based on what I learned from Elliot I think that's correct."

I grimaced. "That just gives both Joe Roswell and Robb Gorham even more of a motive to have killed him."

His eyes met mine. "I came to the same conclusion."

I heard the click of Liz's high heels on the floor outside in the workroom. In a moment she appeared in the doorway. "Well, hail, hail the gang's all here," she said. She was wearing a gray skirt with a cerulean blue jacket and a gray-and-blue-tie-dyed scarf at her neck. I knew the scarf was one of Jess's creations.

"No, the gang is not all here. Alfred and Sarah and I are here," Rose said. "Charlotte is in the shop and Nicolas is at work."

Nicolas was part of the gang? I wondered if he knew that.

"It's a figure of speech, Rose," Liz said.

"Well, it's not a very good one since it doesn't properly describe the situation," Rose retorted.

Liz held up both hands as though she was trying to calm an angry mob carrying torches and pitchforks. "Fine," she said. "But 'hail, hail Alfred, Sarah and Rose are all here' doesn't have the same ring."

I gave her my chair and leaned against Mr. P.'s desk. "What brings you here?" I asked.

"I've been asking around about Joe Roswell," she said. "I thought you might like to hear what I've found out so far."

Mr. P. smiled reassuringly. "Thank you, Elizabeth. We would."

"He's broke," she said flatly.

"That doesn't make any sense," I said. "He's been working on the hotel project for months."

Liz tapped one French-tipped nail on the arm of the chair. "The only reason his business is still afloat is credit and goodwill. He built an office complex down in Portland and got very overextended on that. If he doesn't win this lawsuit, it'll be the end of his company."

I laced my fingers together and rested both hands on top of my head. Liam hadn't given any indication that his friend's business was in this much trouble. Was it possible he didn't know?

"That sounds like a motive for murder," Rose said.

Liz shifted to look at her. "Oh, it gets better. Or maybe I should say worse; I guess it depends on your perspective. Mr. Roswell has an assault charge from several years ago that apparently was dismissed. I didn't get the details."

"I can," Mr. P. said. Given his computer skills there was very little that he couldn't find out.

I tipped my head back and stared up at the ceiling for a moment. "I'm having trouble getting my head around the idea that Joe Roswell might have killed someone over a piece of land. He let us have all the toys and the photos they found to auction off for the hot lunch program."

"It isn't just a piece of land, toots," Liz said. "It's also the man's business. People have killed for a lot less. And by the way, do we know yet how Christopher Healy *was* killed?"

"We do," Rose said. She quickly brought Liz up to date.

"Aconite?" Liz said. "You're positive?" Two furrows had appeared between her expertly groomed eyebrows.

"Yes," I said, dropping my hands onto my lap. "Why? Is there a problem?"

"For Mr. Roswell, maybe."

"We're not getting any younger, Liz," Rose said impatiently. "Spit it out."

"Fine," Liz said. "Joe Roswell's wife is a teacher." She paused for a moment, probably to needle Rose just a little. "She teaches high school chemistry."

I blew out a breath. I could hear Tom Harris's words in my head when he'd explained about extracting the poison: *Anyone with basic chemistry skills could have made it.*

"I think it's time we talked to Mr. Roswell," Rose said.

Liz lifted the teapot and frowned. I was guessing it was empty. "That might not be so easy," she said.

"Why do you say that?" Mr. P. asked.

"Because from what I hear, Joe Roswell is spending most of his time closeted with his lawyers trying to find a way to get this lawsuit settled in his favor." Liz glanced at me. "Even your brother admitted the man hasn't been around much in the past few days."

"You didn't tell Liam that we think Joe might have killed Christopher Healy, did you?" I asked. Liam hadn't taken it well when he had thought I was implying that same thing.

"Of course not," she said, making a dismissive gesture with one hand. "I said I wanted to know more about the apartment idea, which is true because I do want to know more."

Based on what Mr. P. had told me, I wasn't sure that was going to happen.

"I can get us in to see Mr. Roswell," Rose said as though it was a done deal. I'd been subject to her persuasive skills before so I had no doubt she'd find a way to make sure it was.

It was decided—mostly by Rose—that Liz would see if she could find out anything more about Joe Roswell's business while Mr. P. looked into the assault charge. There didn't seem to be anything that needed my skills at the moment.

I walked Liz out to her car. Mac was still working on one of the pink benches. "How long are you two going to keep dancing around each other?" she asked.

"We're not dancing around each other," I said. I felt my face getting warm, which took away some of the credence of my words.

Liz gave a snort of laughter. "Please. All you two

need is tap shoes and top hats and we could sell tickets."

I looked around the parking lot. Maybe a sinkhole would open up, swallow me and I wouldn't have to have this conversation. I glanced down at my feet. No such luck.

Liz poked me with her elbow. "Make a move," she said. "Walk over and lay one on him."

"Lay one what on him?" I asked.

Liz gave a near eye roll. "Oh, for heaven's sake! No wonder this—whatever this is—isn't getting off the ground." She stopped walking and jabbed my shoulder with one finger. Hard. "Kiss him."

I stared wide-eyed at her. "I'm not doing that." She sounded like Liam when he'd been trying to get me together with Nick.

She sighed. "I had two husbands—both good men. Both crazy about me. But if I hadn't stoked the fire, so to speak, I'd still be Elizabeth Emmerson, not Elizabeth Emmerson Kiley French."

I waved both hands in front of my face. "We are not talking about my love life. Not. Not. Not."

We'd started walking again. Liz gave a snort of laughter. "You don't have a love life, missy," she said. "Rose and Alfred have a love life. Your brother is at least pretending to have one. And I'm not sure I want to know what Avery is doing. You, toots? Zippo."

I put my fingers in my ears. That just made her laugh more.

We reached the car and Liz opened the driver's door. I dropped my fingers. Her expression turned serious. "Decide what you want, Sarah," she said.

"And go after it. Before someone else does." She kissed my forehead and got behind the wheel.

I watched her drive away and thought about her advice. Was going after what *he* wanted what had gotten Christopher Healy killed?

Chapter 14

When Elvis and I stepped into the hallway the next morning Rose and Mr. P. were waiting for us. I noticed that Mr. P. was wearing a different shirt but the same pants as the day before. And he'd nicked himself shaving as though maybe he'd been using something other than his dependable double-edged safety razor. I thought about Liz saying Rose and Mr. P. had more of a love life than I did. I decided that not only did I not want to talk about my love life—nonexistent or otherwise—I didn't want to think about anyone else's, either.

"Charlotte called," Rose said. "Stella Hall got back last night."

"You're going to talk to her," I said.

"As my mother used to say, nothing ventured, nothing gained."

"Where and when?" I asked as we walked out to the car.

Mr. P. was leaning forward, talking to Elvis, who seemed to be holding up his end of the conversation.

"Stella volunteers at the library on Wednesday mornings," Rose said.

Mr. P. looked over at me. "You're welcome to join us."

"Thank you," I said. "I think I will."

I hadn't really done anything on the case so far. In the past I would have seen that as a good thing, but I didn't feel that way now. The memory of doing chest compressions on Christopher Healy was still fresh in my mind. Maybe I felt just a little guilt because Nick and I hadn't been able to save him.

We got to the library just as it opened. "Give me a minute," Rose said. "I'll find out where Stella is." She headed over to the front desk. There was an easel just to the right of the stairs to the second floor. A large poster was resting on it and Mr. P. and I went over to see what it said.

The poster turned out to be an artist's rendering of a proposed ice skating oval to be created at the far end of the library parking lot for the coming winter.

"Maybe Rosie and I will come skating," Mr. P. said. He pointed at the drawing. "They're going to have a hot chocolate stand."

"I think I'd like the hot chocolate part better than the actual skating part," I said.

Mr. P. smiled. "You know the building where the Emmerson Foundation has its offices, the old soap factory?"

I nodded.

"When I was young there was an empty field next door. In the winter the owners of the factory would make a rink for the kids. Elliot and I used to skate there all the time." His smile told me the memory was a good one.

I tried to picture Mr. P. as a teenager racing across the ice with his friends. "You two were close back then."

He nodded. "We were. Even though we weren't in the same class, we spent a lot of time together because of Scouts and football. One of us was always coming up with some potential merit badge to challenge the other to."

"Like?"

"Elliot decided we should get our archery badges."

"Wait a minute," I said. "You know how to use a bow and arrow?"

"I do." There was a teasing gleam in his eyes. "Although I wouldn't advise placing an apple on top of your head to test those skills. I'm a bit rusty."

"I will keep that in mind," I said. I glanced over at the desk. Rose was deep in conversation with one of the reference librarians. I turned my attention back to Mr. P. "So what other badges did you get?" I asked.

His mouth pulled to one side as he thought. "Let me see; there were no badges for computer skills back then, as you might guess, but we did receive merit badges in electricity and electronics."

I arched an eyebrow. "Impressive."

"We also received our badges for cooking; camping, of course; stamp collecting; woodworking, leather work—I made a small change purse for my mother and a belt for my father. Elliot and I planted a vegetable garden for our gardening badge and then made a meal with what we grew for our cooking badge."

"I'm beginning to understand where many of your talents come from," I said.

"I hope I still have a few secrets left," he replied with a teasing smile.

From the corner of my eye I saw Rose coming toward us. I made a sweeping gesture with one hand. "Since we're standing in a building filled with books, Mr. P., I'll just say I like to think that you still have many more stories to share."

Rose joined us then. "Stella is upstairs working on a display in the reference section," she said.

"The elevator is right over there," I said, pointing.

Rose looked wordlessly at me over the top of her glasses.

"Or the stairs," I added hastily. "Stairs are good." Rose didn't like even the implication that she needed the elevator instead of the stairs.

We found Stella working on a bulletin board display that listed the various events observed during the month with corresponding book suggestions. Among other things it seemed October was Cookbook Month, National Pizza Month and Family History Month.

Stella smiled when she spotted us. "I figured I'd be seeing you people sooner rather than later," she said.

I smiled back at her. "Gram said she had tea with you last week." Stella and my grandmother had been friends since—as Gram explained it—they were captains of opposing Red Rover teams on the playground.

"It's good to finally have her home," Stella said. "Married life obviously agrees with her. I told her I might have to go looking for a husband if having one would make me look that much younger too." She switched her attention to Rose and Mr. P. "But enough of that. You want to know what I can tell you about Robbie."

"You heard what happened at the reception last week," Rose said.

"I heard," Stella said. "Nora Healy's boy. Well, Nora Casey now. Terrible thing." She glanced at me. "I also heard you tried to save him." She nodded approvingly.

"You probably also know that Christopher Healy was being sued."

"By Joe Roswell. Over that piece of land out at Gibson's Point. Robbie claims he has some kind of system that can stabilize that whole embankment, make it safe to build on."

"Does he?" Mr. P. asked.

Stella laughed. "Depends on who you talk to. If you're talking to Robbie, well, he's going to change the construction industry. Other than Joe Roswell—who rumor has it is feeling the pinch—no one's lining up outside Robbie's door to give this new system of his a try."

"You don't think it will work," Mr. P. said. He and Rose exchanged a look, which Stella noticed.

"I'm not sayin' Robbie is trying to con Joe or anyone else. He's just always been the kind of person who cuts corners and takes the easy way out." Exactly what Charlotte had said.

"The damnedest thing is, women just can't seem to resist that boy," Stella continued. "I'm not giving away any secrets by telling you he has a complicated personal life: an ex-wife, a wife who's probably going to be an ex-wife pretty soon and a girlfriend."

"He certainly has been busy," Rose said.

"And surprisingly, when things fall apart, he manages to stay friends." She shook her head. "Take Leesa for instance. She's Robbie's ex-wife. They were married for about five minutes when they were barely more than teenagers. She's been in town for the past few weeks. I know she was planning on seeing him. She's involved with that Seabed 2030 project."

"The project to map the ocean floor?" Mr. P. said.

"That's the one. I had breakfast with her." Stella held out her right arm. She was wearing a silver charm bracelet. She touched a tiny anchor hanging from it with one finger. "She brought me this and she said she was going to have dinner with Robbie one night. Not a lot of people want to be in the same room with their exes, let alone have dinner with them."

Rose and Mr. P. seemed to have reached some unspoken agreement that the conversation was over. "Thank you," Rose said.

"I'm not sure I've been much help," Stella replied, "but you're welcome."

I gave her a hug good-bye. "How's Lily?" I asked. Lily Hall was Stella's niece by marriage. A spinal injury had put her in a wheelchair and an expensive experimental surgery had gotten her out of it. Stella had stepped in to take care of Lily's children and Lily herself before and after the operation.

"She's good," Stella said. "Better than good. That's where I was. She's so much stronger and healthier and the kids are doing great. It's a new beginning for all of them."

"Another kind of happy ending," I said. "Please tell her hello the next time you talk to her."

Stella nodded. "I will."

We headed out to the SUV. No one said anything until we had pulled out of the parking lot. Rose was sitting next to me and I saw her give me a sideways glance. "What do you think, Sarah?" she finally said.

"Honestly?" I asked.

She frowned at me. "Of course. Why else would I be asking you?"

"Okay. Right now, with what we know, I don't think Robb Gorham is our killer."

"What makes you say that?" Mr. P. asked from the backseat.

I waited for a break in traffic and then turned right. "For one thing, both Charlotte and Stella described him as being the kind of person who takes the easy way out. Poisoning Christopher Healy took work. It took planning. It wasn't easy. And second, it seems like he goes through life coasting on his charm. I get the feeling that if things don't work out here he'll just take his stabilization system somewhere else."

"I agree."

I shot a quick glance at Rose.

"So do I," she said. "It seems that Joe Roswell had a lot more to lose."

I nodded. "That's what I was thinking."

"I don't disagree with you," Mr. P. said. "But I think

we need a little more evidence before we eliminate Mr. Gorham entirely. I think we at least have to find out where he was in that window of time when the poisoning took place."

Beside me I saw Rose nod her head. "As usual, Alfred, you are the voice of reason."

Right before lunch I took the Seagull S6 down to Sam to get it stringed. "This is a nice guitar," Sam said, running his hands over the smooth wood. "Where did Cleveland find it?"

"In someone's basement," I said, taking a seat on the sofa in Sam's office with the cup of coffee he'd brought me. "Guy hired him to clear everything out and said he could keep anything he wanted." I explained that Charlotte was thinking of buying the guitar as a Christmas present for Nick.

"Good to know," Sam said. "I know how he likes the action. I'll set it up that way." He put the guitar back in its case and came to sit next to me.

"What do I owe you?" I asked. We'd had this conversation lots of times before and it always ended with Sam refusing payment. He'd restrung several guitars for me and given me his opinion on even more, but he wouldn't take anything for his efforts. If I pushed he'd remind me we were family.

"Actually, I'm the one who owes you," he said.

I was confused. "You do? What for?"

"Actually, you and Liz. For Cassie Gibson."

"Oh, you mean the job," I said. "Vince told me you knew her dad."

"We went to school together," Sam said. "He died about five years ago. Cassie's a good kid. And she's not afraid of hard work."

Cassie had showed up at the Emmerson Foundation as Liz had instructed and Liz had kept her promise, hiring the bartender to work with *her* assistant, Jane. I took a sip of my coffee. "That was all Liz."

"Then I owe Liz," he said.

I laughed. "That's a little scary."

Sam smiled. "I think her bark is worse than her bite."

I leaned against the back of the sofa. "I think the two of you are a lot alike."

"I'm going to take that as a compliment," Sam said.

"I meant it as one," I said. "You both have huge hearts and you both look out for the people you care about."

"I could say the same about you, kiddo." He gave my hand a squeeze then reached for his own coffee cup on the desk. "I take it that since Liz gave Cassie a job she isn't a suspect in your case."

I shook my head. "She's not. I can't get into details, but she has an alibi."

"I couldn't see Cassie killing someone," Sam said. "She's a good kid who's trying to make the best of being dealt a bad hand. I take it you know about her husband."

"I do." I propped my elbow on the sofa back and leaned my head on my hand. "This whole case is complicated. The only reason Rose got the Angels involved is because Mr. P. is old friends with Christopher Healy's stepfather."

"Elliot Casey," Sam said. "They seem like an odd pair to be friends."

"Hang on. You know Elliot?"

He shook his head. "I know *about* him. Poker."

Sam played poker semi-regularly with Mr. P. and a group of his cronies. Rose claimed they were a bigger bunch of gossips than any stereotypical group of senior women.

"And?" I prompted.

Sam fingered his beard. "It's nothing, really. It's just that Elliot Casey's name has come up a couple of times. Those guys like to talk about the 'good old days.'"

"Now I'm curious," I said. "Are you going to tell me that Mr. P. has a secret wild-child past?"

He laughed. "Pretty much just the opposite. Alfred Peterson has always been a straight arrow, for the most part. His friend, on the other hand, cut a wide swath as a young man—always another pretty young woman on his arm buying him things to hear the guys tell it. It looks like maybe Alfred was a good influence on Elliot, kinda like the way your dad was on me."

"You never told me that about Dad before," I said.

Sam shrugged. "There are some things I did back when I was a kid that I'm not proud of. I drank too much and I used it as an excuse to treat more than one woman badly. If it hadn't been for your father, my life might have gone a very different way."

I didn't know what to say.

He cleared his throat. "I've always tried to live my life so he wouldn't ever have regretted being my friend. I hope Elliot realizes how lucky he is to have Alfred Peterson as his friend."

"For what it's worth, I have always been glad to have you as my friend," I said.

Sam smiled. "Right back at you, kiddo."

I'd been back at the shop for a couple of hours when Liam arrived. Charlotte and I were out in the workroom behind the shop, looking at the last box of photos. We'd decided to group the school photos by five-year increments and were sorting them into piles with Elvis sitting between us watching and occasionally poking a photograph with a paw. Liam came in the back door and stalked over to us, his coat swinging open.

"I need to talk to you," he said, his blue-gray eyes cloudy with anger.

"So talk." I turned to face him.

He glanced at Charlotte. I could see the tension in his shoulders and jawline. "Fine. Why couldn't you just take my word that Joe is a good guy?"

"Because the person he was suing ended up dead at an event he was hosting," I said.

"I told you Joe didn't have anything to do with Healy's death." Elvis picked his way around the stacks of photographs and made his way over to Liam, who automatically began to stroke the cat's fur. "You're acting like he's hiding something. Why can't you just take my word for it that he's not involved?"

"Maybe because you're lying," Charlotte said in

the same tone of voice she might have used to say the sun was shining. "Elvis thinks so and so do I."

We weren't exactly sure *how* he did it, but Elvis could somehow tell when someone was lying. His green eyes would narrow and one ear would turn to the side as his expression soured. Which is exactly how he looked right now. Mac's theory was that the cat was reading the same sort of physical reactions that a polygraph did, which was as good an explanation as any.

"I'm not sure how Elvis came to that conclusion," Charlotte continued, "but I noticed you're rubbing your left eyebrow and you used to do that when you were a little boy trying to pull a fast one."

Liam dropped both hands to his sides. He sucked in a breath and blew it out again.

"What's going on?" I asked.

His mouth worked for a minute before he spoke. "Okay, there is something I haven't told you about Joe, but it doesn't have anything to do with Healy's death. I swear. Joe had no reason to kill the guy. From the beginning he's always believed the judge would rule in his favor and the inn project would be back on."

I propped one hand on my hip. "So what is this something you haven't told me?"

"Joe's a good guy," Liam said. "He's been hiring some people who couldn't get work anywhere else—guys who are homeless or have criminal records—he gives them a chance to support themselves and get some job experience. A lot of these guys he's been paying under the table, which he shouldn't do. Some of them are on the books, but he's sort of had to fudge their background checks."

"That's a really bad idea," I said, making a face.

Liam started petting Elvis again. "I know, I know," he said. "Joe's just trying to give these guys a second chance. He said someone did that for his dad and he just wants to pay it forward. It's the only thing he's hiding." He held up his free hand. "See? No eyebrow rubbing."

I believed him. "Okay. What do you know about an assault charge from a couple of years ago?"

"Joe went after a guy who was beating a dog. You would have done the same thing, Sarah. And those charges were dropped."

"Liam, no one's trying to railroad your friend," Charlotte said. "We're just trying to get some answers for Alfred's friend."

Liam didn't say anything for a long moment. Finally he nodded. "I get it. I'm sorry."

I heard his phone buzz in his pocket.

"I have to go," he said. "I have a meeting to get to." He gave me an inquiring look. "Are we good?"

I nodded. "We're good."

His gaze shifted to Charlotte. "Always," she said, leaning over to give him a hug.

I slumped against the workbench after Liam left. Elvis came and leaned his furry face against mine. I looked at Charlotte. "Nothing Liam said suggests that Joe Roswell couldn't have killed Christopher Healy," I said. "In fact, if Healy had found out about the faked background checks . . ." I didn't finish the sentence.

"I know," Charlotte said. "Rose is on it. She'll make it happen."

"I hope you're right," I said. I gave Elvis a scratch on the top of his head. "Go help Avery," I told him.

He dutifully hopped down from the bench and headed for the shop. I followed to open the door for him.

Charlotte and I started sorting the photographs again. "So what's my tell?" I asked.

She glanced over at me for a moment. "What do you mean?"

"Liam rubs his eyebrow when he's lying. What do I do?"

A small smile pulled at the corners of her mouth. "Why do you think you do anything?"

She'd answered my question with a question. Nick called that "doing the teacher thing."

I turned to look at her. "You don't want me to know," I said.

Charlotte held a photo at arm's length and studied it for a moment before setting it on a pile by her left elbow. "Did we actually establish that you have a tell?" she asked.

"It's not the eyebrow thing like Liam," I said. I put a hand to my hair. "Is it my hair? Do I touch my hair when I'm not telling the truth?"

"You have lovely hair," Charlotte said. "I especially like the layers you added last time you had it cut."

"Wait a minute, what about my nose?" I rubbed my finger along the bridge of it.

"You have your mother's nose. Nice and straight." She gave me a sweet smile.

I spent the next five minutes trying to get Charlotte

to divulge how—if—she could tell when I wasn't being honest, with my guesses getting more and more silly. Was it how I stuck out my chin? How often I blinked? Or burped? She effortlessly blocked every attempt. It was like a fencing match: thrust and parry, thrust and parry, until I was shaking with laughter. It was good not to think about death for a while.

Chapter 15

Elvis and I had been home for about half an hour Wednesday evening when Tom Harris knocked on my door. "I'm sorry to trouble you," he said, "but Rose isn't home."

"It's no trouble," I said. "Please, come in." I opened the door wider.

Tom wiped his feet carefully on the mat and stepped into the living room. He was carrying a long brown envelope. "I've finished the research I was doing for Rose, and she asked me to leave everything with you if she wasn't here when I finished my work." He held out the envelope.

I took it from him. "Thank you," I said. I had no idea what was inside. Rose had neglected to tell me that she'd asked Tom for help.

"I think I found what she was looking for," he added.

"What were you looking for?" I asked. "Rose didn't say."

"I can't imagine her minding if I tell you," Tom said.

"She brought me the specifications for a ground stabilization system. It uses a network of interconnected fibers. She wanted to know if I thought it would work."

Robb Gorham's system. It had to be.

I glanced at the envelope in my hand. "And what do you think?"

Tom shook his head. "Oh, I doubt very much that it will."

Confirmation of what I had suspected. "May I ask why?"

He took off his glasses, bent the left arm out slightly and put them back on again. "I don't know how much you know about this process."

"Not a lot," I said. "I know that the material that is supposed to keep the ground from collapsing or washing away is made from soy fibers and that it's supposed to be environmentally friendly."

Tom nodded. "You're correct. I have several problems with the process, but the biggest one has to do with the tensile strength of the soy fibers." His eye narrowed behind his glasses. "You understand the concept of tensile strength, I assume."

I remembered the conversation I'd had with Mac when I'd managed to get the last caster onto the leg of the mail-sorting table. I'd told him my technique involved estimating the tensile strength of the metal when really all it had been was dumb luck. "I think so," I said. "It's a measure of how resistant something is to breaking when it's being pulled at or made longer."

He smiled at me. "That's it exactly. The success of this stabilization system depends in large part on the tensile strength of those fibers."

I nodded slowly. So far I was following.

"Seawater is alkaline with a pH of about 8.3," he continued. "Shoreline areas that are battered by waves tend to have more alkaline soil."

"Because of the seawater."

"Yes. And an alkaline environment does tend to reduce the tensile strength of the fibers."

He looked expectantly at me, waiting for me to make the connection. "They won't be strong enough," I said. "They won't hold the ground in place." I knew by the expression on Tom's face that I'd gotten it right.

"No, they won't," he said. "Not along the coastline, for certain. Probably not anywhere."

"Thank you so much," I said.

Tom smiled again. "You're very welcome. It was my pleasure. Please tell Rose if there's anything else I could help with I'd be more than happy."

I assured him I would and he left. I dropped onto the couch still holding the brown envelope in one hand. Elvis padded in from the bedroom, jumped up beside me and began to sniff the envelope. He made a face, his whiskers twitched and his tail flicked in annoyance.

"There's no way you can smell dog on that envelope," I said. "What you might be getting a whiff of though, is a motive for murder."

Elvis gave me a look. He wasn't as impressed with my metaphor as I was.

"I knew Tom would be able to get to the bottom of things," Rose said with a satisfied smile the next morning. We were headed to the shop and I'd just shared what I'd learned from our neighbor the night before.

"It gives Robb Gorham a motive. He had to have known. The question is, where did he get the aconite?"

"Yes, we do need to answer that question," Rose said. "Maybe Nicolas will have some ideas."

"You're going to ask Nick?" I said. "I'm not sure that's a good idea." Even Elvis wasn't sure it was a good idea. He was looking at Rose, his tail moving restlessly along the seat.

"Why on earth would you say that?" she asked. "Nicolas is committed to solving this case just like we are. And we agreed to pool our resources."

That wasn't quite how I remembered it.

"What if we took a look at Robb Gorham's social media as well?" I said. "We might find a clue there."

Rose was fishing in her bag for something. "That's a good idea. I'll ask Alfred to do that."

I was out in the workroom about an hour later trying to decide which in our never-ending collection of mismatched chairs I was going to take into the shop when Nick came in.

"Can I help?" he asked.

"I'm trying to get that chair in the corner," I said.

He leaned sideways for a better look. "The one that's upside down or the one that's right side up."

"Right side up. The pale green one."

Nick moved several chairs, squeezed into the fairly tight space and managed to extricate the one I wanted.

"Thank you," I said. "That was your good deed for the day."

He smiled. "It's always good to have a little positive karma in the bank." He looked around. "Rose is working?"

I nodded. "She called you, didn't she?" I started putting the chairs that I didn't want back where they had been stacked. Nick picked up a couple of them and I pointed to a spot where he could put them. "Thanks," I said.

"I gather you have some new information about Robb Gorham," he said.

There were dust bunnies clinging to the left leg of my jeans. I leaned down to brush them off and made a mental note to vacuum this whole section of the workroom. "You know that whole environmentally friendly ground-stabilization system he's been promoting?" I straightened up.

Nick gave a wry smile. "Let me guess. It doesn't work."

"Bingo," I said. I shared what Tom had explained to me.

"I thought it sounded too good to be true," he said. "Liam said I was a cynic."

"You can be a cynic and still be right," I teased.

He stuffed his hands in his pockets and rocked from one foot to another. "So you think this gives Robb Gorham a motive to have killed Christopher Healy?"

"It means he had a lot more to lose than just the chance to be involved in building an inn on the land at Gibson's Point."

Nick shook his head. "Why poison Healy, though? I can see hitting him over the head with a two-by-four or, say, stabbing him with a drywall knife in the heat of anger. But using poison takes thought, effort, time.

I could understand it maybe if the killer had used rat poison for example or antifreeze; those are more spur-of-the-moment. But aconite? How many people even know it's toxic?"

I ran my hand over the smooth back of the green chair. "I think the killer went to a lot of trouble not to be caught. That's why he or she used the aconite. It isn't as common as, say, antifreeze. On the other hand he—or she—must have had easy access to it, otherwise getting it would have drawn too much attention." I picked up the chair. Nick grabbed the other one and we started for the shop.

"I see your logic," he said. "The problem is, the one person who did have fairly easy access to aconite has an alibi."

"You mean Cassie Gibson."

"Her sister does work at that naturopathic clinic."

I pushed my hair back off my face. "Mr. P. checked her alibi," I said. "And even if she hadn't been at her husband's physiotherapy appointment, how would Cassie have been able to get the aconite into Christopher Healy? The only drink of his she would have had access to was that cup of coffee at the reception."

"He didn't have to drink it," Nick said, stepping into the shop. He looked around. "Where do you want this?"

I was still standing by the door holding the other chair. "Umm, over by the bookcase and what do you mean by 'he didn't have to drink it'?"

Nick set the chair where I'd indicated, eyed it for a moment and then shifted it a little to the right. He turned to look at me. "Christopher Healy could have absorbed the aconite through his skin."

I stared at him, my mouth hanging open. Rose had been coming from the storage closet under the stairs. She'd heard what Nick had said. The quilt she was holding slipped from her hands as his words sank in.

"What?" we both said at the same time.

"Nicolas, did I hear you correctly?" Rose was still staring at him, the quilt forgotten on the floor at her feet.

I folded one arm up over my head, digging my fingers into my scalp. I suddenly had a headache. "You're just telling us this now?"

He looked surprised. "I'm sorry. I thought you knew. Aconite can be absorbed through the skin. In Healy's case, he'd been drinking. That dilates the blood vessels, which just would have speeded up the absorption process."

"So that young man didn't drink the poison?" Rose frowned.

"We don't know that for sure yet," Nick said. "Analysis of his stomach contents isn't back. But yes, it's possible he didn't."

Possible.

So instead of looking for someone Christopher Healy might have had a cup of coffee with, or lunch, or even a beer, someone he likely knew such as a business connection, we were really looking for anyone who could have gotten close enough to slip the poison into say, a bottle of hand sanitizer. I wasn't sure if Nick had just made the case simpler or more complicated.

Rose noticed the quilt at her feet and picked it up. I grabbed one end and she held the other and we refolded it. She took it from me and hung it over the quilt rack. Then she brushed off her hands and patted her hair.

"This doesn't really change anything," she said. "We still have a killer to catch." She turned to Nick. "What do you know about Robb Gorham?"

"Probably pretty much what you know," he said. "He has a couple of kids, a wife and an ex-wife. Nobody really has anything bad to say about him."

"Do you have any idea where he could have gotten aconite?"

Nick shook his head. "No. He has a house just outside of town with a pretty generic garden, no monkshood. He doesn't use any so-called natural remedies other than licorice chews for a sore throat and that's because his ex-wife swears by them. And I doubt he made the aconite himself. He barely passed high school chemistry." He shrugged. "I'm sorry, Rose. I don't see how it can be Robb Gorham."

She looked disappointed, but she patted Nick on the arm. "Don't worry," she said. "I'm not giving up."

He smiled. "I'd be disappointed if you did." He looked at his watch. "I'm sorry, there's somewhere I have to be."

"Will we see you tonight at the jam?" I asked.

He nodded. "I think so. Save me a seat."

Once he was gone I squeezed my head between my hands. I didn't make my headache go away. "This just makes things more complicated. How are we going to figure out who killed Christopher Healy when we're not even sure how he ingested the poison?"

"We'll find the answer, dear," Rose said, shifting the chair Nick had set by the bookcase a little more to the left.

What actually happened was that the answer found us. Or at least Mr. P. did. He came through the front door, his face flushed and what little hair he had askew. He looked at both of us and smiled. "Chinese New Year," he said.

Chapter 16

Rose and I exchanged somewhat baffled looks.

"Isn't the Lunar New Year celebrated in January or February?" I asked.

"Yes, it is," Mr. P. said as he lifted the strap of his messenger bag over his head. "Did you know that some scholars believe there are cave paintings in France that are more than fifteen thousand years old containing markings for a lunar calendar?"

"I didn't." I wasn't surprised that he did, though.

"Now really isn't the time to talk about that," he said. "I need to show you something." He fished his laptop out of his bag and set it on the end of a nearby corner desk.

I looked at Rose, who shrugged. I had no idea what we were going to see or what Chinese New Year meant. Mr. P. beckoned us over. A photo of Robb Gorham filled the computer screen. He was grinning at the camera with his arm around a young woman who looked to be in her early twenties.

"What am I looking at, Alfred?" Rose asked.

"A photo of Robb Gorham that I found on social media."

"Who's the woman?" I said. She had to be significant otherwise why was he showing us the image? His wife, maybe? Or ex-wife?

"That's Mr. Gorham's sister."

"Is one of them adopted?" Rose said.

Robb Gorham's sister had dark brown hair, dark eyes and obvious Asian ancestry.

Mr. P. nodded. "She is. Her name is Maya. The photo was taken in Boston during Chinese New Year celebrations. See the caption?"

"Picking up my baby sister from work," Rose read. Her gaze shifted to Mr. P.

"See the window behind them?" he asked.

"I'm looking at it," I said.

"Now look at the awning above the window."

I leaned closer to the screen. There was something written on the blue canvas fabric. I could make out only a few letters of the first word: O, N, A, L. The second word was "Chinese." Again, I couldn't see all of the last word, just the letters M, E, D. That was enough.

"Traditional Chinese Medicine."

Mr. P. smiled. "Yes. Maya Gorham is going to college in Boston and working part-time in that shop. She mentions several times on her social media postings that she knows very little about traditional Chinese medicine. She's working on a degree in women's studies. It seems she got the job based mostly on her appearance. The owners seem to be catering to people's stereotypes."

"So you think Robb Gorham could have gotten aconite from the shop," I said.

"I think it's a possibility."

"Aconite is used in Chinese medicine as a stimulant for the kidneys and spleen," Rose said.

I looked sideways at her, surprised she knew that.

"I've been reading," she said.

"That's what you were doing at the library before we went to talk to Stella. You were looking for books about poison."

Rose smiled. "You're never too old to learn." One eyebrow went up. "And I now know sixty-seven ways to kill a person without getting caught."

Mr. P. leaned toward me. "Don't get on her bad side," he stage-whispered.

I put a hand up to my mouth and leaned toward him. "I'm starting to think that could be a very bad idea."

He closed the laptop and put it back in his messenger bag just as two women came in the front door. "Bring Alfred up to date on what we learned from Nicolas," Rose said. "I'll take care of the customers."

"All right," I said. "Call if you need me."

Mr. P. and I headed for the Angels' office and I explained what Nick had told us about the possibility that the poison hadn't been in something Christopher Healy drank.

"That changes things," Mr. P. said as he unpacked his messenger bag. "There are a lot more possibilities both for where the young man was poisoned and by whom."

"I had the same thought," I said. "I think the only thing we can do for now is try to eliminate the suspects we have before we start looking for more."

Mr. P. nodded. "I agree. I'll do a little more digging to see if I can find any indication that Robb Gorham has visited his sister recently."

I headed back to the shop to help Rose. It turned out the two women were looking for a linen tablecloth large enough to fit a seventy-two-inch round table. The daughter of one of the women was marrying the son of the other and together they were hosting a dinner for the wedding party.

We didn't have any plain white linen tablecloths of that size, so I brought out one with a gorgeous blue rose design and a border of pale blue crocheted lace. The two women looked at each other and smiled. "It's beautiful," the mother of the groom said. "We'll take it," the mother of the bride said. There was a brief disagreement at the cash register over who was paying but Rose quickly settled that by offering to take half the payment from each of them.

"I think you were a diplomat in a past life," I said once the customers had left.

She patted my cheek. "I was a middle-school teacher, sweetie," she said. "It's the same thing, only with hormones."

I grinned at her. "Mr. P. is checking both of the Gorhams' social media, looking for anything that can put Robb Gorham in Boston within the past month."

"We have to talk to him again in person," she said. "But before we do that, I want to talk to Mr. Roswell."

"Have you figured out how to make that happen?" I asked.

"I have," she said with a smile that gave me a twinge of nervousness. "I've been getting the runaround from Mr. Roswell and I've had enough of this dancing-all-around-the-barn foolishness. I decided it was time to call in the big gun."

"The big gun?" I said.

"Bang!" a voice said behind me.

I turned around to find Liz standing there. The twinge of nervousness turned into a knot of anxiety. "You're going to get an appointment to see Joe Roswell? I thought you were the one who said he's spending all his time with his lawyers?"

"What have I always told you?" Liz asked.

I frowned and pulled on one earlobe. "I need to wear heels more often because they make my legs look longer. I should shave my legs more often to go with the high heels. And never say no to cake."

"All true," Liz said. "And how about it's easier to get forgiveness than permission?"

"Ah, so you're going to blindside the man?"

She smoothed a wrinkle from her pumpkin-colored sweater. "That's a rather harsh word. I prefer to say we're going to stop by unannounced. And if the man had just made himself available to talk to us we wouldn't be in this position."

"'We'?" I said. The knot of anxiety had just twisted itself into a very bad feeling.

"We," she replied firmly, as though it was a done deal which, I realized, it was.

I walked over to her and draped my arm around her shoulders. She smelled like lemons. "And when are *we* going to pay this visit to Mr. Roswell?"

"The sooner the better. I was thinking this afternoon."

"And what if I can't go?"

Liz laughed. "What else would you be doing? You work and then you work."

"That's not true," I said, a little more indignantly than I'd intended. "It's Thursday."

Liz waved away my words. "Yes and you're going to Sam's. With Jess and Nicolas. Big whoop. That's not until tonight. One thirty. This afternoon. Be ready."

Big whoop? I struggled not to laugh at one of Avery's expressions coming out of Liz's mouth. "Fine. I'll be ready." I kissed her cheek and dropped my arm. "I'll be up in my office." I headed for the stairs.

"There are cookies," Rose called after me.

"Thank you," I said.

"A little lipstick wouldn't hurt," Liz added.

I smiled. "I love you," I said over my shoulder. I knew what her reply would be.

"Yeah, yeah," she said. "Everybody does."

I was printing out the orders from the website with Elvis randomly poking a paw at the keyboard and generally getting in the way when someone knocked on my door.

"Come in," I said.

I smiled when I saw Mac. "Hey, you're not going to believe this. You know that ugly vase, the one with the big yellow birds?"

"The one you said was so ugly no one would buy it?"

I nodded. "That's the one; it looks like I'm going to have to eat my words. It sold."

Mac smiled. "How about eating those words over a late lunch?"

I groaned. "I can't. Liz and I are going to talk to Joe Roswell. I'm sorry."

"Me, too," he said. "Some other day then."

"I'd like that," I said. "It's just been so crazy lately."

"It really is okay, Sarah," he said. He gestured at the computer. "I better let you get back to it."

He was gone before I could say anything else. I looked at the cat. "Maybe I should listen to Liz. Maybe I should just walk up to Mac and lay a big ol' kiss on him."

Elvis gave an enthusiastic meow and lifted a paw in the air. It seemed everyone had an opinion on my love life.

Liz picked me up right on time. I'd brushed my hair and my teeth, applied my favorite rose-colored lip-gloss and removed the cat hair from my pants. Liz looked me over and nodded her approval. She tossed me her keys. "You can drive," she said.

I adjusted the seat and mirrors and we pulled out of the parking lot. "No jokes about Driving Miss Daisy?" she said.

I shook my head. "I think we're more like Smokey and the Bandit this time."

"So am I Burt Reynolds or Sally Field?" Liz asked.

"Well, I am driving, so technically I should be the Bandit, but we both know in the movie that would be you. So I guess that makes me Sally Field."

"Frog," she said.

I glanced over at her. "Excuse me?"

"You're Frog. That was the name they gave Sally Field's character in the movie. Burt Reynolds was Bandit. Sally was Frog."

"I want a better nickname next time," I said.

Liz laughed, then out of the corner of my eye I saw her expression grow serious. "I met him once, you know," she said.

"You met Burt Reynolds?" The car in front of me slowed down to make a left turn so I looked over at her again. "Why didn't you ever tell me that?"

She shrugged. "I don't know. It's not exactly the kind of thing you just drop into conversation. 'Oh by the way, I met Burt Reynolds.'"

"No. It's *exactly* the kind of thing you drop into conversation. So where did you meet Burt?"

"At a party in Atlanta. It was years ago, right after Jack died." Jack Kiley, Liz's first husband was a history professor. I knew that he had consulted on several movies. That was probably why Liz had ended up at a party where Burt Reynolds was in attendance. "Burt was very charming," she continued.

"This story doesn't end the same way as Rose dancing with Steven Tyler did, does it?" I asked.

"No, it does not," she said firmly. "Although . . . I'm not one to kiss and tell."

"And luckily we're here," I said, pulling into a parking spot that was about as close as we were going to get to where the construction on the harbor front was being done. We got out of the car and I locked it, putting the keys in my bag. I gestured over my shoulder. "I think the fastest way to the offices would be that way."

"Oh we're not going to the office," Liz said. "We're going to Sam's."

"You think Joe Roswell will be at the pub?"

She started down the sidewalk. "I have spies everywhere."

I scrambled after her. I let the spy remark slide; I had a feeling it might be true.

The lunch rush was over so it was quiet at The Black Bear. Joe Roswell was seated at a table near the front windows. He wore brown canvas work pants and a denim work shirt over a gray long-sleeve T-shirt with the sleeves rolled back. I could see that my original guess that he was somewhere in his fifties was accurate. He got to his feet as we approached the table. "Mrs. French, hello," he said.

"Mr. Roswell." Liz gave him a cool, professional smile as they shook hands.

He turned to me then. "And you're Liam's sister, Sarah, aren't you?"

"I am," I said. "Liam warned you we were coming." *How had he known?*

Joe smiled. "He mentioned you'd probably want to talk to me at some point, although he thought it wouldn't be quite so soon."

Just a general warning, I realized.

"May we join you for a minute?" Liz asked.

"Of course," he said.

Liz and I sat down and Joe took his seat again. I hadn't noticed Sam when we walked in, but he was on his way over to the table with the coffeepot.

"Liz, would you rather have tea?" he asked.

"No, coffee is fine, Sam, thank you," she said.

He poured a cup for her and one for me. Then he topped off Joe's cup. He had to have been curious about what we were doing at the table, but he didn't let that show in his face, although his hand did rest on my shoulder for a moment before he left.

Joe added a little cream to his coffee. The nail on the index finger of his right hand was bruised black. There were several half-healed scratches on his arm and what I was pretty sure were a couple of stitches on the back of his hand.

"Broken light fixture," he said.

"I'm sorry," I said, feeling a little confused. "I'm not following you."

He held up his hand. "You noticed the stitches. A light fixture in one of the hotel's meeting rooms slipped when it was being installed. I grabbed for it." He shrugged. "Force of habit. Bruised a finger and got a piece of glass stuck in the back of my hand. Your brother took me to the ER." He took a drink of his coffee, then set the mug down. "So what would you like to know?" he asked.

"I'm assuming Liam told you we're looking into Christopher Healy's death," Liz said without any preliminary small talk.

"I didn't kill him," Joe said, leaning back in his chair. "I had no reason to want him dead."

"You thought he cheated you out of that piece of property at Gibson's Point," I said.

"He *did* cheat me out of that land. So I sued him. That's how the system works. I didn't kill him. I didn't need to. From the beginning my lawyer has been confident that a judge is going to rule in my favor."

Liz took a sip of her coffee. "The whole thing was costing you money and time."

Joe shrugged. "Time I have, and as for the money, you've probably heard the old saying, sometimes you have to spend money to make money."

"Margins are small sometimes in the building business," Liz said.

Joe smiled. "You heard about Portland. Okay, yeah, I got a bit overextended and yeah, things were tight for a while, but there's an offer on the table for my stake in that project and I'm taking it. So I had no reason to kill Healy." He leaned forward. "Bottom line, the guy was a minor annoyance, nothing more."

"Did you see Mr. Healy the day he died?" I asked.

"You mean other than at the reception?" His eyebrows knit together and he stared past us for a moment. "That was a week ago Wednesday. Yes. Yes, I did see him." He nodded at whatever he had remembered. "Healy came by the job site late in the afternoon. I'm not sure what time. He was angry because the judge had ruled that he couldn't do any work on the land until the lawsuit was settled. It was the same old thing. I didn't want to be bothered with him. A couple of my guys walked him out—nobody got hurt. That's it."

Liz traced the rim of her cup with one finger. "You had no idea he was going to show up at the reception?"

Joe shook his head. "If I had, I would have put someone at the door to head him off."

"So when he did show up, why didn't you have him removed?"

"Because I didn't want a big scene, plain and simple. Healy had been drinking. I figured it was just easier to let him think he'd won some kind of victory by embarrassing me and then he'd go without any more trouble."

"Can you think of anyone who might have wanted Mr. Healy dead?" I asked. I didn't really expect him to name names. I was more interested in his reaction to the question.

Joe reached for his coffee cup but didn't actually take a drink from it. "I've been thinking about that and I can't come up with anyone. Healy was a nuisance, like an itch in the middle of your back that you can't reach. Nothing more. I can't believe someone killed him. I keep thinking we're going to find out that it was just an accident. I don't see what anyone gains because the man is dead."

I didn't have any more questions after that and neither, it seemed, did Liz. She got to her feet and I did the same.

"Thank you for your time," she said.

"You're welcome." Joe gestured at our cups. "Coffee's on me."

I thanked him, waved good-bye to Sam on the other side of the room and we left.

Liz was quiet on the way back to the car. I waited until I was in the driver's seat before I spoke. "You picked up on something I didn't. What was it?"

She turned to look at me, one hand playing with a

button on the front of her heavy sweater. "Those stitches on the back of his hand. How many do you think there were?"

I tried to picture Joe's hand again. "Two, maybe three. No more than that."

"Do you think his explanation about the light fixture makes sense?"

It had actually not occurred to me that it didn't. I thought for a moment before I answered. "I do," I said. "A piece of broken glass could have stuck in the back of his hand and he could easily have jammed that bruised finger on some part of the light fixture. And he said Liam took him to the ER. That would be a stupid thing to lie about." I frowned. "Why? Are you thinking he got into some kind of a fight with Christopher Healy instead?" I didn't remember any cuts or abrasions on Healy's hands or face other than the cut he'd obviously gotten shaving.

Liz ignored my questions. "Did you pay much attention to the scratches on his right arm?"

I shook my head. "Not really. If I hadn't seen the stitches I probably would have just figured the scratches came from a cat."

"Not a cat," she said. "Not broken glass. Blackberry canes."

"Are you sure?"

"Of course I'm sure," she said tartly. "A blackberry thorn is straight and sharp and it'll draw blood, believe me. Those scratches look like they're healing now, but they were infected, which happens a lot with those thorns."

I leaned my head against the headrest and closed my eyes for a moment. "You think Joe Roswell was in the woods."

"Probably sometime in the last two weeks."

"Blackberry season is over."

"Has been for close to a month now."

I could hear Tom Harris saying, *all parts of the plant are poisonous.* I didn't want to have to tell Liam he was wrong about his friend. I opened my eyes, looked over at Liz and sighed softly.

She gave me a sympathetic smile. "Sorry, Frog," she said.

We drove back to the shop. Rose was in the office. Liz stopped to bring her up to date while I headed inside to see if Avery and Charlotte needed any help. Charlotte was showing a young man with blue hair a small metal stool. Mac had made a new seat for it out of a Chinese checkers game board. Part of me hoped the man didn't buy it because I was hoping to have it in my office for a while. Mr. P. was standing by the front door with Elliot Casey. He raised a hand in acknowledgment and I smiled hello at them.

Avery had more than a dozen wineglasses arranged on the top of an overturned wooden soft drink crate. "What are you doing?" I asked as I joined her.

"This guy came in and he wants four dozen wineglasses," she said. "So far I have nineteen."

"Avery, we don't have forty-eight wineglasses in the store," I said.

"Oh, they don't have to match. I asked. He said

they just all have to be about the same size." She smiled and set another glass on the upside-down box.

I took a deep breath and let it out. "We don't have that many wineglasses at all. Period. There are maybe two dozen."

"Twenty-eight," she replied. "I counted."

"Twenty-eight is not forty-eight," I said.

"I know that." There was just a touch of teenage snark in her voice.

"So where are the extra twenty glasses coming from?"

"The garage," she said as though the answer was obvious. "There are two boxes out there full of wineglasses and beer mugs. I bet there's more than twenty glasses."

"They haven't been washed. They're covered with dirt and cobwebs and there are dead bugs and who knows what inside at least half of them."

"Yeah, I know. That's why I'm going to wash them. There's a sink in the workroom and Mac says he has some of that dish detergent that has the ad for the dancing bubbles I can use and there's vinegar for the rinse water and three dish towels upstairs that I can use to dry them." She finally took a breath. "And I'm not afraid of dead bugs. I can get everything ready before the guy comes back."

"When did he say he'd be back?"

Avery pulled her cell out of the pocket of her black skinny jeans. She checked the time on her screen. "An hour and eight minutes and just so you know I did get a deposit."

"You thought of everything." I smiled. "Good job."

She smiled. "Really?"

"Really," I said. "If I can help with anything let me know."

"Is it okay for me to bring in a few more of those big glass vases? I noticed him looking at the two I used on the table. I thought maybe I might be able to sell him one or two . . . or six." The smile turned into a grin.

I grinned back at her. "Let me know what happens," I said.

I walked over to join Mr. P. and his friend.

Elliot Casey smiled. "It's good to see you again, Sarah," he said.

I nodded. "It's good to see you as well."

"Elliot found several photographs of the two of us back in our Scouting days," Mr. P. said. He handed me a black-and-white snapshot of a boy in the traditional Scout uniform complete with short pants and knee-socks.

"That's you!" I exclaimed. Mr. P. had the same smile back then, the same intelligent look in his eyes, the same little tilt of his head.

"Yes, it is," he said. He looked at Elliot. "There's been a lot of water under the bridge since those days."

"Do you remember the time we got the canoe stuck on those rocks under that covered bridge?" Elliot asked.

"I remember that somehow you talked me into getting out and pushing and then when the canoe came loose you paddled off without me," Mr. P. said.

"The current pulled me away." There was a mischievous gleam in Elliot's eyes as he put his hand over his heart. "I swear."

"It sounds like you two had a lot of fun," I said, smiling at them.

Mr. P. nodded. "We did."

"Scouting was the best thing that could have happened to me," Elliot said. "I ended up there because of some, well, let's say youthful mishaps. The principal gave me the choice: Scouts or the authorities." He glanced at his friend. "And then I met Alfred, which is a very good thing. He probably kept me from a life of too much wine, women and song."

His expression grew serious then, his smile fading. "Sarah, I already said this to Alfred, but I want to say it to you, too. Thank you for all you're doing to find out what happened to Christopher. I had no idea that the last time that Nora and I saw him truly would be the last time."

"When was that?" I asked.

"The same day he died. Christopher always kept a change of clothes, a toothbrush and a shaving kit at our apartment. Occasionally he'd stay the night. This time he stopped by to change his shirt. He mentioned he had plans for dinner, but he didn't say what they were."

He looked at his watch then. I recognized it as a classic Longines wristwatch. The band was sleek stainless steel and it had elegant Roman numerals against a deep blue watch face. Just another way he was different from Mr. P., whose Timex watch had probably cost less than fifty dollars.

"I need to get back," Elliot said. "I don't like to leave Nora alone too long."

Mr. P. held up the photos. "Thank you for these. I'll talk to you soon."

Elliot nodded. He raised a hand in good-bye. "Take care," he said and he was gone.

"May I see the other pictures?" I asked Mr. P.

"Of course," he said, handing them to me. "That one"—he indicated the top photo—"is Elliot and me outside the first tent we ever pitched." The boys, arms over each other's shoulder, wore ear-to-ear grins. "Unfortunately, the tent listed a little to the left."

"You can't really tell," I said.

He smiled. "Thank you for not noticing."

I looked at the other photo. Once again it was of Mr. P. and Elliot captured in midjump off the end of a dock. Again I thought how happy they looked.

"I'm glad the two of you reconnected," I said.

"So am I," Mr. P. said.

I went upstairs, put my coat and bag away and spent a couple of minutes with Elvis, who seemed to think the top of my desk was his designated napping spot. When I went back downstairs again, Charlotte was arranging the chairs around the square table I had brought in to fill the spot where Mac's sorting table had been.

"Did you sell the stool?" I asked.

She smiled. "I'm sorry. I did. I know you were hoping to take it up to your office."

"I'll get Cleveland to watch for another one for me," I said. I eyed the table. "And you sold one of those chairs."

Charlotte held up two fingers. "I sold two—the navy blue one with the woven seat and the pale green one."

I gave a nod of satisfaction. "We're finally making a dent in our collection."

Charlotte passed behind me and patted me on the

shoulder. "Given your overall weakness for orphaned chairs, I don't think that will last long."

I decided I'd go out to the old garage to check in with Mac. Avery was at the sink, carefully rinsing wineglasses in a mix of hot water and white vinegar. Her earbuds were in and she was singing along almost under her breath. Rose and Mr. P. were in their office, looking at a map on Mr. P.'s laptop.

I found Mac in a paint-spattered T-shirt putting a coat of black paint on a large arched window. We had decided to repurpose the old window into a frame for a mirror. I was looking forward to seeing the final project. If it worked we had several other vintage windows we could repurpose in the same way.

Mac set his brush down and wiped his hands with a rag as he got to his feet. "How'd it go with Joe Roswell?"

"Not the way I'd hoped," I said. I explained about the scratches on the builder's arm and why Liz thought they were significant. "If he's not hiding something, why try to make us think they were caused by the broken light fixture when anyone who looked closely could see that's not what happened?"

"I'm sorry," Mac said. "I know Liam is friends with the guy."

"That's the problem. Liam's not going to believe the worst about someone he thinks of as a friend."

Mac smiled. "I know someone like that."

For a moment I forgot what I was going to say next. Then the words came back to me. "It's uh, Thursday. Why don't you come down to Sam's tonight? Jess will be there and Nick, as far as I know."

He shook his head. "I can't, I'm sorry. I'm going to Rockport right after we close."

"Oh," I said. There was an awkward silence.

"Do you remember that auction we went to this summer?" Mac asked.

I thought for a moment. "In that big barn."

"Do you remember the stove?"

I nodded slowly. "It was yellow." I remembered how Mac had walked around the 1950s vintage range looking for dents and scratches. It had been in excellent shape, but the asking price was way too high for us to make any money and the owner hadn't been interested in negotiating.

"It's for sale again. The price is a lot more reasonable now and I want to see if I can get it. I mean, unless you have any objections."

Mac and I acquired items for the store all the time without checking with each other, although we did try to touch base on the big things. I trusted his judgment.

"Do you have a potential home for it?" I asked.

"I have three."

"Then have a good time." I turned to go.

"Sarah," he said. I turned around.

"I really would have liked to join you."

I nodded. "Maybe next time." I headed back across the parking lot, remembering what Liz had said about Mac and I dancing around each other. *Decide what you want, Sarah,* she'd said. *And go after it. Before someone else does.* Why couldn't I seem to do that?

Chapter 17

I went home after work and shared a bowl of fried rice—with extra vegetables—with Elvis. He had some of the chicken while I had all of the extra vegetables. I showered and changed and headed down to The Black Bear. Jess, as usual, had already gotten us a table. Nick showed up about five minutes after I did.

He dropped onto the chair next to Jess, ran a hand over his stubbled chin and turned his head to look at me. "Can you take me home?"

"Right now?" I said. "Gee, I don't know."

He made a face. "No. After I drink a couple of beers and likely publicly humiliate myself by getting up and singing harmony with Sam."

Jess poked me with her elbow. "Say yes. That public humiliation part sounds like it could be fun."

This time it was Jess who got the face.

"Yes, I can give you a ride home. Bad day?"

He nodded. "I spent the afternoon in court trying to make complicated evidence sound simple. I don't want to even think about anything related to work."

He leaned forward, grabbed a couple of chips and slouched back in his seat again.

"How was your day?" I said to Jess.

She smiled. "It was pretty good. I have a new wedding dress client and she has to be the most reasonable person I've ever worked with. We're redoing her grandmother's dress. It's going to be beautiful."

I looked over my shoulder toward the door. "Is your boyfriend joining us?" I asked.

"Liam's at a meeting," Nick said.

Jess reached for a chip. "I'm starting to think your brother isn't taking this fake relationship seriously enough."

I was about to tell her that all the people Liam was trying to fool were on to him when Sam came from the kitchen, looked around, spotted Nick and beckoned to him.

"You're up," I said.

Nick picked up Jess's beer, drained the last inch in the glass and headed toward Sam.

Jess leaned toward me. "We need to find him a woman. A girlfriend."

"A real girlfriend?" I asked. "Or a you-and-Liam kind of girlfriend?"

"The first kind," she said.

"And how are we going to do that? All Nick does is work." I pulled the basket of chips closer and snagged one.

She shrugged. "I don't know. Maybe a dating app?"

I had a chip in my mouth and I almost choked. I coughed and hacked and Jess thumped me on the back.

"Bad idea?" she asked.

"Very bad idea," I said when I could breathe again. "You know how Nick is. He's surprisingly old-fashioned about some things."

"I just hate the thought that he's all by himself."

"Because you and Liam have each other and I have Elvis?"

Jess laughed. "Okay, when you put it that way Nick doesn't sound so bad off."

People started to clap then as the guys took to the stage and that was the end of the conversation, but I couldn't push away the thought that while being alone didn't sound that bad, living that way didn't always feel that good.

Friday morning Rose knocked on my door about seven thirty. She was carrying a plate with two apple-spice muffins.

"Hello dear," she said. "I just wanted to bring you these."

"Thank you," I said. "They smell delicious." The muffins were still slightly warm from the oven and smelled like cinnamon. "Come in for a minute. I can make tea."

She shook her head. "I can't. I'm getting the slow cooker ready."

"All right," I said. "I was going to leave in about forty-five minutes." Mac had texted me when I was at the pub to let me know he'd bought the stove. I was eager to see it. "Are you coming in early?"

"I'd like to, if you don't mind."

"Elvis and I are always happy to have your company." The cat meowed his agreement from his stool at the counter.

"I'll be ready," Rose said. She paused in the doorway. "What's your day look like today?"

"Sanding, sanding and then probably some sanding," I said. "Is there something you need? I'd be happy to put down my sanding block for pretty much anything."

She smiled. "Alfred and I are going to talk to Mr. Gorham this morning. Would you like to come along with us?"

I'd heard so much about Robb Gorham that I actually was intrigued to meet him. "I would. Do you have an appointment or are we going to try Liz's approach and just surprise the man?"

"I have an appointment," she said. "Liam got me the man's cell phone number and I called him. There's a lot to be said for the direct approach. I told him that we're investigating Christopher Healy's death and that we wanted to talk to him about the lawsuit."

"And he said yes, just like that?" The muffins smelled so good I was having a hard time not to pick one up off the plate and take a bite.

"How could he say no? It would have made it look like he has something to hide. Which he may have, by the way." She brushed some flour off the front of her apron. "Alfred found a reference on Robb Gorham's social media about a visit to see his sister two weekends ago."

"That's interesting," I said.

Rose nodded. "I thought so." She studied my face

for a moment. "You don't seem sold on the possibility of Mr. Gorham being our killer."

I sighed. "I guess I'm not. Both Stella and Charlotte have said the same thing about Robb Gorham: He's the kind of person who takes the easy way out. They're both pretty good judges of character. I keep thinking that murder was not the easy way out."

"All the more reason to talk to the man then." She reached over and plucked a bit of cat hair from my shirt. "If we can eliminate him, we can concentrate our efforts somewhere else."

"I really want to give Mr. P. some answers," I said. "And Elliot and his wife."

"We will," Rose said.

"Did you see the photos of the two of them? And the one of Mr. P. in his Boy Scout uniform? He was so cute in those short pants."

Rose smiled. "Yes he was. Alfred had great legs. He still does." She winked at me and was gone.

Our appointment with Robb Gorham was for quarter to ten. It turned out we were meeting him at McNamara's. Rose had tea, Mr. P. and I had coffee and he convinced me to split a lemon tart with him.

"A whole lemon tart would be a bit of an indulgence," he explained. "This, however, is just sharing with a friend."

I smiled. "I like the way you think."

Robb Gorham was five minutes late. He walked in, looked around and came directly toward our table. "Mrs. Jackson, it's good to see you again," he said.

"Thank you for meeting us," Rose said. She made the introductions and he sat down.

Robb Gorham was a good-looking man; not movie-star handsome, but he had deep blue eyes, thick, dark wavy hair a little overdue for a haircut and a warm smile. I could see his appeal. He put all of his attention on the person he was talking to. It would be very easy to get swept away by that kind of focus.

"Okay, first thing," he said, holding up both hands. "I didn't kill Christopher Healy. I'm not saying the way he stole that piece of land out from under Joe wasn't a pain in the"—he paused for a moment—"neck, but a judge was going to fix that."

"You have as big a stake in all of this as Joe Roswell does," Mr. P. said.

"You bet I do," Gorham said with an easy smile. "This project is the perfect way to show how well my ground stabilization system will work. It's going to change the construction business."

"And possibly make you rich," Rose added.

He laughed. "I sure hope so. I've put a lot of my time and money into this project. I'm planning on it paying off."

"If you don't mind my asking, what makes you so sure this technique will work?" Mr. P. asked. "I mean no offense, but you're not an engineer."

Gorham took a sip of his coffee and set the mug on the table again. "I don't mind you asking and no offense taken. You're right. I'm not an engineer, and given the way the fibers work with the soil the best person to evaluate the technique would be a geologist not an engineer. I've been consulting with one. The system will work and without doing any long-term damage to the environment."

Except it wouldn't. I had faith in Tom Harris's analysis of the science. Did Robb Gorham know his system probably would not do what he was promising or was he in the dark as well? When Gorham had arrived he'd set his keys on the table next to the cup of coffee Glenn had brought him. The overhead light glinted off the key chain and caught my eye. Its oval-shaped tag featured an anchor with something written underneath. *An anchor*, just like the charm his former wife had given to Stella Hall. I couldn't make out the writing but I was certain the words would turn out to be "Seabed 2030."

"The problem is, that geologist is your ex-wife," I said.

Gorham looked at me then. "What makes you say that?" He didn't flush, didn't look away from me, but a tiny twitch pulsed in his left eyelid.

I gestured at his keys. "She gave you that key ring."

For a moment he didn't say anything. Then he shrugged with a bit of an embarrassed smile. "Okay, yeah. The geologist I consulted is my ex-wife. What's the problem?"

"The problem, Mr. Gorham, is there's a conflict of interest," Mr. P. said. "The two of you have a personal relationship."

"*Had* a personal relationship. *Had.* Leesa's my ex-wife." A little irritation had crept into his voice. "And if anything, the fact that she's my ex should give more credibility to her recommendation." Again, that easy little-boy smile.

"But the two of you are on pretty good terms," Rose

said. She gave him her sweet little old lady smile. "You've had dinner together since she's been in town, haven't you?"

Gorham nodded. "Like I said, we were consulting on the Gibson's Point project."

Rose nodded as though she believed what he'd said. I knew better. "Mr. Gorham, I need to ask you where you were the day Christopher Healy died," she said. "Really just late that afternoon between about four and six PM?"

He picked up the spoon he'd stirred his coffee with and turned it over in his hand. "I'm sorry. I don't remember. I had a crew doing some site cleanup at the hotel. I would have been there for a while. And I think that was the day I talked to a possible client about renovating one of those old Victorians downtown. My days are pretty busy. They can all run together."

"We understand that," Mr. P. said. "Luckily, there are a surprising number of security cameras all over the harbor front and most of the downtown core. I'm sure you'll turn up on at least a couple of them so we can confirm where you were."

"Don't you worry about it," Rose added. For a moment I thought she was going to reach over and pat his hand, but she didn't. She pushed back from the table and started to get to her feet.

"Hang on a minute," Robb Gorham said. "Did you say between four and six?"

She nodded encouragingly. "That's right."

"I remember now. I had a . . . meeting with Leesa. I was bringing her up to date on the court case."

"The meeting was at your office then, I'm guessing," Mr. P. said. He gestured at the room with one hand. "Or did you come here?"

"We um . . . we actually met at the Knight's Inn. See, it's one of my former projects. I was there to check on an issue with their hot tub. Leesa was in the area so it was just simpler for her to meet me there."

Rose had reached her limit. She shook her head. "Do you really take me for that big of a fool, young man? I am well aware what kind of 'consulting' you and your ex-wife have been doing out at the Knights Inn. I don't care about your convoluted personal life. What I care about is getting justice for Christopher Healy and I don't want to waste any more time on you and your whereabouts if I don't need to."

Robb Gorham was learning the lesson dozens of middle schoolers had already learned: Don't try to pull a fast one on Rose Jackson.

She pulled her phone out of her pocket and held it up. "If I were to call your ex-wife right now and ask her if she was 'consulting' with you on Wednesday of last week, what would she say?"

I had no doubt that if he didn't give an honest answer Rose would call Stella right now and get his ex-wife's number.

For a long moment Gorham didn't say anything; weighing his options, I guessed. Finally he exhaled loudly. "She'd say yes because I'm telling you the truth. There are security cameras at the motel, too. You should be able to find us on the footage."

"We will check," Rose said.

He looked at a point just past her right shoulder. "You'll find us."

That put an end to the conversation. Rose and Mr. P. headed out to the car while I went to pay for our coffee and the lemon tart. Glenn inclined his head in Robb Gorham's direction. "I know that look," he said. "In fact, I had that look the time Rose caught me smoking in the woods behind the soccer pitch. And no, I'm not going to tell you how many years ago that was."

I grinned at him. "Glenn McNamara, I had no idea you were such a bad boy."

"I wasn't always the stellar member of society that I am now." He laughed. "So what did Gorham do?"

"It's more of a who than a what," I said.

He held up a hand. "Say no more."

I put my wallet back in my jacket pocket. "However, what he didn't do, it seems, is kill Christopher Healy."

"That's a good thing, isn't it?" Glenn asked.

"I hope so," I said.

It didn't take very long for Mr. P. to confirm Robb Gorham's alibi. "I'm sorry," Rose said when she came up to my office to deliver the news. "I know that Liam is going to be hurt if it turns out Joe Roswell is the killer."

"I wanted to save him," I said.

Rose frowned. "Save Liam? From what? From finding out the truth about his friend?"

"No. I wanted to save Christopher Healy." I swallowed the lump in my throat. It was the first time I'd said what I'd been thinking for the past week out loud. "I thought that Nick and I . . . I thought his heart would start beating. I thought he'd breathe again." I looked down at my hands, remembering how I'd linked my fingers and pressed on his chest while Nick breathed for the man.

"He was already dead," Rose said gently.

I nodded. "I know. Nothing either of us did made a difference because it was too late." I raised my head and met her gaze. "I want to find out who killed Christopher Healy for Mr. P. and for Elliot and his wife. But I also want to find out for me. Does that sound stupid?"

Rose shook her head. "No, it doesn't. It sounds kind." She put her hand on top of mine and gave it a squeeze. "We're going to catch this person, whoever it is. I promise."

Chapter 18

Saturday morning I stopped to pick up Charlotte. Elvis moved over as she got in and murped hello.

"Good morning, Elvis," Charlotte said as she fastened her seat belt. She smiled at me. "How do you feel about lasagna?"

"I have nothing but good feelings when it comes to lasagna," I said.

"Merow," Elvis added. I wasn't sure how many words he understood, but lasagna was definitely one of them.

"How would you feel about lasagna at my house tonight? Or do you have plans?"

"Merow," Elvis said again.

"So you're in?" Charlotte said to the cat as we pulled out of the driveway. He bobbed his head. She looked at me. "What about you?"

"Well, I did have plans for a *Star Trek* marathon with Elvis, but since he's ditched me, yes, I'd love to have lasagna with you. Will this be what Liz calls, 'Hail, hail the gang's all here'?"

"I hope so," she said. "I think it would be good to be together for no other reason than just to be together. Rose and Alfred are in. And so are your grandmother and John, and Liz. Nick is a maybe. I have to call Liam. I'll talk to Mac when we get to Second Chance." She was ticking people off on her fingers. "What do you think about asking Avery to bring Greg Pearson?"

Avery had been spending a lot of time with the teen over the past few weeks. They'd met because of one of the Angels' cases early in the fall. She strenuously denied they were dating. Avery was a little gun-shy when it came to any kind of romantic connection thanks to her parents' tumultuous relationship, but I had watched the two of them together and it was easy to see that she cared about Greg.

"I think it's a great idea," I said. "But just how much lasagna are you planning on making?"

"Two of my big pans. Rose is bringing the garlic bread and Isabel is making strawberry frozen yogurt."

I could see her looking at me from the corner of my eye. "And?" I nudged.

"Liz is making a salad."

"Ha!" I gave a snort of laughter. "You mean The Black Bear kitchen is making a salad."

"I'm going to rephrase that," Charlotte said. "Liz is *bringing* a salad."

"I really like the chopped salad that they do. Would it be wrong to call Sam and ask him to make that one?"

"Yes," she said firmly. "It would."

"Fine," I said. "What can I do to help?"

"Come early and help me set up."

I stopped at the corner and looked over at her. "How would you feel about me coming early to help you set up and bringing Avery and hopefully Greg so she can do that thing she does with the table?"

Charlotte nodded. "I like that idea."

Liz was just pulling into the parking lot to drop off Avery when we arrived. Elvis made a beeline for the teen. She bent down and picked him up. "Hey, fur-ball," she said. He licked her chin.

"Are you coming to Charlotte's tonight?" I asked as we headed across the pavement.

"Yeah, I guess so," she said, her tone indifferent.

"Is Greg coming?"

She shrugged. "I don't know. Maybe."

Okay, she was in full teen mode. "I was hoping the two of you—or just you, if Greg can't make it—would do me a favor."

"What do you want?" she asked giving me a suspicious side-eye.

"Would you do the table? I told Charlotte I'd help her get things set up, but I'm not good at that kind of thing. You can use anything you want from the shop."

"Anything?"

I nodded. "Anything."

"Do I have to do the table all fancy?"

I laughed. "We are not a fancy bunch in case you haven't noticed. So no, you don't. Unless, of course, you want to. In which case, we'll all try not to eat with our fingers and to hold back our burps."

"Yeah, funny, Sarah," she said, but I noticed she almost smiled.

I unlocked the back door. "So yes?" I asked.

Avery nodded. "Okay. But I can't promise Greg will come."

"I hope we'll get to see him, but if he has plans, that's okay." I pointed at the end wall, where several large plastic containers with lids were stacked. "You can use one of those bins for whatever you want to take with you. We'll stick it in the car at the end of the day."

"Only one?" she said.

"No," I said. What the heck was I getting myself into? "Use as many as you need."

Avery filled two plastic bins to take to Charlotte's. Greg showed up just before we closed and carried them out to my SUV. Avery also had an armload of birch branches and a linen tablecloth on a hanger.

I helped the two of them carry everything inside when we got to Charlotte's and then headed for the kitchen to let Avery work without an audience—other than Greg.

About twenty minutes later she came to get me to see the finished table. "Wow!" I said. What I'd thought was a tablecloth was actually an unbleached linen table runner. Avery had ironed out all of the wrinkles and stretched the runner down the middle of the table. A rustic wooden charger plate was at each place, set with Charlotte's gleaming white dishes and polished knives and forks. Avery had filled three rectangular vases with what looked like real moss although I was guessing it wasn't. Each vase held a mix of birch branches and clippings from Charlotte's bayberry bushes in the backyard, the red berries bright against the more subdued dishes.

In between the vases and running the length of the table, she had arranged pretty much every brown glass wine bottle we had, plus a few extra ones I suspected she'd gotten from the recycling center. Each container held a cream-colored taper and there were several matching pillar candles interspersed among the bottles. All the candles were lit. The effect was dramatic and cozy at the same time. It took a moment for me to realize that the candles were actually all battery-operated.

Greg Pearson's mother had died in a house fire. Things like candles and fire pits made him nervous. I was touched by Avery's thoughtfulness. She was talking to Mr. P., who had just arrived with Rose and Liz, hands moving wildly through the air. He was smiling and nodding.

Liz came up behind me and put an arm around my shoulders. "She's a pretty terrific kid," she said, "even if she does make me those damn green things for breakfast."

"She's a lot like her grandmother," I said. I reached up, put a hand on Liz's arm and gave it a squeeze.

She leaned her head against mine. "She's got some pretty good role models around her, too."

Everyone showed up and there was more than enough lasagna *and* salad *and* garlic bread. When I took a second serving of salad, Liz smiled across the table. "I made that just for you," she said. "I know how much you like my chopped salad."

"Good to know you were thinking about me, Pinocchio," I said.

Liz just laughed.

I was halfway through my frozen yogurt when Liam dropped onto the chair beside me. I hadn't talked to him in a couple of days.

"I'm glad you came," I said.

He looked around the room. "Me, too," he said. "I forgot how much I miss this kind of thing."

"Even with them all trying to run your love life?" I teased.

He smiled. "Even with that."

"You know that Jess was invited, right? The only reason she isn't here is because she's doing a last-minute makeover of a wedding dress."

Liam picked up my spoon and took a taste of my dessert. "I know," he said. "I talked to her before I came. I tried to talk her into coming."

I arched an eyebrow.

He made a face. "There's nothing going on. Jess is just fun. I'm going to hate fake breaking her heart."

"I thought she was going to fake break your heart," I said.

Liam shook his head. "I don't know. We haven't worked the details out yet." His expression grew serious. "You talked to Joe."

I nodded. "Liz and I."

"So now you see that there's no way he had anything to do with Christopher Healy's death. It hasn't changed anything as far as the lawsuit goes."

I didn't want to lie so I tried to steer the conversation in a slightly different direction. "I wanted to ask you something about that lawsuit," I said.

"Sure," he said. "I don't know a lot of the details, though."

"Why did Joe sue Healy and not the original owner of the property?"

Liam propped his arms on the top of the chair back. "The woman's old. She's likely in the beginning stages of dementia. Joe didn't want to put her or the family through a lawsuit, especially because he was convinced that Healy took advantage of her confused mental state to get her to sell to him."

"That's kind of low if it's true."

"It's true," Liam said.

There was a bite of garlic bread on my plate. He reached over and snagged it.

I looked around the room and caught sight of Charlotte doing something that involved swinging her arms and legs in unison. "Are Mac and Greg trying to teach Charlotte how to line dance?" I asked.

He leaned sideways for a better look. "Either that or she's teaching them how to play 'Chopsticks' on a giant keyboard. I'm not sure." He turned his attention back to me. "Are you going to ask me about the broken light fixture at the hotel? Joe said you noticed his stitches."

"You were there when it happened."

He ran a hand back over his hair. "Yeah. It was just a fluke. They were on the staging lifting a light up to the ceiling in one of the meeting rooms. One of the guys lost his footing. The light started to slip, Joe tried to grab it. It hit the floor. Glass went everywhere. This one piece flew up and sliced into the back of his hand.

It was bleeding a lot. I just wrapped a towel around him and we went to the ER." He shook his head at the memory. "Joe was mostly pissed at himself. If he hadn't have already jammed a finger on that hand, he probably would have been able to grab the light fixture."

My heart began to thump, thump, thump in my chest, echoing it seemed in both ears.

"He told us you took him to the hospital," I said, hoping nothing on my face was giving away the tangle of emotions I was feeling inside. "What did he do to his finger? It didn't look like it was broken but I didn't ask."

"It wasn't broken. He just jammed it. He was out cutting wood. Got some scratches on his arm, too." Liam grinned. "I thought about Mom. You know how she is about chain saws."

I nodded, grateful for the change of subject. "Remember the time Dad was going to take down that tree in the backyard and he rented the chain saw?"

Liam laughed. "I don't think the rental place had ever had a piece of equipment that came back after ten minutes."

Charlotte came over to the table then. "I'm sorry to interrupt," she said, "but I need to borrow Liam."

"He's all yours," I said.

He got to his feet. "What do you need?"

"I'm trying to show Mac and Greg how to do a backward crossover but something's getting missed in the translation. Nicolas says it's because we don't actually have any ice or skates."

Liam stifled a grin and looked at me. "'Chopsticks' was close," I said.

"Show me what you were doing," he said to Charlotte as they started back to the bare area of floor behind the sofa.

I ate the last spoonful of melting frozen yogurt in my bowl and looked up to find Mr. P. watching me. I got up and walked over to join him.

"Is everything all right, Sarah?" he asked. "I noticed you were talking to Liam."

"Do you remember what Joe Roswell told us about the injuries to his hand?" I knew that he did, but I needed to work into what I wanted to tell him.

Alfred nodded. "He said he jammed his finger, which is how he got the bruise and that he was cut by a piece of glass from a broken light fixture, which is why he needed stitches."

"The part about the stitches is true. Liam did take Joe to the emergency room to have the glass removed and get stitches. But Joe told Liam he jammed his finger and scraped his arm cutting wood."

Mr. P. looked past me to where Liam and Charlotte were "skating" with, it seemed, a little coaching from my grandmother. "That is the problem with lying," he said. "It's hard sometimes to remember all the details."

I shifted restlessly from one foot to the other. "Do you think we should go talk to Mr. Roswell again?"

He took off his glasses, adjusted the left end piece out just a fraction of an inch and put them on again. "At some point, yes. But I think it would help if we can figure out where he was, and you may have just given me a way to do that."

"How did I do that?" Did I look as confused as I felt?

He smiled. "You said Liam told you Roswell said he got hurt cutting wood."

I nodded.

"Did Liam seem surprised by that explanation?"

I pictured Liam, straddling the chair next to me. "No, he didn't."

Mr. P. nodded. "Very good." It seemed I'd given the correct answer.

"This may be a bit of a leap," he continued, "but I think we can infer that cutting wood is something Mr. Roswell does on at least a semi-regular basis."

"That makes sense," I said.

"Where is it happening?"

"In the woods somewhere, I guess."

Mr. P. was nodding once again. "Exactly. Which suggest he owns a woodlot or at least has access to an area where he can cut wood."

"Somewhere that monkshood may grow," I said slowly.

"Exactly," Mr. P. said.

"So how do we find out?"

Mr. P. didn't say a word. He just looked at me with a Mona Lisa smile.

"I'm sorry," I said, shaking my head. "I forgot for a moment who I was talking to."

"It's quite all right, my dear," he said. "Now that I know what I'm looking for it's not like searching for a needle in a haystack. We will get to the bottom of this."

I nodded, hoping I wouldn't have a problem with what we found when we got there.

*   *   *

Sunday morning I didn't get up and go for a run like I'd planned. Instead I slept late and had brunch with Gram and John. I spent some time cleaning up the apartment and doing laundry while Elvis sat on the top of his cat tower meowing and muttering at me like a feline Greek chorus.

I debating curling up on the couch for the *Star Trek* marathon I'd put off the night before, but the sun was shining and being outside seemed like a better idea. Jess was still working on the wedding dress. Mac was helping a friend make repairs to his sailboat before it was put away for the season. Michelle had a cold and had lost her voice for the most part. Liam and Nick had driven down to Portland to find hockey skates for Nick, inspired maybe by Charlotte's skating lesson for Mac and Greg, which had ended with Avery and Greg making plans to skate with Rose and Mr. P. once the rink slated for the far end of the library parking lot had ice.

"Looks like it's just you and me, furball," I said to Elvis. He was sprawled on his stomach; he opened one green eye and looked at me for a moment. "C'mon, we might as well go out to the shop and work on that mantel."

He made a grumbling noise in the back of his throat and closed his eye again.

I had been ditched by a cat.

I made sure Elvis had fresh water and a clean litterbox, then I pulled on a hoodie, grabbed my bag and my keys and headed out to my SUV. I turned at the corner and was singing along with the radio when I caught sight of Mr. P. heading down the sidewalk carrying one of Rose's tote bags. I pulled over to the curb and rolled down the window.

"Would you like a ride?" I asked.

"Hello, Sarah," he said with a smile. "Thank you, but I'm not going home. I'm going to see Elliot and Nora." He held up the bag. "I found an album from our Scouting days."

"I'll take you," I said. "The only thing I'm doing is going to the shop to do some sanding."

"In that case, yes, a ride would be very nice."

He climbed in and I waited until his seat belt was fastened before I pulled away from the curb.

I waved a hand in the direction of the canvas tote. "Are those photos of you and Elliot or of your whole Scout troop?" I asked.

"The whole troop," he said.

"When you get the album back from Elliot . . ." I began.

"You'd like to look at it," Mr. P. finished.

I glanced sideways and smiled. "I would, if you don't mind. I like looking at photographs. They're a moment from someone's life, captured forever."

"I'd be happy to share them with you," he said.

I found a parking spot on the street right in front of Legacy Place. Elliot and his wife were sitting on a bench in front of the building.

"Do you mind if I come say hello?" I asked Mr. P.

"Of course not," he said.

I got out of the car and we walked over to the Caseys.

"You found the pictures," Elliot said as we came level with him and his wife. He looked at me and smiled.

Mr. P. took the photo album out of the canvas tote bag and handed it to his friend. Nora got to her feet. She patted the back of the bench. "Have a seat, please, Alfred. I need to stretch my legs."

Elliot looked up, concern in his eyes.

Nora put a hand on his shoulder. "Don't fuss," she said. "I'm just going to walk along the front of the building." She looked at me. "Sarah, would you mind coming with me?"

"Of course not," I said.

We walked slowly along the concrete path. As soon as we were out of earshot Nora turned to me. "I, uh, I have a question."

"What is it?" I asked.

She cleared her throat. "Do you think Christopher suffered?"

I shook my head. "No, I don't."

She looked down at the ground, kicked a small rock and sent it skittering along the walkway. "I want to know the truth," she said. "Not something sugar-coated because I'm his mother."

I stopped walking, and turned my head to look at her. Her grief was etched into every line on her face. "That is the truth, as far as I know it," I said. "I looked over at the bar where your son was standing, just watching people. Suddenly he put a hand to his chest, his body shook for a moment, he made a choking sound and he went down. It took seconds for Nick and me to get to him. But he was already . . . gone." I put a hand on her shoulder for a moment as I swallowed down the lump that was pressing at the back of my throat. "I don't think he suffered. There just wasn't time."

She pressed her lips together and nodded.

We walked to the end of the brick building, turned and started back to the men. "I'm glad Elliot reconnected with Alfred," she said, finally breaking the silence. "He needs a friend like that. I hope he'll still be Elliot's friend when I'm gone."

"He will," I said, my voice tight with emotion.

We'd reached the bench and Elliot looked up at his wife. "What were you and Sarah talking about?" he asked. "You looked so serious."

Nora's gaze shifted to Mr. P. "I was telling her that I hope Alfred will continue to be your friend once I'm gone."

"You're not going anywhere," Elliot said. He got to his feet. He was noticeably upset by his wife's words. His jaw tightened and there was an edge to his voice. "We're going to find a way to fight this. I don't care what it takes. I will do anything."

Nora caught his hand. "I know. I'm sorry. I didn't mean to upset you. I'm just happy that you and Alfred are back in each other's lives."

"So am I," Mr. P. said. His eyes met Nora's and whatever she saw in them seemed to put her mind at ease.

"I have to get going," I said. "It was good to see you both."

Nora smiled. "It was good to see you again, Sarah. I'm going to get Elliot to bring me over to your store. I've heard so much about it from Alfred."

"You're welcome to stop in anytime."

"I'll see you tomorrow, Sarah," Mr. P. said.

I nodded and headed back to the car. Talking to Nora had just reconfirmed how much I needed answers. All I had to figure out is where to find them.

Chapter 19

I spent about an hour and a half out in the sunshine working on the fireplace mantel. Then I headed home. Elvis was still sprawled on top of the cat tower. The only hint that he'd moved while I was gone was the two cat treats missing from his bowl.

We had supper—cat food for him and leftover lasagna for me—and had just settled in to finally watch our favorite *Star Trek* movie—*The Voyage Home*—when there was a knock at the door. I lifted Elvis off of my lap and set him on the couch before I went to answer it. The cat leaned sideways as though he wanted to know who it was but not enough to jump down and walk over to find out.

It was Mr. P. He was carrying his computer in one hand and a plate with three cupcakes in the other. He held out the cupcakes. "Rosie sent these," he said. "They're mocha fudge."

"Please tell her thank you," I said. I resisted the urge to take a swipe of frosting from the top of one of them.

"Do you have a minute?" he asked.

"You found something?"

"I did."

"Please, come in and show me."

He set his computer on the kitchen counter and tapped the touchpad. A map of Maine's midcoast region filled the screen. "Amanda Roswell owns a woodlot in Waldo County," he said.

"Joe's wife," I said.

Mr. P. nodded. Then he tapped the screen near the bottom-left section of the county on the map. "It appears to be property she inherited when her grandfather died."

He brought up another smaller map of the entire state. "This is a Biota of North America map of the state. See those purple shaded areas?"

I nodded.

"Those are areas where monkshood has been reported to grow." He clicked back to the first map.

"The woodlot would be in one of those purple areas," I said.

"It appears so."

I linked my fingers and rested my hands on the top of my head. "So what do we do?"

"I think you should treat Elizabeth to a late lunch at Sammy's," he said, pushing his glasses up his nose. "What do you think?"

I nodded. "I think that sounds like a wonderful idea."

Joe Roswell was at the same table at The Black Bear that he'd occupied the last time Liz and I were there. We'd thought about getting there ahead of him, but Liz had decided that a "dramatic entrance" might unsettle the man a little. Not to mention she liked making dramatic entrances. She was dressed for one, in black trousers, a deep crimson sweater and a black faux leather jacket. Her nails were a vivid shade of red.

There was one empty chair at Roswell's table. Liz sat down without being invited. I stayed standing like I was the bodyguard for some celebrity, which in a way I was.

"I didn't expect to see you again, Mrs. French," he said.

"You should have, Mr. Roswell," she said. "I consider myself a very tolerant woman. I don't care whether you shave your head or choose that unfortunate style known as a man bun. I don't care whether you name your child after a piece of farm equipment or your grandfather. But I do loathe being lied to. It's an insult to my intelligence. And *you* lied to me."

He didn't even flinch, although he should have. "I don't know what you're talking about."

"How did you get the scratches that were on your arm?" Liz asked. One leg was crossed over the other, her foot bobbing as if to some piece of music only she could hear. It was the only indication of her annoyance.

"I already explained that," he said.

The foot's tempo increased. "And which explanation should I go with? The one you gave us or the one you gave other people such as the ER doctor?"

It was a bluff but a good one based on the way the color rose in Joe Roswell's face.

"Your wife owns a woodlot in Waldo County," Liz

continued. "It turns out, in a happy little coincidence, that the plant that poisoned Christopher Healy grows in the same corner of the county where that woodlot is located."

Roswell went rigid. The muscles along his jawline tightened and his mouth pulled into a thin line. "I told you that I didn't kill Christopher Healy."

Liz eyed the man the way I'd seen her look at something that had stuck to the bottom of one of her expensive pairs of shoes. "Mr. Roswell, at the moment you have zero credibility with me. And I see no reason not to share what I know with the police." She continued to look at him. He stared back at her without speaking.

I knew he was going to lose. Liz waited less than half a minute, then she got to her feet. As she turned toward the door, Roswell jumped up as well.

"Wait," he said, holding up a hand. "Just wait a minute. I didn't kill Healy. I swear I didn't."

Liz looked at him over her shoulder. "Same song, same verse—sing something else."

He looked down at the table for a moment. I counted in my head, *one, two, three.*

"Okay," he said. "Okay, yes, I got the scratches in the woods, but I wasn't looking for anything to poison Healy with." He paused again.

"You're burning daylight and my patience, Mr. Roswell," Liz said, the warning obvious in her voice.

Roswell ran a hand back over his hair. "The centerpiece of the hotel lobby is this massive reception desk made of reclaimed wood from the old hotel and some other businesses that were torn down for the harbor front development," he said.

I remembered Liam telling me about that. It was a way to acknowledge the history of the waterfront and the town. Liz nodded as though she was aware of the plan as well.

"The problem is most of the wood went missing."

"What do you mean, missing?" I asked.

He put both hands flat on the table. "We have a contract with a company that has a wood gas generator. They take whatever wood can't be recycled. It saves us money and overall it's less stuff that ends up in the landfill. That wood—the stuff I wanted to use on the reception desk—was sent to them by mistake and by the time I realized what had happened—"

"Your front desk had gone up in smoke," Liz said. She pulled out her chair and sat down again.

Roswell took his seat as well. "That reception desk was a contract item. There'd be a substantial penalty if we didn't deliver it."

Liz made a motion like she was shooing away a fly. "I understand all of that, but what does it have to do with Mr. Healy's death?"

Roswell picked up his coffee cup then set it back down again. "I've been . . . appropriating wood from different buildings to make up for what's missing. It's not easy to find the right . . . vintage. There's an old barn on a piece of land next to my wife's property. I tried to track down the owner—I swear I did—but the man lives out of state and I was running out of time."

"So you stole what you needed."

"Borrowed," he said sharply. "I was going to pay everyone back."

Liz shook her head. "No. The word you're looking for is 'stole.' You took something that wasn't yours."

His expression hardened. "I wasn't in the woods looking for a plant to poison Christopher Healy. I didn't try to kill him. That's the truth. That's always been the truth."

I had been listening to Joe Roswell's voice and watching his body language looking for a sign that he still wasn't being straight with us. I didn't find it.

"Do you want me to show you the barn and the wood? Is that what it will take for you to believe me?" he asked.

Liz stood up again. "This is enough. For now," she said. "But you do need to come clean with the hotel management about the reception desk. And find the man who owns that barn so you can pay him for the wood you 'borrowed.'"

Roswell stiffened and looked away. "The penalty is several thousand dollars."

"The truth is worth more than that," Liz said. "Your *word* is worth more than that."

For a long moment he said nothing, then finally he met her gaze. "All right," he said.

Liz nodded, seemingly satisfied. Then she turned and walked away. I followed.

"Do you believe him?" I asked as we drove back to Second Chance.

"Do you?" she countered.

I checked the traffic and made a left turn before I answered. "I do. I didn't see any signs that suggested he was lying. He looked you in the eye. He didn't fidget. He didn't shade his words. On the other hand, as we know from the last time, he is pretty good at shading the truth."

I saw her nod out of the corner of my eye. "Yes, he is, but I believe him as well. Lying to us the first time was self-serving. This story, however, doesn't get him anything. I think it's the truth."

And that's what we told everyone when we got back to the shop.

"It should be possible to match the boards to their source," Mr. P. said. He glanced at his laptop, which was next to his elbow.

"I don't think that's anything we need to concern ourselves with, Alfred," Liz said. Rose had brought her a cup of tea and she took a sip of it. "Let's face it: If Joe Roswell wanted to kill that young man there were easier ways to do it. In my opinion, he just doesn't benefit enough to be our killer."

"This isn't a complete surprise," Rose said. She patted her white hair. "We just need to widen our investigation and take a closer look at Christopher Healy's life. And we will. First thing in the morning."

I was sitting on the edge of Mr. P.'s desk. Rose put an arm around me and gave me a hug. "At least now we don't have to tell Liam that his friend is a killer."

I nodded. It wasn't a lot, but it was better than nothing.

The rest of the afternoon was quiet. I checked the online auction and was happy to see that most of the toys had more than one bid on them. The response to the photos was better than I'd hoped for as well. It looked like this was going to turn out to be a good fund-raiser for the hot lunch program. That was one thing Joe Roswell had done well.

Right before we closed for the day I went out to the garage work space to see what Mac was working on. He had the top attached to the ice cream table and was cleaning the glass. I stood in the doorway and studied the finished piece. "I have to say that turned out better than I expected," I said.

Mac turned at the sound of my voice and smiled. "You had a good idea," he said. "The piece is different enough to catch people's eye, but it has a purpose as well. And we kept an old chair from going to the landfill."

"That always makes me feel good."

He set down the cloth he'd been using to polish the glass and came over to stand in front of me. "I heard what happened with Joe Roswell."

I nodded, tucking a wayward strand of hair behind my ear. "I really did think he killed Christopher Healy. The pieces almost fit together. On the other hand, now I don't have to tell Liam that his friend murdered someone."

"That's something," Mac said.

"That's it?" I said. "I was hoping for one of your rah-rah pep talks."

His dark eyes narrowed. "I give rah-rah pep talks?"

"You say things like, 'The Angels are good at what they do.' 'People always underestimate Rose.' 'Liz has a way of ferreting out people's secrets.'"

Mac took a step closer to me. "The Angels *are* good at what they do," he said, his eyes locked on mine.

"People *do* underestimate Rose, probably because she looks like everyone's idea of a grandmother. And Liz is better at digging up people's secrets than anyone I've ever met. In fact, she scares me just a little tiny bit."

I smiled.

"They will figure this out, Sarah. *You'll* figure this out."

We continued to stare at each other and I had the sensation—not for the first time—that we were moving toward each other, so slowly the motion couldn't be seen, but it was happening.

Then Avery stuck her head around the doorframe.

"Sarah, Charlotte needs you," she said.

I jumped, shook my head and turned to look at her. "I'm sorry. What?"

"Charlotte needs you," she repeated, carefully enunciating each word as though I couldn't hear well or didn't understand the language.

"What for?" I asked.

"Some guy wants to buy a couple of guitars." Avery was singing just under her breath even though she didn't have her phone out or her earbuds in. Like her grandmother, it was like she was tuned in to music no one else could hear.

"I'm coming," I said. I smiled at Mac. "Thanks for the rah-rah pep talk."

He smiled back. "Anytime."

For supper that night, Elvis and I cooked a potato in the microwave and topped it with tomato sauce, chopped leftover broccoli, chicken and cheese. Comfort food. He had some of the chicken. I had everything else. After we'd eaten I wandered around the apartment putting things away and picking up cat hair. The book I'd been reading didn't hold my attention and I ended up sprawled across the bed watching *Jeopardy!* with the cat.

I couldn't stop thinking about the case, about Nora asking me if her son had suffered. What Liz had said earlier kept looping through my mind: Joe Roswell didn't benefit enough to be the killer.

In the kitchen I found a box I had flattened and put in the recycling bin. I cut it open along one side to make a big rectangle of cardboard, which I spread out flat on the counter. I got a couple of markers and started mapping out what I knew about the murder and everyone connected to it.

Elvis jumped up and walked over the cardboard, looking at what I'd written. I propped my elbows on the counter. "Who benefits?" I asked the cat.

He wrinkled his whiskers. He didn't seem to have any answers either.

I looked at the names I'd written down. I remembered the cut on Christopher Healy's chin and how he smelled like he'd been drinking. I went over what Nick had said, that Healy hadn't necessarily had to drink the aconite to get it into his system. Elvis leaned against my arm and I reached over to scratch behind his ear as I studied my handiwork. Everyone was connected to the lawsuit in some way, directly or indirectly, I realized. I thought about how Mr. P. had told me that while Elliot wanted to settle the lawsuit Nora didn't.

Who benefited?

I got my laptop and looked up aconite poisoning.

Halfway down the screen my stomach lurched. I sank onto the closest stool. Elvis cocked his head and me-owed inquiringly. I picked him up and pressed my cheek against the top of his head.

"I know who it was," I whispered. Just saying the words made bile rise in my throat.

I knew who had killed Christopher Healy and that truth was going to hurt someone I loved.

Chapter 20

I sat with Elvis for a while. Then I went down the hall, knocked on Rose's door and stood in the middle of her kitchen floor as I told her what I'd figured out. She asked several questions. I had answers for all of them. Finally she looked at me with sad eyes. "You're right," she said. I hugged her and wished that she'd told me I was wrong.

Rose made tea and the two of us sat at her kitchen table and worked out what we were going to do with what I'd figured out.

"This is the right thing, isn't it?" I said.

She nodded. "The right thing is never the easy thing," she said. "That's why so many people don't do it."

When I got back to my apartment, Elvis was sitting just inside the door as though he was waiting for me. I bent down and picked him up. He nuzzled my chin. I sat down on the sofa, settled the cat on my lap and pulled out my phone.

Mac didn't answer. Then I remembered that he was

still helping his friend with the repairs to his sailboat. He'd probably left his phone in the truck. I didn't bother leaving a message.

When I came out of the apartment in the morning Rose was just coming out of hers. She locked her door and came down the hall to join me. "You don't have to do this, you know," she said. She reached for my hand.

"Yes, I do," I said. "I owe it to Nora."

The two of us had agreed that even before I talked to Michelle or Nick, Nora Healy-Casey deserved to hear the truth. So we weren't going to the shop. We were going to pick up Mr. P. and head to Legacy Place.

"I am at a loss for words," Mr. P. said when he got into the backseat of the SUV. Rose reached an arm over. He caught her hand and gave it a squeeze.

"I'm sorry it turned out like this," I said.

"I know, my dear," he said. "So am I."

Mr. P. had used the pretext for the early visit that he was dropping off more pictures. This wasn't the kind of thing any of us felt comfortable talking about on the phone. He'd actually found a photo album and brought it with him.

"Please, all of you, come in for a few minutes," Elliot said. "Nora's resting. She'll be sorry she missed you." He took the album and sat on the arm of a chair, flipping through it. He grinned at a page of photos. "We were so young, Alfred. So full of life."

"Yes, we were," Mr. P. said. "So was your stepson. Why did you kill him?"

I waited for a denial, an expression of outrage. It

didn't come. Elliot set the album aside and looked at his friend.

"You don't understand, Alf," he said. "Christopher didn't use the money he'd inherited from his father to buy that piece of land. Most of that inheritance is long gone, wasted on pipe dreams and pie-in-the-sky schemes. He convinced his mother to give him the money." He looked down at his hands for a moment before meeting Mr. P.'s steady, nonjudgmental gaze. "We needed that money. There are treatments in Europe that could help Nora. I told him that. I begged him to settle the lawsuit, to get the money back."

"What happened?" Mr. P. asked. His voice was steady.

Rose was beside me on the sofa. I felt for her hand and, when I found it, linked my fingers with hers.

Elliot swiped a hand over his mouth. "I couldn't just do nothing. Not with Nora's life at stake. I went to see Christopher. We got into an argument. I admit I hit him." He kept his eyes fixed on Mr. P., almost as if he thought that if he could explain things to his friend, then everyone else would understand. "We were talking about his mother. I asked him what the hell was wrong with him."

I could feel his anguish. See it on his face. He'd killed his stepson and yet I felt a twinge of sympathy for him.

"He called me an old fool. He said I needed to accept that Nora was going to die and that these new treatments were nothing but a waste of time. He said he was going to turn the nature preserve into a lasting tribute to his mother." Elliot's voice was ragged with emotion now. "He cared more about a piece of ground than he did about his own mother."

I swallowed hard against the sudden press of tears. I looked at Rose. Unshed tears shone in her eyes as well.

"You understand, Alf, don't you?" he said. "I had no choice. It was Nora or Christopher and I chose her."

"You remembered about the wolfsbane from our Scouting days," Mr. P. said, "and you put it in his aftershave."

Christopher always kept a change of clothes, a toothbrush and a shaving kit at our apartment, Elliot had told us.

He nodded now. "I don't know how he could have been Nora's child and been so selfish."

I remembered the story Sam had told me about the person Elliot used to be and, it seemed, still was deep down inside. My throat tightened. There was a noise behind us and I turned to see Nora standing in the doorway. Her arms were wrapped tightly around her body. Tears slid down her face.

"Elliot, what did you do?" she asked in a shaky voice.

"I took care of you," he said, getting to his feet. "The way I've done from the moment we met. The way I will always do." He started toward her and she recoiled. Mr. P. and I stepped in front of him at the same time. He leaned around us. "Nora, please," he begged.

Mr. P. put a hand on his friend's chest.

Elliot looked at him. "Tell her, Alf," he said. "You understand. I didn't have a choice. Tell her."

Mr. P. shook his head. "You did have a choice. There's always a choice, Elliot. And you made the wrong one."

Nora stood there, silent tears dripping off her chin. Rose went to her, put an arm around her shoulders. I stepped away from them all, swiped at my own tears and called Michelle.

Chapter 21

The police took Elliot into custody. "I need the two of you to lay this out for me," Michelle said, as he was being led from the apartment, her voice still raspy from her cold.

I nodded. "Is it okay if we meet you at the station? I just need a couple of minutes."

"All right," she said.

I turned to Mr. P. I wanted to cry, but I knew it wouldn't help either one of us. Rose had taken Nora into the kitchen. The two of us were alone. I saw for the first time how painful this had been for him.

"I'm so, so sorry," I said.

Mr. P. nodded. "At one time he was my best friend," he said. His whole body seemed to sag.

"I know," I said. And then, because I didn't know what else to do, I just wrapped my arms around him and let him lean on me.

Mr. P. and I spent a lot of time at the police station explaining how we'd eliminated everyone else and how I'd figured out that Elliot had killed his stepson.

"Next time, call me first," Michelle said when she finally let us go.

Rose had stayed with Nora until her sister arrived. Liz had picked Rose up and taken her home and that's where I took Mr. P.

Before he got out of the car he turned to look at me. "You did the right thing, Sarah," he said. "Don't doubt that for a moment."

I headed back to the shop. My head ached and my stomach hurt. I'd called Mac when we first got to the police station. He met me at the door. Charlotte was with him.

"Forget about the shop," he said. "You're going home with Charlotte."

I shook my head. "I can't." It registered that he was worried. I could see it in his eyes, in the lines pulling at his mouth.

"You can. Avery and I can take care of things here."

"I can't leave Elvis all night." Gram and John were in Portland and I didn't want to disturb Rose and Mr. P.

Mac put his hands on my shoulders. "I'll go feed him. And I'll watch *Jeopardy!* with him. I'll read him a bedtime story if he wants one. Go with Charlotte. Let us take care of you for a change."

I didn't have the energy to argue with him. I took my house keys off of my key ring and handed them to him.

He put the keys in his pocket, then he leaned over and kissed my forehead. "Go," he said.

I went.

Charlotte made me tomato soup and a grilled cheese sandwich. She listened while I talked and put her arms around me when I started to cry. Then we watched *The Great British Baking Show* and I was asleep by eight thirty.

Mac picked me up in the morning to take me home to shower and change. Elvis seemed happy to see me. I picked him up and he nuzzled my face as I stroked his fur. There was a knock at the door.

"I'll get it," Mac said. "It's probably Rose."

It wasn't Rose. It was Mr. P. He was holding a small blue cardboard box with a lid. I recognized it at once.

"Hello, my dear. How are you?" he asked.

"I'm all right," I said. "How are you?"

"I'm all right as well," he said.

He indicated the box. "Rosie gave me this last night." He glanced at Mac. "It's a View-Master. I had one as a boy."

"That was a thoughtful thing to do," Mac said.

Mr. P. nodded. "Yes it was." He looked at me. "She told me it was really you who bought it."

I smiled. "When we were at the reception it seemed like it brought back happy memories."

"It did," he said. He reached over and laid his hand against my cheek for a moment. "And now I have another one."

Over the next couple of days we settled back into our normal routine at the shop. Mr. P. had made the decision to help Nora in any way he could, which didn't surprise me, and while he was horrified by what Elliot—who had been sent for a psychiatric evaluation—had done, he wasn't abandoning his friend, either. That also didn't surprise me.

Nora's stepdaughter, Chloe, had come from Phoenix. She was taking Nora home with her. Chloe's two daughters were eager to see their grandmother and Nora had secured a spot in a very promising drug trial being conducted in the city.

Nick had once considered going to medical school and I knew he had connections in that world. I suspected that he'd had something to do with Nora's last-minute invitation to join the drug trial. Like the rest of us, he'd do anything for Mr. P. When I'd asked Nick, he'd just shrugged and said, "I don't know what you're talking about," which pretty much confirmed my suspicions.

Late Saturday afternoon I was in the workroom trying to decide which table to move into the shop when Clayton McNamara called. "Sarah, I'm sorry to put you on the spot but a friend of Beth's stopped by. Seems Beth showed her a picture of that china cabinet in the dining room. She seems interested."

Glenn and his cousin had hired us to help clear some of the clutter out of Clayton's tiny home. He'd had some beautiful pieces of furniture and an extensive collection of Pyrex bowls and casserole dishes among other things.

"Do you want to sell it?" I asked. The piece of furniture was 1920s vintage and had been well taken care of. The door had the original leaded glass and there were several different kinds of wood used in the inlaid door design. Clayton had bought it as a tenth anniversary gift for his wife.

"Well, it's not exactly Beth's style," he said. "I guess

it all depends on how much money she wants to give me. I don't have a clue what the thing's worth. I don't want to cheat her but I don't want to get cheated myself if you know what I mean."

"Is she there now?"

"No. She'll be back in about half an hour. So what do you think? What should I put for a price on it?"

I didn't want to see him be ripped off. Glenn had been a good friend to me, and Clayton was the only family he had in town. And I liked the old man.

"Why don't I come over?" I said. "We can figure out a fair price before she gets there."

"I hope it's not too much trouble because I'm going to say yes to that. If the woman hadn't been a friend of Beth's, I would have sent her on her way." He laughed. "Glenn says I got to stop acting like a cantankerous old coot."

"Glenn is wrong," I said, keeping my voice serious. "You're not old."

Clayton laughed. "Well, I walked into that one," he said. "I appreciate this. I'll see you in a bit."

I explained to Mac and Charlotte where I was going. It was a beautiful day with just a few clouds overhead and I was happy to be out of the shop. Clayton was out in the yard when I arrived. I gave him a hug and he gave me a cup of coffee. The two of us settled pretty quickly on what I felt was a reasonable asking price for the china cabinet.

"What about your percentage?" Clayton asked.

I held up my mug and smiled. "I just take that out in coffee," I said.

Clayton had a couple of his big Adirondack chairs still out in the backyard. We took our coffee outside to sit in the sunshine and wait for Beth's friend.

She didn't show up.

"I'm sorry," Clayton said. "I'm an old fool for not getting her phone number. I brought you out here for nothing."

"The coffee was good and the company was even better," I said. "It wasn't for nothing."

He shook his head as he got to his feet. "I remember when a handshake deal meant something." He smiled and smoothed a hand back over his bald head. "If Glenn was here, he'd remind me that was back when I still had hair, which sadly wasn't yesterday."

I finished my coffee, made Clayton promise that if he heard from the woman again he'd call his nephew or me and then I headed back to Second Chance. It was about five minutes past closing time when I pulled into the parking lot. Mac had pulled in ahead of me and was getting out of his truck.

"Hey, where were you?" I asked.

"Glenn called right after you left," Mac said, walking over to join me. "Remember that old icebox he bought at that auction in Belfast?"

I nodded.

"Someone offered him a few dollars more than he paid for it and he decided to sell it. Problem was, he needed help to get the damn thing up the basement stairs."

"So he needed your muscle." I smiled.

"Something like that," he said. "Anyway, the guy had supposedly gone to get the cash because Glenn didn't want to take a check, but it must have been some sort of scam because he didn't come back."

I felt a prickling sensation up my spine as though a cool breeze had just blown down my neck. "So you didn't see the person who wanted to buy the icebox?"

Mac shook his head. "No. And what happened at Clayton's? Did he sell the china cabinet or is he going to keep it?"

I glanced over at the shop. "No," I said slowly. "The woman didn't show up."

Mac looked at me. "Rose," he said.

I rubbed the space between my eyebrows. "I know. This has her sticky little fingerprints all over it."

He put a hand on my arm. "No. I mean Rose is at the back door. They all are."

I looked across the lot. He was right. They were standing there: Rose, Mr. P., Charlotte, Avery, Liz and my grandmother as well, all smiling at us, lined up like the receiving line at a wedding. Or a funeral.

I closed my eyes for a moment and raked both hands through my hair. "What has she done? It has to be something massive because she went to a lot of trouble to get both of us out of the shop."

Mac tipped his head in the direction of the building. "We could go find out or we could just stay out here. I'm pretty sure I have a granola bar in the glove compartment. I'll share." He smiled.

"As tempting as what is likely a six-month-old granola bar sounds, I need to know what Rose and her band of merry outlaws has been up to." We started for the back door.

"Okay," Mac said. "But my granola bar offer still stands if you change your mind at any time."

I bumped him with my hip. "I'll keep that as a Plan B."

He smiled. "It's probably not as bad as you think. They probably just painted the walls black or something like that."

"Do you remember when they were filming that reality show down the street? You know what Rose is like. What if she signed us up for something like that?"

"I could see her doing that," he said.

I winced. "On second thought, that granola bar in your glove compartment is starting to sound good."

He laughed. "Whatever it is, we'll work it out. It won't be that bad."

I pointed over my head. "From your mouth to the Big Guy's ear."

"What did you do?" I asked Rose when I reached her.

"Goodness, so suspicious," she said, patting my arm. Then she smiled. "We just wanted to give the two of you a little break. You've both been working so hard."

"What kind of break?"

"Honestly, Sarah, it's just dinner. There's chicken stew with dumplings keeping warm in the slow cooker upstairs and dessert is in the refrigerator." She held out both hands. "That's all."

"Don't even think about the dishes," Charlotte said.

"Or the table or anything else," Mr. P. added.

Avery was holding Elvis. "And don't worry about the furball," she said. "We're having a sleepover."

"Heaven help us," Liz said.

Gram smiled at Mac and gave me a hug. "Remember what I told you," she whispered. "There aren't nearly as many chances to be happy as you might think. When one comes along, grab it with both hands." She pulled back and gave me a mischievous grin. "Or at least whack it over the head with a book."

They headed across the parking lot toward Liz's car. I hadn't even noticed Gram's parked beside it.

"I love you," I called after them.

"Yeah, yeah everybody does," the six of them replied in unison, something else that had obviously been planned.

"So do you want to see what they've done?" Mac asked.

I ran a hand back through my hair. "Truthfully, that old granola bar of yours is starting to look pretty good."

"Dumplings, Sarah. And dessert." He raised an eyebrow.

I blew out a breath. "All right. Never let it be said that I turned down a dumpling. Let's go take a look."

Rose and her cohorts had closed the store early and transformed the space. A blue Oriental rug was spread on the floor in the middle of the shop. I had no idea where it had come from. A square table sat in the center, set for two with a crisp white tablecloth, matching napkins, and a centerpiece of pink pillar candles. The blinds that covered the front window were down and music was playing in the background. "I Don't Want to Miss a Thing." Aerosmith. Of course.

It was the last thing I had expected to walk into. Color flooded my face. "This is supposed to be a date," I said, closing my eyes for a moment and shaking my head. "They set us up."

Mac nodded. "I know." He didn't look nearly as uncomfortable as I felt; a little nervous, maybe but not mortified, which is what I was feeling.

"So what do we do?"

He gestured at the table. "We have dumplings and dessert. I would like to change the music if you don't mind. I kind of feel like I'm at the prom."

"I don't mind," I said. "No offense to Steven Tyler but it's not as though this really *is* a date or anything." *Why had I said that?*

Mac nodded. "That's true." His brown eyes never left my face.

I felt my cheeks getting warm again.

I took a step backward. "I should go up and get our food, then." I made a gesture in the general direction of the stairs with one hand.

"That's a good idea," he said. He took a step toward me.

"I uh, I'm guessing the dishes are upstairs." I backed up again.

"Makes sense." He moved closer once more.

"So I'll just . . . go do that," I said. I stepped backward and felt a chair behind me. There was nowhere else to go.

Mac reached over and caught my hand. "Before you do that . . ." he hesitated and then he leaned in and kissed me.

It felt for a moment as though we were the only two people in the world. And because we were the only two people in *our* small corner of the world, I slipped both of my arms around his neck and kissed him back.

Love Elvis the cat?
Then meet Hercules and Owen!
Read on for an excerpt of the first book in
the Magical Cats series.

CURIOSITY THRILLED THE CAT

by Sofie Kelly. Available now!

The body was smack in the middle of my freshly scrubbed kitchen floor. Fred the Funky Chicken, minus his head.

"Owen!" I said, sharply.

Nothing.

"Owen, you little fur ball, I know you did this. Where are you?"

There was a muffled "meow" from the back door. I leaned around the cupboards. Owen was sprawled on his back in front of the screen door, a neon yellow feather sticking out of his mouth. He rolled over onto his side and looked at me with the same goofy expression I used to get from stoned students coming into the BU library.

I crouched down next to the gray-and-white tabby. "Owen, you killed Fred," I said. "That's the third chicken this week."

The cat sat up slowly and stretched. He padded over to me and put one paw on my knee. Tipping his head to one side he looked up at me with his golden eyes. I sat back against the end of the cupboard. Owen climbed onto my lap and put his two front paws on my chest. The feather was still sticking out of his mouth.

I held out my right hand. "Give me Fred's head," I said. The cat looked at me unblinkingly. "C'mon, Owen. Spit it out."

He turned his head sideways and dropped what was left of Fred the Funky Chicken's head into my hand. It was a soggy lump of cotton with that lone yellow feather stuck on the end.

"You have a problem, Owen," I told the cat. "You have a monkey on your back." I dropped what was left of the toy's head onto the floor and wiped my hand on my gray yoga pants. "Or maybe I should say you have a chicken on your back."

The cat nuzzled my chin, then laid his head against my T-shirt, closed his eyes and started to purr.

I stroked the top of his head. "That's what they all say," I told him. "You're addicted, you little fur ball, and Rebecca is your dealer."

Owen just kept on purring and ignored me. Hercules came around the corner then. "Your brother is a catnip junkie," I said to the little tuxedo cat.

Hercules climbed over my legs and sniffed the remains of Fred the Funky Chicken's head. Then he looked at Owen, rumbling like a diesel engine as I scratched the side of his head. I swear there was disdain on Hercules' furry face. Stick catnip in, on or near anything and Owen squirmed with joy. Hercules, on the other hand, was indifferent.

The stocky black-and-white cat climbed onto my

lap, too. He put one white paw on my shoulder and swatted at my hair.

"Behind the ear?" I asked.

"Meow," the cat said.

I took that as a yes, and tucked the strands back behind my ear. I was used to long hair, but I'd cut mine several months ago. I was still adjusting to the change in style. At least I hadn't given in to the impulse to dye my dark brown hair blonde.

"Maybe I'll ask Rebecca if she has any ideas for my hair," I said. "She's supposed to be back tonight." At the sound of Rebecca's name Owen lifted his head. He'd taken to Rebecca from the first moment he'd seen her, about two weeks after I'd brought the cats home.

Both Owen and Hercules had been feral kittens. I'd found them, or more truthfully they'd found me, about a month after I'd arrived in town. I had no idea how old they were. They were affectionate with me, but wouldn't allow anyone else to come near them, let alone touch them. That hadn't stopped Rebecca, my backyard neighbor, from trying. She'd been buying both cats little catnip toys for weeks now, but all she'd done was turn Owen into a chicken-decapitating catnip junkie. She was on vacation right now, but Owen had clearly managed to unearth a chicken from a secret stash somewhere.

I stroked the top of his head again. "Go back to sleep," I said. "You're going cold turkey . . . or maybe I should say cold chicken. I'm telling Rebecca no more catnip toys for you. You're getting lazy."

Owen put his head down again, while Hercules used his to butt my free hand. "You want some attention, too?" I asked. I scratched the spot, almost at the top of his head, where the white fur around his mouth and up the bridge of his nose gave way to black. His green eyes narrowed to slits and he began to purr, as well. The rumbling was kind of like being in the service bay of a Volkswagen dealership.

I glanced up at the clock. "Okay, you two. Let me up. It's almost time for me to go and I have to take care of the dearly departed before I do."

I'd sold my car when I'd moved to Minnesota from Boston, and because I could walk everywhere in Mayville Heights, I still hadn't bought a new one. Since I had no car, I'd spent my first few weeks in town wandering around exploring, which is how I'd stumbled on Wisteria Hill, the abandoned Henderson estate. Everett Henderson had hired me at the library.

Owen and Hercules had peered out at me from a tumble of raspberry canes and then followed me around while I explored the overgrown English country garden behind the house. I'd seen several other full-grown cats, but they'd all disappeared as soon as I got anywhere close to them. When I left, Owen and Hercules followed me down the rutted gravel driveway. Twice I'd picked them up and carried them back to the empty house, but that didn't deter them. I looked everywhere, but I couldn't find their mother. They were so small and so determined to come with me that in the end I'd brought them home.

There were whispers around town about Wisteria Hill and the feral cats. But that didn't mean there was anything unusual about my cats. Oh no, nothing unusual at all. It didn't matter that I'd heard rumors about strange lights and ghosts. No one had lived at the estate for quite a while, but Everett refused to sell it or do anything with the property. I'd heard that he'd grown up at Wisteria Hill. Maybe that was why he didn't want to change anything.

Speaking of not wanting change, Hercules was not eager to relinquish his prime spot on my lap. But after some gentle prodding, he shook himself and got off. Owen yawned a couple of times, stretched and took twice as long to move.

I got the broom and dustpan from the porch and swept up the remains of Fred the Funky Chicken. Owen and Hercules sat in front of the refrigerator and watched. Owen made a move toward the dustpan, like he was toying with the idea of grabbing the body and making a run for it.

I glared at him. "Don't even think about it."

He sat back down, making low, grumbling meows in his throat.

I flipped open the lid of the garbage can and held the pan over the top. "Fred was a good chicken," I said solemnly. "He was a funky chicken and we'll miss him."

"Meow," Owen yowled.

I flipped what was left of the catnip toy into the garbage. "Rest in peace, Fred," I said as the lid closed.

I put the broom away, brushed the cat hair off my shirt and washed my hands. I looked in the bathroom mirror. Hercules was right. My hair did look better tucked behind my ear.

My messenger bag with a towel and canvas shoes for tai chi class was in the front closet. I set it by the door and went back through the house to make sure the cats had fresh water.

"I'm leaving," I said. But both cats had disappeared and I didn't get any answer.

I stopped to grab my keys and pick up my bag. Locking the door behind me, I headed out, down Mountain Road.

The sun was yellow-orange, low on the sky over Lake Pepin. It was a warm Minnesota evening, without the sticky humidity of Boston in late July. I shifted my bag from one shoulder to the other. I wasn't going to think about Boston. Minnesota was home now—at least for the next eighteen months or so.

The street curved in toward the center of town as I headed down the hill, and the roof of the library building came into view below. It sat on the midpoint of a curve of shoreline, protected from the water by a rock wall. The brick building had a stained-glass window that dominated one end and a copper-roofed cupola, complete with its original wrought-iron weather vane.

The Mayville Heights Free Public Library was a Carnegie library, built in 1912 with money donated by the industrialist and philanthropist Andrew Carnegie. Now it was being restored and updated to celebrate its centenary. That was why I had been in town for the last several months. And why I'd be here for the next year and a half. I was supervising the restoration—which was almost finished—as well as updating the collections, computerizing the card catalogue and setting up free Internet access for the library patrons. I was slowly learning the reading history of everyone in town. It made me feel like I knew the people a little, as well.

ABOUT THE AUTHOR

Sofie Ryan is a writer and mixed-media artist who loves to repurpose things in her life and her art. She is the author of *No Escape Claws*, *The Fast and the Furriest*, and *Telling Tails* in the *New York Times* bestselling Second Chance Cat Mysteries. She also writes the *New York Times* bestselling Magical Cats Mysteries under the name Sofie Kelly.

CONNECT ONLINE

sofieryan.com